DUNCAN McGEARY'S
LED TO THE SLAUGHTER
THE DONNER PARTY WEREWOLVES

BOOKS of the DEAD

BOOKS of the DEAD

Cover Design by Andy Zeigert
Map by Andy Zeigert
Book Design by James Roy Daley
Edited by Lara Milton

LED TO THE SLAUGHTER
THE DONNER PARTY WEREWOLVES

Copyright 2014 by Duncan McGeary

For more information, contact: Besthorror@gmail.com
Visit us at: Booksofthedeadpress.com

Dedicated to my wife, Linda,
who I met in writer's group and who has always
understood my need to write.

She has been my amused,
bemused muse from the beginning.

CHAPTER 1

James Reed, Sierra Nevada, November 1846

They had been led to this place, led to the slaughter. James Reed could see that now. He'd been a fool, always looking for shortcuts, manipulated and coerced into bad decision after bad decision, until they had ended up here, on the side of a mountain, unable to go forward or go back, without food, frozen and abandoned.

By now, he'd left hunger behind, buried beneath the snowdrifts. Starvation had hollowed him out, leaving nothing but the determination to move forward, foot by foot. Fear froze over him like a sheet of ice, but inside, he was burning. His family was still behind him, in the company of monsters.

The dry snow squeaked like a needle going through leather. His frozen, bunched-up coat and his poncho, hastily constructed from a blanket, moved separately from him, chafing his shoulders and thighs.

Beneath the frozen shell of clothing, Reed was a dying husk of skin and bone. He ducked under the poncho as the wind blasted his face, and in the diffused light, his jutting collarbones and sticklike arms horrified him. When he poked his head out again, the glare of the snow was blinding.

Through slitted eyes, he tried to make out the path, but was forced to close his eyes and move forward blindly, holding his arms up defensively. He walked into branches, and the snow fell onto his head and flowed like water into the cracks of his shell. He told himself he mustn't become snow blind, or he would flounder and sink into the drifts like a drowning sailor, never to come up for air again. His heart pounded and his chest heaved as he gasped for breath.

In the morning, the slope had seemed like nothing more than a slight incline, but as the hours passed, the hill grew ever steeper, until it was as though he was clinging beneath an overhang, in danger of falling backward. Yet still he shoved his legs through the snow, slowly digging his way forward.

Reed tripped and fell to his knees. He had an overwhelming urge to simply fall over into the comforting bed of white and go to sleep. *Let them find me in the spring*, he thought; *I have done my best.*

If he had been alone, he might have given up. But Walter Herron was keeping up with him, step by frozen step. They lent each other what little strength they had, even if it was only their strength of will. They were proud men, neither wanting to admit defeat before the other. They took turns breaking trail. They'd been the strongest of the company, and if they couldn't make it, no one could.

Reed looked back at Herron, and it was as if he was staring at a doppelganger. They were both animate scarecrows, with black button eyes in gaunt white faces, patchy black beards, and emaciated bodies.

I will survive, Reed vowed. He felt as if he was almost gone, as if all that endured was an open flame, melting the path before him, as if he was nothing but spirit and raw will, his body burned away so that nothing physical—not the snow nor the slopes of the mountain—could stop him.

Only those... *creatures*... could stop him now. He could feel them watching him, could feel their flames burning to match his.

The huge cliff loomed above him. He stared tiredly up at the broken, reddish rock and the splintered remains of small trees shattered by the winds.

Reed felt Herron's hand on his shoulder, and it steadied him. The other man pointed to the left, and there, barely noticeable in the gathering dark, was a small deer trail. They trudged toward it and began climbing—no, *crawling*—upward, sliding back a foot for every slippery yard they managed to gain, grabbing hold of each other when one of them started to slide backward. The nearness of the summit gave them the will to go on, here at the last of their strength.

Looking west, Reed saw that there was still some light left in the sky. Below the cliff, it had been nearly dark; on top of the cliff, the day's last rays of sunlight struck him with the force of hope.

But the fading light also revealed the dark shape of the creature looming above them—a wolf that was not a wolf, a man who was not a man. The monster was taller than any human Reed had ever seen, with gangly arms and legs and a wiry trunk, and was covered in reddish, stringy fur matted with blood and gore. It had a long muzzle with razor-sharp teeth that jutted out, and huge red eyes. Its body appeared to waver and dance like a candle's flame even when it was standing still, and when it moved, it was so quick that it became a dreamlike blur.

Half man and half wolf, yet more than the sum of both.

It stood waiting for them, but made no move to attack. *Retreat*, it seemed to be saying. *Go back.*

The monster was terrifying. What chance did Reed have against such a creature? Just the sight of it drained the strength from his limbs, and they had thrown away their rifles before beginning this final climb, useless dead weight, the gunpowder completely soaked.

Still, every ounce of Reed's spirit rebelled against defeat. He pushed upward, drawing his Bowie knife. He couldn't feel his fingers, and had to look down to be certain he was still grasping the knife's handle.

It didn't matter. He would die if he turned back. His whole family would die. Someone had to get out. Someone had to bring help.

He raised the knife, knowing the creature could be on him before he had the chance to use it. In his mind's eye, he saw the thing rush at him, slap the knife out of his hand, push him over the cliff, and land on top of him, then start ripping great shreds of flesh from his bones and eating his steaming insides while he yet lived and screamed.

Herron faltered behind him, slipping backward with a cry. Reed crawled upward until the creature's legs were within striking distance. He stabbed out, but his target wasn't there anymore: instead, those filthy, gore-encrusted legs were straddling him. The sharp points of claws dug into his sides.

The monster loomed over him, staring down with baleful eyes that gleamed with malevolent intelligence. There was something familiar in that gaze, as if he'd met this creature before, somehow, somewhere. Its claws came slicing down on his arm, and Reed felt a slashing pain even through the numbing cold. He dropped his Bowie knife with a cry. Out of the corner of his eye, he saw Herron cowering below him, too terrified to either help or run away.

James Reed waited for death. A strange sense of peace settled over him. He had done his best, and at least it would put an end to his suffering. His thoughts went to his family—his wife, his two young boys, and his daughters, precious Patty and brave, resourceful Virginia, his stepdaughter and yet his favorite. She would fight to the end to save his family, he knew. She had his spirit and more.

The creature bent over him, and the gunge from its fangs dripped onto his face. The wolfman's foul breath smelled of death and carnage. The slime seemed to burn where it oozed onto Reed's cheek. He retched, and his body tried to vomit up food he hadn't eaten in days. It was a dry heave, for there was naught but bile left in his disintegrating body.

The abomination reached down with exaggerated slowness and picked him up by his neck, raising him into the air while it made huffing sounds. Below, Herron was screaming, whether from fear or pain, Reed couldn't tell. His mind tried to reject the thought that came to him: that the sound the creature was uttering was laughter—gloating, scoffing laughter, that the last thing he would ever hear was mockery.

Closing his eyes, Reed roared out his defiance, a wordless shout that contained everything left of his human spirit. The world went dark as his scream rent the air.

Then there was an awful silence. There was no sound except for the wind blowing through the trees and the creak of branches shifting.

Strangely, Reed felt as though the earth was moving slowly toward him; then he realized he was being lowered down, until he was resting on his back on the ground. It was almost a gentle motion, but Reed sensed it was a show of strength, and of disdain.

He lay there waiting for the creature to rend his flesh and devour him alive. He couldn't breathe, though he heard his throat rasping with the effort. It seemed as if this one awful moment was frozen in time. Reed was aware, but his mind couldn't form coherent thoughts. He felt the wind blowing across the snow, the pellets of ice striking his face.

"Ja... James?" he heard Herron's stuttering voice say, breaking the silence. "He... that *thing*... is gone."

Finally, Reed opened his eyes and turned his head. He stared at the jutting, muscled back of the beast as it moved away and disappeared into the trees. A gust of wind blew snow over its strange tracks, and then it was as if the creature had never been. Why had it let him go?

Reed stared up into the sky and started laughing.

"What's so funny?" Herron asked.

Reed couldn't answer. He simply lay there, chuckling mirthlessly as panic and adrenaline washed over him. He recalled how he'd fished with his father on the humid summer banks of the Mississippi, and how his father had unhooked the small fish and thrown them back into the swirling waters. And as this thought became clear in his mind, so did the words his father used to say.

In unison, James Reed and the ghost of his father said, "Throw 'em back; they're too scrawny."

* * *

The monster watched the two pathetic humans tumble down the gentler western slopes on the other side of the mountain. They looked back at him with a fear that was palpable. Feeding on their terror was all he would do on this day.

Let them go, he decided at the last moment. It was going to be a long winter. *Let them bring others...*

CHAPTER 2

The Reed family, Independence, Missouri, May 18, 1846

Our time in Independence, Missouri, reminded me of the last afternoon of the county fair—my favorite time, when the merchants were relaxed and inclined to lighten their loads on the way home by offering good deals to the locals. It was so vibrant, so different from stodgy old Springfield.

"Don't wander too far, Virginia," my mother shouted after me as I joined the flow of the crowd.

I pretended not to hear her. She treated me like a little girl, but I was thirteen, old enough, I had heard, to be courted in the West. Springfield was in our past, old and staid. Our future was going to be a journey into the new and undiscovered.

The town was built to cater to this season-long fair, this festival, this leave-taking and ongoing farewell party for those headed west. Reputable merchants were practiced in helping the wayfarers; disreputable merchants who fleeced travelers had mostly been run out of town by this late in the season. The laborers were well trained, the preparations for the journey to the West by now routine. The residents were starting to relax, flush from a successful spring.

For me, it was the beginning of an exciting adventure. There was anticipation and elation in the air, reflected in my fellow travelers' eyes and in the freshness of everything, the newly painted wagon wheels, the clean whiteness of the wagons' canvas tops, the smell of recently planed wood. Many of the wagons bore the family names of their proud owners in bright colors along their sides. Some of them also included their destination. "Willimete," one said in spelling that was only guesswork. "Oregon," said most of them; "California," said a few. Their owners were beginning an ambitious and dangerous venture—and most of them had only a vague notion of their destination.

All in all, it seemed a grand event.

Over the past few days, I'd explored all the little shops that served the travelers. Now I wandered into one that was filled with glass cabinets of all shapes and sizes piled on top of each other, each filled with bulk goods and scoops. The merchant eyed me suspiciously at first.

"We owned a store just like this back in Springfield," I announced. Our store had been a pale shadow of this well-stocked shop, but I couldn't help but try to make it bigger in my memory. The shopkeeper seemed to find something reassuring in my claim. He nodded and smiled, and went back to counting nails in a box. Along the walls hung hardware and wheels, and watching over all of it was the head of an antelope. It was to be many years before I'd again see a shop so filled with merchandise.

I left the bustling store and rejoined the flow of the crowd, letting it take me where it would. I looked up at the bluffs above the river and felt a pang of nostalgia.

Those of us still preparing to leave had been enviously watching the wagon trains that left before us, miles of wagons, their white canvas glowing in the sun. We'd sit on top of the bluffs and imagine we were going with them. At night, campfires lined the Missouri River, glittering like a fairy city, miles and miles of sparkling lights, as if the entire country was moving westward. Lately, there had been fewer of the campfires. It was getting late in the season.

"Why, I think perhaps the Indians are going to believe you are a princess," I heard a voice say. I might have thought the comment was friendly, even flirtatious, but it dripped with disdain.

I turned in surprise. The speaker was Bayliss, the young man Father had hired to drive our third wagon. He was leaning against the wheel of that wagon, a bale of flour at his feet. He was little more than a boy in appearance, but the knowing look on his face made him seem years and years older than me. He was tall and slender, with shaggy black hair and the beginnings of a beard. He had high cheekbones and wide eyes, and—I hated to admit it—I thought him handsome, when he wasn't scowling.

I looked down at my fine primrose dress. Everyone was dressed in their Sunday best—that is, those of us who owned Sunday best. Bayliss's clothes were worn and muddy. His hat was battered and torn, and there was a thick smudge on his face, axle grease he'd smeared across his cheek and forehead.

Whatever he might have thought, I do not believe I looked down on him. Father had told me that most worthy men start at a low station, and that here in America, any man could rise through hard work.

I smiled at Bayliss uncertainly, unsure if he was mocking me. I'd only been introduced to him once back in Springfield and I couldn't remember having seen him since, though he must have been present during all those miles we had already traveled away from home. Before leaving, Father had given me a small pony, whom I called Paint, and I had ridden him most of the way, no doubt looking as if I was lording it over everyone else.

I blushed a little, realizing I'd probably been ignoring Bayliss the whole trip. I pretended not to understand that his words might have been mocking, and curtsied prettily. "Why, thank you, kind sir!"

His hard grin didn't soften. He *was* mocking me. I couldn't help it: I turned up my nose and sniffed, knowing as I did so that I was coming across as a prig. "Some of us are excited to be on our way," I said loftily.

"Oh, and what do you know? Do you have any idea what is ahead of us?"

"I have read all the books there are to read," I proclaimed. In truth, I had read one of the accounts of westward migration, but I suspected it was more than this boy had. "Do *you* have any idea what's ahead of us?"

A cloud passed over his face. "My uncle Frank left last season. He was going to send for me when he was established in Oregon. He had great plans for my family." Bayliss shook his head. "We have not heard from him since. Mother has sent me to find him."

"I'm sorry," I said, feeling vaguely ashamed of my pert response.

"Sure you are," Bayliss muttered. He pushed off from the wagon and walked away, his face stiff with anger.

Why is he mad at me? I wondered angrily. *I've done nothing to him!* But even as I thought that, I realized that was the problem. I'd had nothing to do with him all these many days. I'd probably acted like a conceited, spoiled brat to him, all unknowing.

I vowed to do better. After all, we were all beginning anew. We were all lowly pilgrims to a new land.

* * *

I progressed farther into the crowd, feeling less exuberant after my encounter with Bayliss, but the festive mood soon had me smiling again. I was passing by a giant tent that was set apart from the others when I heard what sounded like a cry for help. There was much shouting on this day, for everyone was excited, but this had sounded like the scream of someone in pain—a scream that had been cut off.

I moved close to one corner of the tent and listened. I heard another cry, which was also choked off, followed by the growling of animals.

There was a gap in the canvas between the ties. I dared to peek through the narrow gap, but couldn't see anything. Scarcely believing my own brashness, I forced the opening larger and stuck my head in. At first, it was too dark to see anything; then I made out a tight knot of animals, shifting and snarling as they milled around something. They looked like dogs. This was probably a kennel, I decided, owned by someone selling the pioneers dogs to help protect the wagon trains.

I must have heard one of them yelp, I thought. I began to pull my head out of the gap, but something about the movement of the dogs made me look more closely. Perhaps it was an illusion, but I suddenly realized the dogs were huge, larger than any I had ever seen. Their frenzied movements, amplified by their shadows on the canvas behind them, were wild and terrifying.

They were fiercely devouring something; something that, for a moment, looked like...

No, I thought. *That is not possible.*

Whatever creature was being consumed swatted feebly at the dogs, then fell to its side, as if offering itself up to its attackers. Its head, which had been thrashing frenetically, now lolled in defeat.

My mind denied what my eyes were seeing. I realized too late that I had cried out in alarm.

Across the tent, one of the dogs lifted its head. Then, with a movement so fast it froze me in place, the animal broke away from the others and sprinted in my direction.

Run, my mind told me, but my body had turned to stone. I stood there, struck dumb with fear, waiting for the nightmare to take me. I wanted to scream, but could only shake my head in denial of what was happening.

Then, thankfully, my body reacted and I managed to pull my head out of the tent and step back. I stood blinking in the sunlight, letting the warmth soak into me, trying to comprehend what I had just witnessed. I must have been mistaken, I decided. It was dark in the tent, and I had been too frightened to understand what I was seeing.

A man stuck his head out of the gap in the tent, forcing the opening wider. His chest was bare and covered with scars, and I sensed that he was just as naked below the flap of canvas. His red hair was long and wild, and his dark eyes seemed to glow.

"What do you want, girl?" he snarled. "Why are you snooping around?"

"Forgive my intrusion, sir." I tried to sound innocent. "I thought I heard something."

"What business is it of yours if you did?" he asked. He spoke words, but I could have sworn I heard them as guttural growls. "Anyway, I am only feeding my dogs the carcass of a pig."

I didn't respond at first. He was lying. But why was he bothering to lie to me? And who was he?

"I'm sorry, Mister...?" I was shaking and still had the urge to flee, but I sensed it was important not to show fear to this man. My voice was calm, and my inquiry had been surprisingly matter-of-fact, given the circumstances.

He hesitated and then gave me a humorless grin, as if to say, *I don't care what you saw; if you speak of this, you will be the next pig I feed to the dogs.*

"Aren't you a brave girl," he said mockingly. "My name is Keseberg. So now that we are friends, why don't you come in? You can pet the dogs."

"No, thank you, sir," I said. "I have very important things to do. I have to... " I tried to think of something impressive, but failed. This man gave me an uneasy feeling on several counts. Whatever had happened in that tent had been bad. It couldn't have been what I'd thought at first, but I knew it had been wrong. "I have to get back to my family," I finished lamely.

He reached out suddenly, and for a moment I imagined his fingers were blood-covered claws. I blinked and leapt back, just managing to avoid his grasp. I heard a snarl behind me as I hurried away, but when I looked back, the flap of the tent was closed and there was no one pursuing me.

CHAPTER 3

From the personal notes of Jacob Donner, Secretary of the Wolfenrout, Independence, Missouri, May 18, 1846

The Wolfenrout met today and voted for a Foregathering of the Clans to take place in the last week of October in the mountains of California. It will be the first Foregathering of Our Kind in fifty years. Before that, there wasn't a full Foregathering for more than a hundred years. Before that, it had been a millennium since we'd gathered enough of Our Kind to pass laws.

The Wolfenrout meeting started well enough, possibly because the ceremonial sacrifice satiated the bloodlust of the more aggressive among us.

My daughter, Marilee, went to a local tavern and enticed the town drunk back to our tent. He was a disgusting, smelly creature.

"What's this, then?" the man slurred when he saw the gathering. "You want me to meet your family, do you?" He looked a little uneasy, but did not yet understand the danger he was in.

He laughed, then faltered as the silent gathering closed around him. "Get back!" he cried, grabbing Marilee's arm. "What... what're you doin'?"

She shrugged him off and began to undress. She had a calm look on her face, dispassionate, as if she was undressing for bed. He could only stare. A few moments before, he had wanted nothing more than to see her naked, but now the coward averted his eyes.

Solemnly, the other twelve members of the pack disrobed and surrounded the sacrificial offering.

"What're you folks doin'?" he cried. "Stop it! This ain't natural!"

I don't know what shocked the human more: our nudity, or when we began to Turn.

My daughter transformed first. Her arms distorted, her fingers becoming sharpened claws; her legs lengthened, became thicker at the haunches, and narrowed to paws. Her torso elongated and her chest widened. Finally her head changed, her face squeezing outward, her teeth getting longer, her eyes growing larger, and her ears moving to the top of her head and becoming pointed.

Marilee stood upright, like a wolf standing on its hind legs. The man fell to his knees and began to cry.

"Please… I don' unnerstand this. But I won' say nuthin' to no one. If you be devils who reckon to punish me, I swear I won' never steal or hurt no one, ever again. I won' never have another drink. Jus' let me go."

Marilee reached down and, putting one long claw beneath his chin, gently lifted his head. She leaned toward him, growling as she bent her head to his as if to give him a lover's kiss. Instead, she licked his face with her long tongue.

He squeezed his eyes shut. "God, please God," he chanted. "Please God, forgive me. I don' wanna go to hell."

My daughter's barking laugh misted his face with spittle. He voided himself. In my human form, I would have been disgusted, but when Marilee began to eat the hand the man was holding up in self-defense, I was overwhelmed by the smell of fresh blood.

He was screaming, and even as I became wolf, I worried that someone might hear. Keseberg, as usual, transformed faster than the rest of us. He leapt on the drunk and clamped his jaws around the man's neck, and his cries faded to a low, horrid hum. We fell upon his bleeding body.

The man was barely aware that he was being eaten alive. The shock to which humans succumb is a blessing of nature, and proof that they are meant to be our livestock. Mercifully, the man soon fell unconscious. I say mercifully, but only in hindsight. At the time, I wanted him alert, aware of what was happening, his eyes open so that I could stare into his soul as he died.

Each time I think we have progressed beyond our primitive nature, these sacrifices remind me of the satisfaction of tasting the flesh of humans, of eating their essence, of watching the life leave them, the horror of it shining in the blackness of their eyes. Each time, I feel as though I have eaten their souls, and that as they vanish from this Earth, I grow stronger. The God they call on to save them never comes, and as I devour them, I always think, *If He did, I'd eat Him as well.*

In the middle of the carnage, there was a small gasp near the front of the tent. We paused in mid-meal. Keseberg instantly transformed back into human form, and again I was impressed by his control. Bloody and naked, Keseberg went to see who it was.

He came back a few minutes later. "It was just some nosy little girl," he growled. "Hey, save some of that for me."

He transformed back to wolf and pushed aside some of the weaker members of the Wolfenrout. It troubles me that they let him. Keseberg is even stronger than we have been led to believe.

We resumed feeding on the now-dead man.

It is at such times that I fear my brother's plans to reform the Wolfenrout are hopeless.

Duncan McGeary

One thing I know for certain: if my dear brother is smart, he will delay the Wolfenrout vote until well after the ceremonial sacrifice. I suspect that with blood on our muzzles, even the most civilized among us will vote with Keseberg and his brethren's more aggressive solutions to the problem of humans.

We have attached ourselves to a small wagon train, one of the last of the season. It was always our plan to join a human party, one that we could delay and control. Inevitably, there are those who fall by the wayside on these long, dangerous migrations. We will be well fed while we travel, without the need to reveal our true natures.

I fear, however, that the daily proximity of Keseberg and his followers to humans who are unaware of the danger is only asking for trouble.

CHAPTER 4

Virginia Reed, Independence, Missouri, May 19, 1846

The unpleasant incident at the tent was still running through my mind the next morning as we got ready to leave. I'd dreamed all night about heaving shadows on the canvas of a tent, blurry canine shapes surrounding me, and the mocking voice of Mr. Keseberg. I could not shake the memory of that forlorn cry.

It was only a pig, I told myself. *Nothing more.* What I thought I'd glimpsed in the shadows was impossible, of course. The dogs were probably just in a feeding frenzy over that poor pig, as Mr. Keseberg had said.

I was reluctant to voice my suspicions to anyone. I'd vowed to myself that this trip would be a new beginning: no more of the type of exaggeration and storytelling that made my mother roll her eyes. From now on, I would only tell the strictest of truths, without any imaginative flourishes. By the end of the journey, Mother and the rest of my family would take me seriously, as a proper young woman.

Still, I wanted to tell someone about the strange things I'd seen. I certainly couldn't tell Mother. She would think her overly imaginative daughter was just making up stories again. Father might believe me, or pretend to, but he seemed so happy that I was behaving myself that I decided to keep what I had seen secret for now.

I had slept late, which was unusual for me—*and of all the days to do it on, too!* I thought ruefully. My nightmares had kept me up most of the night. I rolled up my bedroll and gave the room one last cleaning. We were one of the few families who possessed the money to escape the wagons, and had rented a room in a boarding house. It was to be the last time we had a solid roof over our heads until we got to California. My mother, sister, and I, my brothers, and Grandy had all crowded into the small room. Father had slept with the wagons, to keep them safe. The sleeping arrangements had been uncomfortable, but we all knew there were much greater privations ahead of us on the trail.

The framework of the bed Mother and Patty had slept in and few other pieces of crude furniture had been pushed aside in the cramped space. The walls were bare wood, and there were names carved on them: the names of those who had gone on to Oregon and California before us. I wondered how many of them had arrived safely. I wondered if any of them would ever return—if *we* would ever return.

Most of my family had already left the boarding house. Our luggage was already gone as well, except for two small cloth bags. Only Grandy was still in the room, perched like an old owl on a chair in the corner, blinking at me. She seemed perfectly happy to be doing nothing at all, but I could see the disquiet in her watery eyes. Underneath her calm exterior was a welter of silent fear and pain. For as long as I could remember, she had been ill, her life slipping away.

I helped her get dressed, and she smiled at me and reached out with a shaking hand covered in paper-thin skin. Even if she didn't quite know who I was, I was grateful for the gesture.

I had always been her favorite, before she disappeared into silence. To Grandy, at least, I wasn't a relative half-removed: I wasn't a half-sister, as I was to my siblings, or a stepdaughter, as I was to Father—though he accepted me with all his heart. I had been her first grandchild, and she had showered affection on me.

I was checking the room one last time when I noticed a small locket on top of the dresser, its tarnished brass blending in with the wood. It was the locket that my mother always carried, containing a lock of little Frank's hair: Frank, my infant brother, whose sudden death had finally compelled mother to give up our home and travel to a new land for a fresh start. She would be frantic if she found it missing. I slipped the locket into my cloth bag and helped Grandy down the stairs, and we set out to find the others, moving at such a slow pace that I wanted to shout in frustration.

We wound our laborious way through the excited crowd. Amid the festive mood, my misgivings receded, and soon I was smiling at everyone.

I heard Father's booming voice before he came into view. He stood at the back of our magnificent wagon, the sun burnishing his dark hair and long beard. This is the image of him that I carry with me to this day: Father looking down on me with an indulgent smile. He was forgiving of my mistakes. When I told a story that seemed to stretch the truth—well, it *was* the truth as I saw it!—he commended me for my imagination. When I wasn't quite the lady my mother wished me to be, all prim and proper, he supported me with the words, "She has spirit! Let her be, Margret!"

As Grandy and I shuffled our way those last few yards to join the rest of the family, Mother turned and saw us. She rushed toward us and embraced Grandy, kissing her on the cheek. "Oh, Mother, you're going to see a new land with us!" she cried. I dug into my bag for the locket. Mother's eyes opened wide in surprise when she saw it, and she smiled at me gratefully as she took it from me and slipped it around her neck.

Here, at the beginning of our long quest, Father was quivering with energy, his voice overly loud with excitement—but his listeners forgave such enthusiasm. Indeed, his fervor was contagious. He had attracted a crowd. He was tall and lean, with a thick black beard, and had a ramrod posture that made him seem even taller. His eyes were deep-set and piercing. He rarely smiled, and yet he always gave the impression that he was amused by what was happening around him.

We gathered at what the young men called "the jumping-off place." I loved the sound of those words. We were jumping off into the unknown. Our journey was to take about four months, we were told. There were few among us who really knew for sure, strange as that may sound. We were relying on guidebooks that would prove to be inaccurate, sometimes nearly fictional. Some of our guides meant well, but what was possible for a lone traveler on horseback often proved impossible for a heavily laden wagon. Others were little more than charlatans, only interested in selling their books, or in selling routes they had a financial interest in.

"It is our duty to settle these lands," Father declared. "It is America's destiny to stretch from the Atlantic to the Pacific, and no one must stand in our way. The savages will have to give way before us. Foreign nations must be warned to get out. It is our land on both coasts and everything in between, and by God, we will take it!"

There were murmurs of agreement, even a couple of cheers, but George Donner shook his head. He was scratching his ample belly thoughtfully, his white hair and beard making him seem wiser than his actual years—he was only slightly older than the rest of the family patriarchs. His round face was guileless, his manner slow and thoughtful.

"I'll be satisfied with a plot of land with good, fertile earth," Donner said. "And I will not care if I have to pledge allegiance to the Brits or the Mexicans or the Russians—or the damn savages, just as long as they leave me and my family alone."

There was laughter from some among the crowd. Mr. Donner was well liked and seemed to enjoy puncturing Father's pretensions. I knew from overhearing conversations around the camp that not everyone liked Father's outspoken opinions, or his support of Abraham Lincoln and the abolitionist movement. Nor did everyone enjoy the lectures about Manifest Destiny that were ever on Father's lips.

"Hear, hear," Patrick Breen said. He had joined us at the last minute when he realized our group wouldn't reject him because of his Catholic faith. "As for me, I only wish for a chance to worship without interference. In California, we will be free; we will live as good Catholics should live."

"Indeed, it is by divine will," Father said.

"Oh, let's just get on with it!" Keseberg shouted.

"Well… " Father said, looking a little deflated. "We all have our reasons for heading west." He regained some of his enthusiasm as he continued, "It doesn't matter why we are going, as long as it we get there. We Americans are a blessed people. It is our destiny to remake the wilderness, to turn it into the paradise of our ideals."

"Hear, hear," someone said. Father frowned, for there had been a mocking tone to the words.

"It is a worthy goal, Mister Reed," Walter Herron said. Mr. Herron was constantly at Father's side these days. They seemed to see eye to eye on the importance of this great national migration.

By now, almost everyone who intended to join us on our journey had gathered. We were ready, and seemed only to be waiting for someone to give us the word.

Father shook off his gloom and smiled. "Shall we get started?" he asked.

The crowd cheered. "On to Oregon!" someone shouted.

Then it was all business. Our party was not a large one, only about twenty wagons at the beginning. We would join larger groups along the way. Toward the end of the journey, when we took our ill-fated turn, there would be more than seventy wagons.

The wagons were lined up in the agreed-upon order: the largest wagons first, to break trail, followed by the smaller ones. This had the unfortunate result of the bigger wagons kicking up dust into the faces of the smaller, poorer families. Father's huge palace was the worst offender of all.

Later, our giant wagon would cause much resentment. The party would break up and reassemble into smaller parties, again and again, until everyone had settled into the group with which they were most compatible.

At the beginning, none of this mattered. All that counted was that we were finally on the move.

CHAPTER 5

From the personal notes of Jacob Donner, Secretary of the Wolfenrout, Independence, Missouri, May 20, 1846

"Are you sure you want to do this, George?" I asked, not for the first time. It was the first night of the journey, and we were already committed. Still, I couldn't help but question the wisdom of our actions, even now that it was probably too late to turn back.

"We don't have much leeway in the matter, Jacob," my brother said. "We have been arguing about this for weeks, to no avail. I am certain that if we can get enough of Our Kind in one place and get them to sit down together, we can reason with them, make them see the sense of the old laws... and make the strictures even stronger."

George said "we" as if certain I agreed with him, and as if it was also my decision. I am not yet ready to tell him how I really feel.

I sometimes wondered if George was making too much of it. Humans thought of Our Kind as myths. Those that believed in us thought we only Turned during the full moon. They had no real concept of our true natures. We weren't supernatural beings—but simply a cross between man and wolf.

My brother needed seven votes by members of the Wolfenrout—and a quorum of all thirteen members—to approve the Foregathering of the Clans. He quietly arranged for the five members who already agreed with him to meet in what he thought was an out-of-the-way place: the far West. He thought that no one who disagreed with him would show up. Counting my vote, he had the seven he needed.

Unexpectedly, Keseberg and the German contingent of the Wolfenrout arrived at the last minute. They are the most militant of Our Kind. They have been hunted to near extinction in their home country, but instead of making them cautious, this has emboldened them. Their arrival was not a good sign. It meant that someone had told them about the meeting, which meant the betrayer had to be one of the six members whom George had expected to vote on his side. Since the Germans also had seven votes, that meant the matter could have gone either way.

But to our surprise, the Germans also voted in favor of a Foregathering of the Clans for the purpose of reforms, though I don't believe they have the same reforms in mind. Even more surprising, they also agreed that the gathering should be held in California, which means that they are confident they have the votes to carry the day. To George's dismay, they have decided to join us on our long journey west, as part of the very same wagon train.

"Perhaps we should delay the Foregathering," I said.

"What choice do we have?" my brother asked. "The Wolfenrout has already voted. Besides, we must do something soon. The humans become ever more numerous. Their expansion increases rapidly. They are invading territories that have always been ours. Confrontations between humans and Our Kind are inevitable."

"Oh, I agree," I said. "But I am not at all sure you will get your way in this, nor that you can impose order through a set of rules—even if you succeed in getting approval. Our Kind do not follow rules well. A Foregathering can suggest guidelines, but cannot enforce them."

"That is what I mean to change," George said adamantly. "We must make the rules mandatory."

"George," I said, trying to sound reasonable. Yelling at my brother only makes him more stubborn. "You know if it was up to me, I'd go along." Inside, I winced at the lie, but there was no point in getting George riled up. He has never liked it when I disagree with him. "As you always say, if it was important to avoid confrontation in the past, it's even more important today."

"Exactly," George said.

"But you must understand," I said, trying not to couch it as an argument, "the humans keep increasing while Our Kind decreases. The rules you are advocating about not creating more of us may have protected us from detection, but they have made us fatally weak in numbers."

As I spoke, I looked down at my journal, where I have written down the guidelines the last Foregathering of the Clans established. I have listed them here because I wonder if the day will come when there will be no one left to remember them. They have served us well up until now, but I fear they have become outdated, obsolete. My brother wants to make them mandatory, but I wonder in my Wolfen heart if they shouldn't be scrapped altogether—not that I would ever say that in front of George.

The Rules of the Foregathering of the Clans

1. Do not eat humans except in emergencies; hunt animals instead.
2. Do not create more of our kind, except through natural reproduction or with the approval of the Wolfenrout.
3. In our ceremonies, only sacrifice humans who won't be missed.
4. Leave no witnesses to our acts.

Keseberg and his cronies only agree with rule number four, naturally. As for the rest, Keseberg wants us to do the opposite: to expand, to confront, to reproduce in greater numbers, and to act on our ancient instincts.

George believes such a response will almost certainly mean the inevitable demise of our species. He wants to make all the rules compulsory and have them enforced on pain of death.

Word has gone out to all the clans of the world that a Foregathering is to be held in late winter, in the territory of California. Some of Our Kind will likely travel there by ship, others overland like ourselves. George had hoped to encourage his supporters to attend while discouraging his opponents from going, but now the German contingent has arrived and disrupted those plans.

"I'm worried about the Germans," I said. "Keseberg has a strong following among the younger Wolfen. You should know: even my own children are in sympathy with his more aggressive ways. Even *your* children are, dear brother."

"What choice do we have?" George repeated, as if he wasn't really listening to me. "Those times when we have been revealed, we have been slaughtered. We are faster and stronger, one on one—that much is true—but the humans are more organized and have much greater numbers. They have won every time we have come into open conflict. Their weapons have neutralized our brute force."

Again, I dared not disagree with my brother, though I worry that he does not see that he is in danger of being outvoted. "Keseberg sees no reason why we cannot use human weapons as well as brute force," I said.

My brother has forgotten who and what we are. He is too old to remember the fire that runs through the veins of our young ones. He dismisses the dangerous possibility that their instincts will override their reason. I disagree with George on what path Our Kind should take, but instead of telling him so, I have been trying to get him to see that his attitudes are considered old-fashioned.

"We simply do not have the numbers to defeat the humans," George said with a finality that brooked no further argument. "We'll never catch up, no matter how much we breed. Nor do we have the financial resources. If we are revealed, we cannot win."

With a sense of foreboding, I let my objections rest.

CHAPTER 6

Virginia Reed, The Oregon Trail, June 1846

We made good time at first. The trail was well worn—indeed, almost too rutted for some of the wagons—but additional, parallel trails had been created that were less pitted and grooved, with the happy result of moving the lagging wagons to the side and out of the dust.

Those first few weeks stand out strongly in my memory, though little of consequence happened. I shall never forget the smell of canvas broiling in the summer heat. Even now, a whiff of this pungent smell can send me into a state of overpowering but unwanted reminiscence. Some of these memories are pleasant, but most are not.

We soon broke away from the Missouri River and began to follow the Platte River instead. It was a shallow, dirty river with shifting sands and treacherously soft banks. No one had much luck catching fish in its muddy waters. Somehow, it had turned out that there was not a fisherman among us.

So many wagon trains had already passed this way this year that the water was too polluted to be drunk, except by the livestock. We were forced to seek out tributaries along the way to find clean water for drinking and bathing. Yes, the Platte was an ugly river; but it was easy to follow, and it went in the direction we desired.

Our family had eight oxen pulling our large wagon, so it didn't matter if we rode in it or walked, as they were unlikely to grow too tired. I walked for most of the first few days, simply because I wanted to see, hear, and smell everything there was to see, hear, and smell. But my feet started getting sore on the fourth day, and the oxen I was walking next to or behind began to stink, and after the second week, I started spending more time drowsing inside the wagon, under the canopy.

All of us—men, women, and children—settled into daily routines. Some things were done without comment, as when women would wander off to the side of the trail and disappear into the bushes or tall grass for a short time. When there was no cover at all, several of the women would go off together and make a kind of privacy screen with their outstretched skirts, taking turns. Men were slightly bolder, sometimes simply turning their backs and watering the trees, but again, no one said anything. Modesty was a luxury we no longer had.

I soon found that I had little in common with the other girls my age. Father had always called me a tomboy, but until this journey, I hadn't really understood what he meant. I chatted occasionally with one of the Donner family's servant girls, Eliza Williams, but even she seemed more interested in domestic activities than in the adventures of the trail.

So I spent most of my time alone. I noticed one boy my age, early on, and tried to approach him, but he practically ran from me. He was a little waif of a fellow, with untrimmed hair and huge brown eyes that never looked you in the face. I found out later that he was an orphan named Luke Halloran. No one seemed to know where he had come from. He had attached himself to our wagon train, and would drift from camp to camp, begging for food. Most of us gave him what we could, out of pity.

Most days, I would sit in the back of the wagon, writing in my diary, and sometimes the wind would whip up and rock the wagon back and forth, as you can see from the scribbles that pass for entries. When it rained, we would tie the canvas tight around the wire canopy rungs, but no matter what we did, moisture got in anyway. When we traveled too long bundled up in such a fashion, it became so stifling inside the wagon that even the rain was preferable.

What I remember most about those first ten days was Grandy's passing.

For days, I'd been expecting it, watching the spirit drain from her eyes. I thought—feared—I would soon see them dim, unsure how I would endure it.

It seems strange now that Grandy's death could have affected me so. I was to see many more deaths, more than anyone should have to bear, but this was the first. The only blessing was that the whole family was with her at the end, as she coughed up blood for the last time, relaxed her bent body, and became still.

"She is at peace," Father said with a sigh. I understood his sad relief. I remember those last few years with Grandy; her eyes had always shown alarm and fear, as if she couldn't believe she was dying. She'd frowned at us when we had loaded her into the wagon, but had said very little since. Now she was forever quiet, her eyes closed, and indeed she seemed finally to be in harmony with her fate.

As it happened, the wagon train had passed a small graveyard of the earliest pioneers the day before. Father pleaded for the others of the party to wait while we went back to bury Grandy.

"We don't have time," Patrick Breen argued. "We are going to be late getting to Fort Laramie as it is. We don't want to be caught in the mountains when winter comes."

"Oh, let them have their ceremony," George Donner said. "It may be the last time any of us has the luxury of a formal funeral."

For once, Keseberg did not offer an objection. He just shrugged. "I wouldn't mind a day of relief from this cursed dust."

We took one wagon to carry Grandy back in. The rest of us rode horses. Out of respect, many of our fellow travelers joined us, though most of them barely knew us. Grandy was the first to die on the trail, and it was as if everyone knew that it was important to mark the occasion—as if it was understood that, as Mr. Donner had said, we would not always have a chance to pay proper respects to our loved ones.

We buried Grandy beside the trail. The men dug a grave, but when my mother asked if it was six feet deep, to keep away the wild animals and Indians, they were silent. In her grief, she jumped into the grave and started digging with her bare hands. The men begged her to desist, and dug the grave deeper.

Mother was never the same after that day. She was a good wife and companion to Father and always did as he asked, and she did her duty to us children as well. But the light had gone out of her eyes, for one of the reasons she had agreed to this difficult journey was now buried along the trail. She had hoped that the mild climate of California would improve Grandy's health.

The following night, William Eddy, a handsome man with a pretty wife and two small children, presented my parents with a loose board he'd pulled off his wagon and spent several hours carving on. It read:

A precious one from us is gone
A voice we loved is stilled
A place is vacant in our hearts
Which never can be filled.

We were all quieter after that, and there were fewer occasions of Father proclaiming our Western destiny.

* * *

The beast slipped away from the others in the darkest hour of the night. He easily found the graveyard and its newest grave, and quickly dug up the old woman's body. Dead meat was distasteful, but it was too early to start feeding on the living.

He didn't want to scare them away too soon, or put them on their guard. Better to guide them gently to their doom; to lead them to the slaughter in such a way that they never knew what was happening until it was too late.

* * *

Grandy's was far from the last gravesite we saw along the trail. Every day, it seemed, we would pass another gravestone, cairn of rocks, or crude wooden cross. Sometimes they lined the trail like silent sentinels, miles and miles of them.

Led to the Slaughter

At first, the entire wagon train obediently stopped to observe the Sabbath, but as we fell further and further behind schedule, we continued traveling throughout the week, stopping only before our midday meal on Sunday to pray. We believed that God would forgive us, for he saw the difficult road we followed.

At the beginning of the journey, the landmarks were well established, and the watering holes came in a timely and orderly sequence. It appeared that most of the Indians had been driven away. The livestock of earlier wagon trains had closely cropped the grasslands, but in those days, there were not yet so many that the earth was completely denuded. We were on an established trail, and because many thousands had traveled it before us, we believed it was safe and that its dangers had been tamed.

In retrospect, this was the easiest part of our migration, though we didn't know it then.

At the time, the journey seemed endless. Already the drudgery of the day-to-day routine was setting in. The great American desert stretched out before us, and the summer heat was oppressive and draining. Our water never seemed to last as long as we thought it would. Dirt and grime got into everything.

I feared for my mother, but she stood up to the hardships surprisingly well. Grandy's death was difficult for her, especially so soon after the loss of dear little Frank, who died the year before we left Springfield. But Grandy had been fading for a long time, and though no one said it aloud, we all felt a sense of completion. After all, she'd been an older woman— almost sixty-seven years. Mother was not happy, by any means, but she seemed reasonably content.

So our family carried on, though somehow all seemed different. Before, we had been both pulled by the West and pushed to the West: pulled by the desire to save Grandy and pushed by the death of baby Frank. Now half of our motivation was gone.

As we pushed onward, I could not help but reflect on how different things were from the grand adventure we had imagined when we'd first set out for the West.

CHAPTER 7

The Reed family, Springfield, Illinois, May 1845

Before we began our journey, we were a very different family. Back then, it seemed to me that we were firmly settled, that Springfield, Illinois, was where we would spend the rest of our lives. It never occurred to me that we might move, or that we would join the ranks of the uprooted, the wanderers, the adventurers.

Then, one morning, Father stayed home instead of going to his office above the hardware store in town, which was unusual for him during any season, but especially during the spring. I remember watching him sitting in the rocking chair on the porch, which was usually Grandy's spot. He was brooding, whittling a stick with his prized Bowie knife, which was also surprising, because he normally wouldn't have dulled the blade in such a way. Back then, everyone from hunters and trappers to established landowner wanted a Bowie knife: if not one made by Jim Bowie himself, then one that looked the same.

I lingered near the house, though the eggs needed to be gathered and the cows needed milking. I was twelve years old, and it was my duty to take care of the livestock. Soon, I thought, Mother would call me in to help her start preparing dinner. But on this particular morning, it was as if my mother saw me but didn't really notice me. Both of my parents were distracted.

At noon, a tall man arrived on horseback. My parents stood to greet him, and by that, I understood that he was important. They rarely acted so formally with our neighbors or other visitors. He was the ugliest man I had ever seen, and at first he scared me.

I sensed a deep melancholy in the man, but as he and my parents settled on the porch, drinking lemonade, the folksy cadence of the stranger's voice hinted that he was telling some droll story, and indeed, I soon heard laughter. This, too, was unusual. Father rarely laughed, and it seemed that Mother never laughed at all.

I moved closer to the porch, pretending to weed the vegetable garden. Somehow, though the vegetables were withering, the weeds still thrived. When the tone of the conversation grew serious and the adults began speaking in earnest, I dropped all pretense of doing my chores and sat silently on the bottom step to listen.

"I've been offered the position of Secretary of the Oregon Territory," the tall man said. "I have been assured it will eventually lead to the governorship."

Father said, "They want you out of the way at the statehouse, Abe. They are afraid of you."

"Perhaps. Still… I must admit I am tempted. Oregon and the West will be the future of our great nation, I think. But it is the 'far corner of nowhere' to Mary, and she doesn't wish to go. So I've decided to run for Congress instead. I have assured Mary I have no chance of winning."

"You have our full support, of course, Abe," Father assured him. "Anything you need from me, you shall have."

"I hoped and expected you would say that. I pray you will not mind, James, but I have put forward your name as Oregon Secretary in my place," said the visitor. "I've come to call upon you because I thought you should be informed of the possibility. I must warn you, however: your abolitionist leanings make the appointment unlikely."

Father looked surprised but pleased. "Thank you, Abe. That you even thought of me is a great honor."

"As I say, you are an underdog for the position," Abe said, smiling. "But then, my sympathies and hopes have always been with the underdog, even though he is often the dog that starts all the fuss."

"Are you not an abolitionist, Mister Lincoln?" my mother asked. She sounded both curious and gently mocking.

"I abhor slavery, Mrs. Reed," he answered quietly. "But it is clearly allowed by the Constitution."

"Oregon," I heard Father say wistfully. "I've always wanted to see if it is as beautiful as they say… "

"May I get you another glass of lemonade, Mister Lincoln?" my mother interjected.

"Thank you most kindly, Mrs. Reed, but I must be moving on." The visitor stood up, rising ever higher until his head plunked against the roof of the porch. He had a skinny frame that, from where I sat at the bottom of the steps, seemed to stretch into the sky. He looked up, grimaced, then looked down at me and shrugged. "I sometimes think I wasn't made for this world," he said ruefully.

The tall man walked down the steps. I stood aside to let him pass, but he suddenly stopped. "Do you see what I see, under yonder nest?" he asked me, and I turned to see that a bird had fallen out of a nest in the dead birch tree and was flopping about in the dry grass.

I ran over to the fallen bird, then hesitated, squeamish about picking it up. Mr. Lincoln followed me with long strides, reached down and took the bird tenderly in his hands, then lifted up the poor, helpless creature and settled it back into its nest.

"Now we will both sleep better tonight, will we not?" he said to me. His eyes were so liquid and deep that I felt myself falling under his spell. Mr. Abraham Lincoln was an almost biblical figure. I couldn't think of anything to say that would not sound silly or shallow. He smiled sadly and turned away.

"It was an eagle," I blurted. "I saw it!"

What was I doing? Warning bells were going off in my mind, but something about this man made me want to impress him.

"An eagle?" He frowned.

"Yes," I continued, determined to go through with it. "I saw an eagle try to snatch the poor birdy."

"Virginia!" I heard my mother cry in horror. "You know that isn't true! I'm sorry, Mister Lincoln. Virginia always has to have stories like that for the things that happen."

He stared down at me gravely for a moment, then smiled. "Nothing wrong with a good story, is there, Virginia? A story does not have to be fact to be true."

Mr. Lincoln got on his black horse, which looked far too small for him; his legs seemed to nearly reach the ground. He tipped his tall hat to Mother and Father and waved to me, then trotted off. *A nice man,* I thought. At the time, I didn't think anything more of his visit, but strangely, the vision of his dark eyes often came to me during our trip out West, and it was somehow reassuring.

I went back to my hot, sweaty chores, dreaming of the wild forests of Oregon, where I imagined there were brisk, cool breezes and Indians lurking in the shadows. When I played with my young brothers, Tommy and Jimmy, I became an Indian princess and they my captives.

* * *

"Oregon," Father declared that night at the dinner table, after we said grace but before we could start eating. My mother winced as if she knew what was coming. "The future of this country is in the Oregon Territory. I was talking to Abe, and he agrees that the West must be conquered."

"James," Mother said, "you must know that Mister Lincoln is overly ambitious under all his melancholy."

Father made a fist and started to strike the table, but changed his mind at the last moment. The oak table we were eating on had been transported all the way from Pennsylvania and was dinged and stained from use. The whole house had lost the newness I remembered, the fresh whitewash and the smell of freshly hewn wood. The birch tree in the front yard, planted on the day of Patty's birth, which had shaded the porch for so many years was dead. The sun glared down unimpeded on the weathered white paint of the house.

Everything was drying out, inside and outside our house. The fence posts were cracking and splitting; the banks of the creek, which had widened and flattened and stunk of cow pies from the constant encroachment of the cattle, and the ruts in the road, which I remembered as always being muddy, were crumbling and turning to dust. At night, I would sometimes be awakened by the crack of a tree limb, the thud of a falling fence post, or the creaking of the walls slowly splitting apart.

It seemed as though the more the house creaked, the more Father wanted to leave, to find a new place, a new home, and a new life. I'd been an infant during the family's last move, yet I remembered being excited, just as this possible new adventure excited me. I always wanted to see what was on the other side of the hill.

Oregon was a storybook land of lush rains and verdant fields, salmon runs, and virgin forests, so different from the flat, dry plains of the Midwest. The drought in Illinois was in its fourth year, and the crops withered no matter how hard Father worked.

I watched my younger brothers, Jimmy and Tommy, shoveling down their beans and gnawing on their chicken legs. Their eyes were gleaming at the prospect of traveling west. I could almost hear them thinking, *Indians! Buffalo! Grizzly bears! Streams filled with leaping salmon!*

These boys are never going to be farmers, I thought. Unexpectedly, before their eyes, the possibility was unfolding that a life of drudgery would be transmuted into a grand adventure.

Grandy broke the silence at the table with one of her coughing fits. Mother quickly rose, took one of the linen napkins, and put it to Grandy's lips. "Here, Mother. Cough into this." The red blood soaked through the white material like a blooming flower, a terrible, deadly red rose.

The hacking set little Frank to crying in his high chair at the other end of the table. I got up and cradled the infant, tending to him as was my responsibility as the eldest daughter.

"Hush, little baby. All will be fine," I said.

I felt a tremor pass through the baby, and a chill down my spine mirrored it. I had a foreboding of the future at that moment. It was as if everything had changed in the blink of an eye, though we didn't know it yet.

* * *

Later that night, I heard my parents arguing in bed. The house creaked in the wind. Underlying everything was the sound of dust blasting against the windows, the topsoil of our once-fertile farm blowing away. I imagined it blowing all the way to Oregon, waiting for us there.

Over the sound of the wind, I could hear my mother crying.

"Mother is too ill for the journey," she pleaded. "She will never survive, James."

Father's firm voice rumbled through the house despite his low tone. "But Margret, the weather in the West will be idyllic for her! If you don't favor Oregon, we will go to the Southwest, to California. I'm told that it is a wondrous place for those suffering from consumption."

"She will not survive."

"Abe says—"

"'Abe says! Abe says!' What is that man's hold on you, James? He will lead you into disaster with his high-minded ambition."

"Abe says that the West must and will be developed. He envisions railroads from sea to sea. That's why he became a lawyer; so he could represent the railroads' interests. Those who are there first will prosper from this great expansion. Can't you see, Margret? We would not be Irish immigrants anymore, but the founders of a new state!"

My mother didn't answer, and I knew she didn't care if we were founders of a new state: she wanted only to be safe and secure, and comfortable. I also suspected Father was completely unaware of her feelings.

As I drifted off to sleep, the foreboding I'd felt at the dinner table returned.

* * *

My baby brother, Gershom Francis Reed, dear little Frank, died that night in his crib.

He looked perfectly natural in death, as if he was merely sleeping. I couldn't bear to see him taken away to be buried, for I was certain that at any moment he would look up at me, his blue eyes shining mischievously.

Mother took to her bed and didn't come out of her room for weeks. It fell upon me to cook the meals and do the chores she would have done, but I didn't mind. My brothers even pitched in, which was unusual for them.

Father endured it as he endured all setbacks, with a grim and determined air, a stiff, upright posture, and a headlong dive into activity. The farm almost recovered that spring, but then the weather—which, even with the drought, had always provided a few inadequate sprinkles of rain here and there—suddenly dried up even more, into an absence of all moisture.

That summer, Abraham Lincoln won the seat of the Illinois Seventh Congressional District in the Thirtieth Congress. My father never brought up his name again, and I wondered if he thought the tall man's visit had been a harbinger of ill. Still, Father did not stop speaking of the West.

On the first hot day of summer, my mother came slowly down the stairs, dressed all in black, her hair carefully coiled, her eyes dark and somber. She was much thinner, and her lips turned downward at the corners, whereas I remembered them being a prim, straight line across her face.

Led to the Slaughter

She sat at the head of the table while I served dinner. The entire family was quiet, even the boys, as we waited for her to speak. Finally, she looked directly into Father's eyes and said, "I want to leave this place. I want to leave as soon as we possibly can."

Father stood up and nodded. "We are going to California."

Then, in a rush of commands, Father established the roles we were to play during our long trek west. Even though he was only five years old himself, Jimmy was given the task of watching over three-year-old Tommy. The eldest daughter at twelve, I should have been Mother's helper, but more often, I found myself helping Father. That left Patty to assume the responsibilities I should have had.

"Virginia, help me harness the horses," Father said. "I'm going into town to see if Mister Hopkins still wants to buy this place. We'll drop by the Browns' house and ask them to start building us a wagon. Jimmy, you need to look after Tommy. Patty, you help your mother."

* * *

To my father's great frustration, it was not until the next season that we were finally able to sell our house, have our wagons built, and gather supplies—but the decision to go West was made that day.

CHAPTER 8

The Reed family, Oregon Trail, 1846

After Grandy's death, I decided not to ride my little pony anymore. Most of the emigrants walked beside the wagons instead of riding gaily ahead of them. Father seemed surprised, but I think he also approved.

The terrain was so flat that we could see the few houses that had sprung up along the trail miles before we reached them. There was always brisk business being done at these solitary homesteads: eggs and chickens, beef and pork, bread, pies and produce of all sorts were being sold for many times the going rate back in Springfield. There was also commerce among the inevitable wagons camped nearby. I often wondered why we didn't stop at one of these homesteads and make our fortune by catering to the settlers headed west.

I remember the heat, but there were also days of pouring rain, when we had to keep the wagons moving for fear of getting stuck in the mud. On those days, we were forced to stop well before dusk if we found firm ground to camp on. Each river crossing became more difficult than the last. We slowed down, and at times it seemed as if we were the only humans in this vast land. I pictured all the wagon trains ahead of us entering Oregon and California while we sat in the middle of the great desert. Behind us, I imagined emptiness.

We traveled 450 miles that first month, which put us behind schedule with the most difficult parts of the trail still ahead. I wasn't yet aware that we were falling behind, though in hindsight I remember my parents talking in worried tones late at night. Still, I remember this part of the journey as being mostly a happy and peaceful time.

Because of the unpredictable rains, the covers of the wagons were left on most of the time, and it got hot and musty inside. Mother and Patty got motion sickness from the wagon's constant swaying, but I did not mind it.

A week into this leg of the journey, I climbed up onto our third wagon and stood on the buckboard across from Bayliss. Though we were the third wagon in line, the dust was already almost unbearable. I could only imagine what it was like for the smaller wagons bringing up the rear.

Bayliss was wearing a red bandana over his nose and mouth, but I could still see him scowl. I was sure he didn't like me, and I was determined to change that.

"Well, are you going to move over for me or not?" I demanded. I stared at him until he shrugged and removed his canteen and leftover lunch from the seat next to him. I clambered into it.

"Why, what can I do for you, miss?" His words were polite, but his tone wasn't.

"It's time for me to learn how to drive one of these wagons."

"You want to take my job?" He sounded aggrieved.

"Oh, no, I assure you! I merely thought that with such a long journey… that… " I trailed off as I noticed that his eyes were crinkled up at the corners and realized he was teasing.

Then I could sense the smile under the bandana disappearing. "Mister Reed would horsewhip me if I let you near these oxen," he said.

"Oh, he's not so bad as that," I said.

He just stared at me.

"He is a fair man," I said stoutly. "He was a colonel in the Black Hawk War, you know." I cringed as I said it, wondering, as always, why I felt the need to exaggerate. Father had been a volunteer in the war, and an enlisted man.

Bayliss snorted and called out to the four oxen with a series of whistles and trills. They responded by pulling harder. We'd fallen a few yards behind while conversationally dueling, but we quickly caught up.

"How did you do that?" I asked.

"Nothing to it, really," he said. "These brutes follow whatever is in front of them. Indeed, it can be a more difficult task to stop them. The hardest part of my job is harnessing them in the mornings and taking care of them at night. I imagine you'll be wanting to do that, too?"

I did not answer him. He was probably well aware that I had my own duties during those times.

I was surprised when he handed me the reins. We awkwardly changed places, and he showed me the rudiments. I could hear the men in the wagon behind us, who'd been observing all this, laughing at the idea of a woman driving oxen.

"Show me how to use the whip," I ordered. He hesitated, then passed the whip to me, put his right arm around me, and showed me how to snap the end of the leather lash. After several lame attempts, I succeeded in creating a sharp sound that made the oxen start and speed up. It was unexpectedly thrilling.

We reached a low point in the road that was covered by small logs, which squished into the mud as the wagon clattered across them. I started to say something, but the jouncing made me bite my tongue, so I decided to wait. It was hard to converse in the wagons at the best of times. The road was always rutted, and as we lurched here and there, the groaning and rattling of the wagons swallowed our words. It was no better off to the side of the main trail, because others who had had the same idea had churned up that ground as well.

"Did you go to school in Springfield?" I asked when I could safely speak again.

"School?" he asked in disbelief. "Do I *look* like I went to school?"

No, I thought with annoyance, *if you had gone to school, you might have learned some manners.*

Bayliss and I sat next to each other in awkward silence for a time, and finally, I excused myself. That might have been the end of it, but a week later, as I was walking along the trail, I happened to look up, and saw him staring down at me from his perch on the wagon. His bandana was around his neck, and he was smiling. He gave me a jaunty wave. He seemed almost friendly.

I blushed and gave him a quick smile in return, but that was all, for I couldn't be certain he wouldn't turn cold on me again.

As we continued on, I often found myself walking next to his wagon. I'm not sure he noticed, but I suppose he must have. During some of our meals, he sat near me—on purpose, I thought. Though he never sat close enough to converse with, I took it as an invitation. One night, I got up the courage to sit next to him. "Hello, Bayliss."

"Miss," he answered politely. The firelight flickered on his face, and I thought I caught a quick smile. Someone on the other side of the fire threw a fresh buffalo chip on the flames, and soon we were coughing and laughing at the sudden smoke and stink.

We exchanged a long look, then looked away when neither of us could think of anything to say. The Dutch oven was nearby, and I got up and gave the coals a quick stir. I saw Mother raise her eyebrows, because I avoided cooking whenever possible.

I sat down next to Bayliss again, and this time I felt pretty comfortable, as if he was already on old friend. But it wasn't quite like that, either, for I also felt a strange thrill.

"Have you driven the big wagon yet?" I asked. "What do you think of it?"

"I admit, your family wagon is the biggest I have ever seen," he said. "I have been hoping Mister Reed will give me a turn at driving it. The other drivers can't stop talking about how fancy it is."

"Well, it isn't because we are being ostentatious," I said defensively. "The builder decided that Father deserved a grand wagon, because he so obviously has a grand future, so he insisted on building it that way." In truth, I suspected that the builder Father had engaged didn't know what he was doing and had accidentally built it using oversized proportions.

"Os... osten... tatious?"

"I mean, we are not showing off. Really, we aren't! My mother is sickly, and you know how ill my Grandy was. Father promised them back in Springfield that he would make the journey as comfortable as possible."

"But he did not promise *you*?" he asked, smiling.

I didn't know what to say to that.

"He treats you almost like a son," Bayliss said admiringly. "I don't think he worries much about you. I believe he thinks you can take care of yourself."

Now I was even more speechless.

"I can see why he thinks that," Bayliss continued.

"The promise was to Mother," I insisted, finding my tongue. "It was the only way he could get her to agree to this journey."

"He should never have promised that," Bayliss said. "This is not an easy journey for anyone. Rich or poor, we'll all get thirsty and tired, dirty, and hungry before we reach California. Indian arrows aren't picky. Rivers drown highborn and lowborn alike. It will take hard work and luck for all of us to survive."

"I am not afraid of a little hard work," I said, ready to take offense. "I was in charge of the milking back at our farm." Well, I *did* milk most mornings, even if I wasn't really in charge.

Bayliss backed down, nodding agreeably. "Oh, I can see that you don't mind doing your share," he said. "I've been watching you. You are not the little princess I thought you were."

Well, I never! I wanted to jest. I could see he had meant it as a compliment.

"Your daddy shouldn't have been so *ostentatious*," Bayliss said. "The bigger the wagon, the slower it goes. Many wagon trains wouldn't have allowed it."

I didn't respond, even to his mocking use of the word "ostentatious," because I knew he was right. Smaller wagons made good time, and as it turned out, many of the extra supplies we had brought along thinking to sell along the way were already rotting on the side of the trail.

We sat companionably after that. The adults were having another one of their arguments, and as we fell silent, their words drifted over to us: angry words. Instead of having dinner with their families, as usual, the leaders of all the households were gathered beside our giant wagon. Blame was being cast for something, and Father seemed to be the focus of much of the anger.

It was high summer by then, and extremely hot. Hailstorms had pounded down on us over the past week, pelting us with huge balls of dirty, frozen water. Everyone was tired from the constant river crossings and the necessity of repairing broken wheels and axles every evening.

Every day, the scenery was both the same—mostly flat and dirty—and different, sometimes breathtakingly spectacular. One day, we came upon the grand pinnacles of Chimney Rock rising over the endless plains, and not long after that, we saw Courthouse Rock and Scott's Bluff. Even the barren desert had unexpectedly wondrous curves and surprising colors, reds and greens and yellows.

Every day was much the same, beginning with a chilly and often rainy morning spent trying to start a fire to cook with and eating cold food if that was impossible. If it wasn't raining, the sun was beating down on us. No matter the temperature, the high winds never seemed to abate. We rode in the wet or stiflingly hot wagons, or walked in the mud or dust, and though the days seemed endless, darkness would always come sooner than we expected, and we never traveled as far as we hoped.

The next morning, the women would again try to start fires, and if successful, would cook over them. Cooking over open fires was a new experience for most of us, and we'd often end up eating black cinders mixed in with our food, but at the end of a long, hard day, it would always taste good anyway.

Mother tried at first to keep up appearances, but eventually she settled on one black dress, which trailed in the dust and constantly needed to be mended. Her one vanity was a cameo brooch she wore at her throat. I, too, settled on one dress, and though mine started off a more colorful blue, it soon looked as black as Mother's.

There were an endless number of rivers to cross, all of them different, but all depressingly similar. When one blocked our way, we'd first have to unload the wagons. A few of the wagon beds were watertight, sealed with tar from the barrels that hung from their sides. That smell, the smell of the tar, is one that has never left me. I can smell it even now.

We would then launch these wagon beds into the river, reload them, attach a rope to each side, and laboriously pull the makeshift rafts back and forth across the river until all the supplies were on the other side. Then all the wagons would have to be reassembled and the contents loaded back up.

It was the women who did most of the loading and unloading, the men who made the perilous crossings. It still frightens me to think of it. Our party was lucky; we didn't lose any of our menfolk to the rapids, but other parties had men swept away in full view of their horrified loved ones, and most times, there was nothing anyone could do to save them.

We often heard stories of the trail from the wagons ahead of us or the ones behind, for wagon trains were constantly passing each other, shedding members and adding new ones, depending on how fast or slow the travelers were going.

And always, there were graves by the side of the road. Sometimes there would be one, alone and forlorn; other times there would be a bunch of them. Often, the graves were dug up: by Indians or wolves, we never knew. Our fear of wolves began with those dug-up graves and grew with every passing mile, as if they were pursuing us in both life and death.

Led to the Slaughter

My diary entries from this time often consist of little more than a record of the miles traveled and the number of graves passed. If I sometimes seem unemotional about such things, it was just the way we were back then. To dwell on tragedy was to admit weakness, and there was no room for weakness on the trail. Everyone trudged on stoically, and everyone was equally in danger.

I open my diary at random:

June 5: Traveled sixteen miles today. Passed a new graveyard of ten graves. Father is sick, coughing, but refuses to rest.

June 7: A good day. Three dead cattle. Traveled twenty miles, and no gravesites. Father is still looking wan, but I heard him laugh today.

June 10: Traveled fifteen miles, passed a single grave. The marker was gone and the dirt was turned up. I saw a pretty red fabric, dusty and torn, peeking out of the dirt. Next to the grave was a piano, and I wondered if it was discarded because the member of the family who could play it was gone.

There are not only graveyards for humans, but for their possessions as well: stoves that had been dragged for hundreds of miles, now tipped on their sides beside the trail; dressers and cabinets and tables, undoubtedly precious heirlooms, now left to their fate.

June 12: Traveled eighteen miles. A dead mule, half eaten by animals. Passed four graves, new, with cairns for headstones. Patty seems to have caught Father's illness, but she is not so stoic as him. She asked to ride in the back of the wagon today, and Mother let her. Found an entire set of china plates, carefully placed on top of a flat rock as if on offer, but no one stopped to take them. I wonder how long they will sit there unbroken before some child dashes them against the rocks.

CHAPTER 9

The Reed Family, The Oregon Trail, Spring, 1846

After a discouraging day in which we traveled only eight miles, we camped by the banks of a wide, unnamed river. We were falling further and further behind on our schedule.

The elders gathered to discuss the matter, and we younger ones were left with the chores, or in my case, with trying to eavesdrop without being noticed. The wagons were arranged in a circle around the fire, and most of the men and women were sitting on the tongues, which was cleaner than sitting on the ground, though not as comfortable.

"We are still two weeks from Fort Laramie," Patrick Breen was saying, pacing next the bonfire. The smoke seemed to follow him wherever he went, and his reddened eyes were blinking frantically. "That pace will put us at the base of the passes in late October, which may be too late."

"I've been told it doesn't snow until late November," Jacob Donner said. "We should be able to make it."

"Then again," Breen said, "you never know with the weather, now do you?"

Father's voice boomed over the others. "What of the Hastings Cutoff? I have met Lansford Hastings, and he claims he has a route that will shave weeks off the journey."

"Then why has no one taken it, if I may ask?" This was the Widow Murphy, who was the head of a family that numbered thirteen. Her daughters were married, but there was no doubt who spoke for the family, and it wasn't any of the menfolk.

"Because they're too *timid*, that's why." This was Dutch Charley, who was the driver for the Wolfinger family. Because the German couple could not express themselves well in English, he had become their spokesman. "Most folks just keep following the other sheep on the longer route because it's safe. But nothing was ever gained in this world by playing it safe. I've read *Emigrant's Guide to Oregon and California* from beginning to end, and I tell you, this Hastings fellow knows what he's talking about."

"I would not mind saving a few miles of hard travel," said Lewis Keseberg, the man I'd encountered in the tent that day in Independence. He was also a German, well spoken, though he had a strong accent. He had a young wife and two small children, one of whom, a boy, had been born on the trail. One thing he did not have, I noticed for the first time, was a kennel of dogs. I wondered what had happened to them. I wondered if they had ended up in some of the evening meals.

Keseberg was an ugly man, not unlike Mister Lincoln, I suddenly realized. But whereas Mister Lincoln's ugliness concealed a kind spirit, Keseberg's disagreeable appearance was almost certainly the outward manifestation of the meanness within.

I had caught him staring at me more than once on the trail, then looking away when I glanced at him. He was wondering what I had seen back in Independence, I believe, which only made me wonder more myself. But there was more to that offensively speculative look. I was becoming a young woman and was well aware of what that stare meant. From the boys and younger men, I expected it, but not from a married man with a family.

"I intend to go to California, not Oregon," Father was saying. "The more I travel westward, the more I want to see it. We will have to split up at some point. I would rather not have to detour to Oregon first."

"Even so," the Widow Murphy said, "there is a well-beaten path to California, even if you do have to go a little ways north first."

"I begrudge any delay," Father said. "I do not believe the Mexicans can hold onto California much longer, but must soon relinquish it. I want to be there when that happens."

"Really, Mister Reed." Tamsen Donner, who didn't usually speak at these meetings, sounded exasperated. "I have no wish to arrive at my new home in the middle of a war. I say we should stick to the proven trails and not stray. We are making adequate time."

"Adequate?" Father exclaimed.

Tamsen ignored him. "I have to say," she continued, "if this is all the worse it gets, then most of the difficulties were in the getting started. We are on our way. Let's stick to the plan."

It wasn't a new argument. The adults had been wrangling back and forth over the route for days.

I yawned. Bayliss bumped me with his shoulder and I turned to look at him. He nodded toward one side of the camp. He got up, and a few discreet minutes later, I followed him.

It was a black night; the moon was but a sliver. I almost stumbled into him. He was standing so near me, I was glad of the darkness that hid my reddened cheeks.

"I wanted to get away from all that stuffy talk," he said in the softest voice I'd ever heard him use. A thrill went through me as I realized he was courting me. We were alone in the dark and he was courting me, and he was a handsome boy, if a little rude.

He reached out with his callused hand and took mine, and led me down the trail. We walked hand in hand for what seemed like miles. Once our eyes became accustomed to the darkness, the little bit of moonlight was enough for us to see the trail.

He wants to kiss me, I thought with a shiver of delight. *I want him to kiss me!* But I wasn't going to encourage him. I was enjoying the anticipation, waiting to see what he would do. To my great disappointment, he kept delaying the attempt. *Don't be afraid*, I wanted to say, but I knew it would embarrass him.

Eventually, we started back. Bayliss's shoulders were slumped, and I wished I could be the one to initiate a kiss. *No*, I decided. I was a little miffed that he hadn't made his move. *The first boy brave enough to try to kiss me is the first boy who will kiss me.*

I chattered nervously about not much at all, and he stayed silent. The fires of the camp were only a few hundred feet away when he whirled me around to face him. I caught my breath.

The howl of a wolf interrupted that nearly happy moment. It sounded as if it was only yards away. I suddenly realized that I had moved into Bayliss's arms and was clutching him tightly.

"What was that?" he whispered. I knew by the fright in his voice that the moment had passed and that my first kiss would have to wait.

"It sounded like it came from the German encampment," I whispered, not certain why we were whispering. Apparently, the big meeting had broken up and the different factions had gone back to their own camps. The Wolfingers and Kesebergs and their drivers, Dutch Charley, Augustus Spitzer, and Joseph Reinhardt, had set up camp together. Hardkoop, the Belgian, was also with them.

We hurried to the side of the trail so that we would bypass the stretch where it intersected the German camp. From a distance, we could hear the sound of voices and could see movement.

"The others are waiting for us." It sounded like Keseberg speaking. "They should all be gathered by now."

His voice was even more heavily accented than usual and more guttural, almost grunting. Their fire had gone out and I strained to see them in the dim moonlight. Why were they meeting in the dark?

"We can pull some of them away from the main group, I'm sure of it." It was Dutch Charley, and he too sounded different, as if he was snarling. They were moving in an odd way, circling each other, almost as if they were dancing. I could see their outlines, and it seemed they weren't wearing clothing—no, that wasn't it; it was more like their clothing was torn and hanging in shreds from their bodies.

"I think that pompous ass Reed is already half convinced," Keseberg said. "He speaks loudly and often. I think with a small nudge, he will end up do the convincing for us."

"I'll work to persuade him," said a new voice, and I thought it sounded like Spitzer. "Best let him take the blame when everything goes wrong. James Reed is the kind of man people like to blame: sure of himself and sure he knows what's best for everyone else."

There were grunts of agreement with Spitzer's words. I was furious. Bayliss grabbed my arm tightly, tugging me backward. I resisted, wanting to march in and set them straight about Father, to tell them that he only wanted what was best for everyone.

"Don't!" Bayliss whispered in my ear, holding me by both arms now, pulling at me insistently.

"Then we are decided," Keseberg said. "Time to eat, boys."

I saw several shapes lift something from the ground and start tearing it apart. I thought I saw limbs, oddly shaped. Had they shot a deer? No one had said anything about a kill. It was impolite for them not to have offered venison for the communal meal.

Then I caught a whiff of what they were eating and gagged. Whatever it was was long dead. Beside me, Bayliss covered his nose and mouth with one hand. We staggered away, not sure what we had just seen and heard, but unsettled by it nonetheless.

What had *we seen and heard?* I wondered as we neared the safety of our own camp. *Nothing, really. Nothing that can't be explained.* It had to have been the darkness, and the nervous energy from our interrupted moment of romance, that had cast things in a sinister light.

Late that night, just as I was about to fall asleep, I heard the howl of another wolf, this one sounding even closer, as if it was staring into my tent.

Father stirred and his hand drifted toward to his rifle, but he didn't awaken.

I dreamed that night of creatures that sounded like humans but were shaped like animals. I vowed to tell Father everything in the morning.

CHAPTER 10

The Reed family, Fort Laramie, 1846

"Father?" I hesitated at his elbow while he hitched the oxen to the wagons.

"Yes, Gina?" Only he called me Gina. Once Patty had called me that, and I'd nearly torn her hair out.

"I saw something yesterday," I began.

"Is this another one of your tall tales, Virginia?" he asked. His using my full name was a warning that he wasn't in the mood for tomfoolery.

Was it a tall tale? I wondered. *What did I hear, after all?* I asked myself. I had simply heard the Germans making the same arguments amongst themselves that they had made in front of the rest of the party. I'd been offended by how they'd talked about Father, but I saw no point in wounding his pride further.

The rest of what I thought I had seen and heard, the uneasy sensation that something unnatural was happening—I could not talk about that. Father would scoff. And also, I was a young girl who'd been on a moonlight walk with a boy unescorted, which I knew that Father would not approve of. Whatever I had sensed could be attributed to the wild imagination my mother was always telling me I had. My parents would say, "There goes Virginia, telling stories again."

"I saw a flock of crows attack a hawk," I said.

He nodded. "Some birds will do that, if their nest is threatened. But crows, they might do that just to be ornery." He smiled at me, and I tried my best to summon a genuine smile in return.

We lost another week, bogged down by the rains, before we reached Fort Laramie. It only took one wagon getting stuck in the mud to delay us all, and all too often, it was my family's big wagon that caused the problems. Sure enough, within sight of Fort Laramie, it slid into a culvert, and it took all the able-bodied men in the wagon train to pull it out.

Keseberg started shouting at Father, who, for once, didn't respond, but turned his back on the German. I saw Keseberg reach out to grab Father's shoulder, and for a moment I imagined his fingers becoming claws. Then Keseberg thought better of it and walked off.

Led to the Slaughter

It seems amazing now to realize that at that point, we were only halfway to our destination. As we reached the end of our stamina and our tempers grew short, the men argued and the women watched them fearfully. All along the way, there had been rumors of shortcuts, of ways to avoid the most difficult parts of the trail. At this moment, we were most susceptible to these illusions.

That night at the campfire, Mother sat with her head down, toying with the locket containing Frank's hair, as she did when she was worried. "We must get there soon," she said. The fire had died down, and I got up so I could stir the coals—and so I could get close enough to hear my parents' quiet conversation. "Mister Hastings told us we could save time if we took his route."

"Yes, Margret," Father said gently. He always talked in a low voice with Mother these days, as if afraid she would shatter if he spoke loudly. "But the route is unproven."

"I don't care," she said petulantly. She held the locket up to her lips and kissed it. It was a superstitious gesture that I noticed her making more and more often. "I want this journey to be over."

Father didn't answer. I had to move away before I was noticed, but after that night, he became the strongest proponent for the shortcut.

After a short rest in the safety of Fort Laramie, the main group of wagons went on without us while our smaller contingent decided to take the short detour southwest to Fort Bridger. We could delay the decision about which direction to go for a short time longer. It would cost us only a few days to go to Fort Bridger, and if we chose the new route, it might save us time. Or so we hoped.

* * *

After our brief dalliance, Bayliss seemed to be avoiding me. He wouldn't meet my eyes or converse with me. I did not know if he was embarrassed, or whether he disliked me, or... I didn't know what to think. Was he ashamed of having shown fear in front of me? Surely he didn't think I cared that he'd been frightened, for what kind of fool would not have been?

I spent more than one afternoon lying in the back of our wagon, dreaming of another walk with Bayliss, imagining how it would have been if we hadn't heard that wolf howl. If only he would speak to me, or even smile in my direction. But he was usually nowhere to be seen, and when we crossed paths, he didn't acknowledge me.

* * *

I walked beside our huge wagon most mornings, because I liked the smell of the new dawn. On our first day out of Fort Laramie, I sensed someone walking up next to me and glanced over to see that it was a handsome young man I had begun noticing a few days before.

"My name is Jean Baptiste Trudeau," he said, giving his name a good French twist, though I never heard him speak a word of his native tongue, and the more I spoke to him, the more his accent faded. I suppose he had hoped to intrigue me.

Without thinking why, I looked around to see if Bayliss was near. The wagon he was driving was far ahead of us, so my conversation with Jean could not be overheard. I still felt a twinge of guilt, as if I already understood that this new boy in my life was going to be important.

Had I been a year older, I would perhaps have flirted with Jean Baptiste—or perhaps I would have given him the cold shoulder. At thirteen years old, I was already considered a young lady, and I would soon be fourteen. But I was still young enough not to play games, and I gave him a straightforward smile. "I am Virginia Reed.

"I know," Jean said, then added bluntly, "We should not take this new route. You should tell your father so."

I could not hide a frown at this. "What do you know of it, sir?" I asked, quickening my pace and hoping he'd fall behind. "Father is an expert on the Oregon Trail."

"I worked for a man at Fort Laramie," Jean said breathlessly, catching up. "A Mister Bryant. He was a reporter, and he checked out the Hastings Cutoff on horseback and found it to be unused and unusable for wagons. He said that if we stick to the regular route, it will be difficult, but if we stray from it, it will be impossible."

"Then why did he not speak up?" My voice was shrill with both alarm and irritation as I faced him, heedless of the rumbling wagons creeping past. "Why did he not warn us?"

Jean stopped too, frowning. "He said he was going to leave cautionary letters. Perhaps he forgot."

Or someone intercepted the messages, I thought. It seemed suspicious, and for some reason, an image of Keseberg's shrewd, calculating face popped into my mind. I couldn't imagine why he would steal the letters, but I suspected him nevertheless.

I wished I could talk to Bayliss. I wanted to know if he had heard the same thing I had when we were hidden outside the German camp. Was it my imagination that they were trying to delay us? That the route they wanted us to take—for Father to advocate—was some kind of trap?

But Bayliss still wasn't speaking to me, and I couldn't fathom why Keseberg would want such a thing.

There was no help for it. We were on our way. No one was going to listen to a thirteen-year-old girl and a destitute orphan boy. *Besides,* I told myself, *it will not be too late to join the regular trail even after we reach Fort Bridger.* We would have gone out of our way by only a few days. I suppose that even then, I hoped the adults would make the right decision. I decided to speak with Father at the first opportunity.

I promptly forgot that resolution, so enamored was I with this new and intriguing young man. Jean Baptiste was not as tall as Bayliss, nor as lanky, but he had fine, sharp features—a narrow nose and sharp chin—and dark brown eyes. He was the handsomest boy I had ever seen. Furthermore, he was a mature and worldly sixteen years old. We seemed to understand each other from the start, though we came from very different backgrounds. He was an orphan, and was already an experienced traveler of the West, having come from New Mexico for the trip to California.

As Bayliss continued to ignore me, I found myself seeking out Jean Baptiste's company more and more. We were of like mind, both seeing the world through stories. We told each other tales around the campfire at night, making each other laugh with our outrageous imaginings.

He told wild stories about Indians and the trails out West that I suspected were fanciful, but he didn't mean any harm by it. I liked that he told stories—it made me feel less alone, and he never shamed me for my own exaggerations.

Three days out of Fort Laramie, the families of the wagon train decided, almost independently of one another, it seemed, to stop for a full Sunday. The weather was mild, and it appeared we were getting back on schedule. We were perhaps a little behind, but not so much so that we couldn't catch up.

We camped by a lake where the mosquitoes were so bad that the only relief to be found was in hiding beneath a blanket or walking until you got away from them. Jean and I found ourselves on the other side of the small lake, where we were forced to climb a hill, as the banks of the lake were impassible because of the thick bushes that grew there. For the first time in days, we were out of sight of the wagon train.

We both stopped dead in our tracks at the same moment, staring in stunned amazement at the majestic vista before us. More than at any other time during the long journey, I had a true sense of the immensity of the wilderness. On the other side of the hill rose distant mountains, and leading up to them were dark foothills, rolling like the waves of an ocean, with huge valleys between them, each large enough for our wagon train to become lost in. There were mists in those mountains, even on this hot day. I sensed that man had never walked on some of those hills.

As we contemplated this soaring vastness, Jean Baptiste's hand reached out for mine, and I clasped it eagerly, my heart giving a sudden leap. We were but two small humans confronting the enormity of nature. As we continued to gaze around us, our fingers interlaced and his hand slowly squeezed mine.

This is the moment for us, he seemed to be saying with his touch. *These are the sights we must never forget.*

We heard the howls of the wolves before we saw them. There is a primitive instinct in man that knows from whence danger is approaching, and we quickly spotted the animals. They were running through the small glade below us, moving so fast through the undergrowth that I couldn't count them. *A dozen or more*, I thought. They were mostly gray or brown, with a few of mixed colors. I felt an instinctive rush of fear and a desire to flee, but Jean held me still with another squeeze of his hand.

"Don't make any sudden movements," he whispered. "They will leave us alone if we leave them alone." He was trying hard to sound calm, but I heard the nervousness in his words.

The lead wolf caught sight of us and stopped, the pack coming to a halt around it. With great casualness, the wolves sat on their haunches and gazed up at us. And then, from the other side of the glade, there came a lone wolf, emerging silently out of the brush. He was bigger than the others, with a solid black pelt. He stopped and bayed to get the pack's attention. The lead wolf responded with a low growl and the others joined him, their fur bristling and fangs showing. Fear washed over me as I realized that nothing would stop these creatures from tearing us apart if they chose.

The lone wolf was silent now, seeming nonchalant. He sat with his tongue lolling.

The pack attacked en masse, no doubt expecting the stranger to run. But he leapt up and streaked toward the other wolves, and all at once he was in their midst, and their growls turned to yelps. A big gray wolf flew through the air and hit a tree. Another wolf lay unmoving on the ground, its neck at a strange angle. The pack's swarming attack fell apart, individual wolves flying in every direction. It seemed there must be more than a single wolf battling them. The lone wolf appeared to be in several places at once, moving faster than my eyes could follow.

The pack broke ranks and ran, until only their leader stood facing the strange wolf. He growled one last time, then lowered his head. His tail drooped and he rolled onto his back. The larger wolf trotted over and sniffed at the belly of the submissive wolf dismissively, then raised his head and howled in triumph.

Then the lone wolf started back the way he had come. Before he left the glade, he stopped, turned, and looked directly at me. His eyes were a bright orange, almost red, and there was an almost human intelligence in them. *I know you are there*, the creature seemed to be saying, *and I don't care. I will attend to you later.* He raised his muzzle into the air and howled, and the sound seemed to strike directly at my heart and mind, stopping both for an instant. From the distance came other howls, answering. With one last toss of his head, the wolf loped out of sight.

We walked back to camp in silence. Jean Baptiste held my hand the whole way.

CHAPTER 11

Virginia Reed, Fort Bridger, 1846

We reached Fort Bridger a few days later. There, our party had to make a final decision about which path to take. We could go back to the main route through South Pass in Wyoming and north to Fort Hall, and from there, take the well-established trail to California. This was the safer and better-known route. Or, we could take the new, unproven shortcut. On the map, the former option appeared to take us far out of our way, whereas the latter, which ran due west, looked as if it would cut weeks off our trip.

The temptation to follow Lansford Hastings's new route was almost irresistible.

All the adults were on edge, so much so that the children noticed and grew subdued. It was dangerous to be traveling so late in the season, whichever trail we took. We needed to cross the mountains soon, or we would be forced to wait until spring. I suspected that most of those in the party did not have the money, supplies, or inclination to spend another season on the trail. Most felt there was no choice but to push on.

I trusted that the adults—especially Father—would arrive at the right decision and deliver us safely to our destination.

* * *

That evening, our leaders gathered to make the final decision. The fateful meeting was held inside the walls of Fort Bridger. They called it a fort, but it was barely more than a hovel surrounded by crude mud bulwarks. It was owned by Jim Bridger and his partner, Pierre Louis Vasquez, who ran a small trading post within it.

As he had many times before, Father spoke strongly in favor of the Hastings Cutoff. I wanted to stop him, to take him aside and tell him what I'd heard, especially when I saw Keseberg exchanging a smirk with another German, but I hesitated to interrupt Father in front of the others, especially when he was so certain of his position.

The argument seemed to go on forever, and my attention started to stray. I looked for Bayliss in the crowd, but he was nowhere to be seen.

Jean Baptiste caught my eye, then rolled his own in exaggerated exasperation at how long the meeting was taking.

The adults' discourse was insistent and intense, but as the discussion
dragged on, their voices became merely a droning in my ears. Then, suddenly, some of those voices were being raised in anger, and I began to pay
closer attention.

"We should go with the others," Hardkoop was arguing loudly. He was
an older man, and his Belgian accent made it hard to understand him. He
had missed the chance to join the bigger wagon train, and now he was stuck
with us.

"You old coward," Keseberg snapped at him. "Why didn't you leave
with the others, if you wanted to go that way?"

"You know why!" Hardkoop yelled. "I gave all my money to you. You
will not give it back!"

"I would never have agreed to carry your old carcass if I had known you
were so feeble," Keseberg growled, looming over the smaller Hardkoop as
if ready to strike him down. Keseberg was a big, harsh man, and as the trip
went on, he was becoming harsher.

Father stepped between them, and Keseberg backed away. I was never
so proud of Father as at that moment. He looked so tall and handsome, and
had such a commanding presence compared to these petty-seeming, bicker-
ing men.

"I believe we should take the alternate route," Father reiterated. "Mister
Hastings has promised to meet us along the trail and show us the way. We
will save weeks."

Tamsen Donner spoke up. "I do not trust that man," she said. "I think
he's nothing more than an adventurer." Her husband frowned at her, but
she ignored him. Several of the other women were listening and nodding
silently. Her servant girl, Eliza, was sitting next to her, wide-eyed at her mis-
tresses' forwardness.

"What do you think, Mister Bridger?" George Donner asked. "How
passable is this route?"

Old Jim Bridger spoke up. "I think you will find it an easy trip," the rug-
ged-looking mountain man said. And who could doubt him? You could tell
just by looking at him that he had a wealth of wilderness experience. His
face was wrinkled and weathered, with lively blue eyes whose intensity was
piercing when he looked at you directly.

Of course, if any of us had thought about it, we would have realized his
"fort" would make much more profit if more emigrants chose the southern
route.

"There are few hostile Indians left in the area," he said in a cracked, dry,
but confident voice. "Best of all, there is water along the way."

"What about the desert?" Breen asked, tension making his voice hard.

"I admit, there are two small deserts," Bridger said. "But you should be able to cross those in less than two days."

"If that is true," said Breen, "why haven't others taken this route before us?

"They have," Bridger said. "As a matter of fact, Mister Hastings left Fort Bridger with a group of forty wagons only ten days ago. You need only follow his tracks to get where you want to go."

Doubt still filled the air. I could see that even Father sensed that something wasn't quite right. Bridger was making it sound too easy.

"You will save 350 miles." Bridger dropped the words into the ensuing silence like meat to a pack of hungry dogs.

The men exchanged glances, and the women looked momentarily hopeful.

"If it is so easy, why has it taken so long to be discovered?" Breen persisted, raising the question that was on everyone's minds.

There was some muttering at that, and the enthusiasm that had begun to build for the new route began to dissipate. Once again, it appeared as if there would be a stalemate. Without a nearly unanimous decision, we would probably turn back to the established trail. No one was fool enough to strike out on his or her own.

It was at that moment of indecision that Charles Stanton stepped forward. He had been with the wagon train almost from the beginning, and had hired three wagons to carry goods westward. He was a prosperous businessman, plump and a little older than most of the men, but with great stamina. He was also a very thoughtful fellow, rarely expressing an opinion without strong, hard evidence to back him up, so when he spoke, the others listened.

"My goods are growing stale on this trek; some of the merchandise is beginning to rot," he said forcefully. "I simply cannot wait to take an extra month to get to my destination. I say we take a chance on the shortcut."

That seemed to sway the tide of opinion. It wasn't long before the rest of the family groups decided to join the expedition through Hastings Cutoff.

* * *

"Well, that's it, then," Father announced, breaking the silence that had followed the party's decision. "All that is left is to name our leader." He propped a booted foot up on the log next to Tamsen Donner, who looked affronted. "What say you?" He nodded at George Donner as if expecting a show of support. His face fell when no one spoke up. There was an awkward silence.

At this point in the journey, the party was divided into two main camps. There were the German families, who stuck together, and there was everyone else, and no clear leader had emerged.

Outside these two groups was the Reed family. Father seemed to feel that our family was different from the others, and everyone else seemed to share that feeling—but for a different reason. There was no doubt in Father's mind that he was the best equipped to lead. There was no doubt in anyone else's mind that he was overbearing and overconfident. The slow progress of our giant wagon had often delayed the entire party, and more than once, some of our fellow pioneers had threatened to leave us behind. Father had antagonized too many people. I knew that he was the right man for the job, but that didn't seem to matter. It was obvious that few would support a German leader, but neither would they pick Father.

Finally, Jacob Donner, in his diffident way, suggested that his brother, George, should be elected leader. From the relief that swept through the others, it was clear that this was a popular choice.

For reasons I couldn't explain, I did not trust George Donner. He came across as good-natured and easygoing, but I saw something cold and calculating in his eyes. It was the first time I realized that people will trust the friendly more than the stalwart, the mild-mannered more than the righteous. The choice, however, was not mine to make.

It wasn't even put to a vote, the decision was so clear.

Our leader having been decided by the adults, we were to leave early the next morning.

Everyone went back to his or her own camps, resolute and hopeful now that a route had finally been decided on. When I returned to the shadows of our great coach, I found Father alone. He was eating some of the pie that Mother had managed to bake in her spare Dutch oven. She and Patty had spent hours picking bucketsful of berries in the gullies around the camp.

Mother had gone to bed early, as usual, joined by Patty, as was her wont. Tommy and Jimmy were underfoot of the younger drivers and single men, who were drinking hard cider around their own fire. The boys had become something of a good-luck charm to them.

Father was stirring the coals with a frown on his face, the piece of pie neglected in his hand. He glanced up and gave me a tired smile. "Hello, Gina."

I sat at his feet. "They are fools, Father."

He looked ready to deny it, then shook his head ruefully. "Being right isn't always enough, Gina. Remember that. A pleasant and agreeable demeanor can take you much farther in this life. As you likely know by now, being spirited isn't always appreciated either, especially in a woman."

He saw that I was about to take offense and quickly added, "You have a pleasant demeanor *and* a strong will, dear girl, which is the best combination of all. As for myself, well... I never learned to say the right things."

His compliments gave me a warm glow. I leaned closer to him, and he reached out and put his hand on my head. It was comforting, something I'd been missing. Sometimes I was too independent for my own good.

"Father?" In that moment of closeness, I found myself daring to speak of my worries.

There must have been something in my tone, because he looked me in the eye and said sternly, "Yes, Virginia?"

"Can we not wait for another group to join?"

"Why would we do that?" he asked.

"I don't trust Keseberg and the others."

"Don't trust them?" he asked. "Whatever do you mean, Gina?"

"I... I don't think they are... quite human," I said hesitantly.

A look of disappointment crossed his face, which I could not bear. "I've tried to teach you, Virginia," he said, and sighed. "Just because they are foreigners doesn't mean they are not deserving of respect. It's true that we don't always agree; but remember, all men are equal, and should be treated equally."

"I mean, Father," I persisted, "I don't think they are *men* at all!"

"Not men?" He looked at me with puzzlement, which quickly turned into exasperation. "I thought we were done with your wild flights of imagination, Virginia. You are getting much too old for that."

I wanted to tell him what I had seen—or what I thought I had seen—but the disappointment in his voice stopped the words on my lips. "I'm sorry, Father. They just... make me uncomfortable."

He softened immediately. "I understand, Virginia. They are rough men. But we couldn't join another party even if we wanted to. I think we are the last group on the trail. We will simply have to try to get along."

"Yes, Father." I was far too old to climb into his lap, as I used to do, but that didn't keep me from longing to. Instead, I sat next to him and leaned my head against his shoulder. Sitting with him thus, I felt secure, and was almost relieved that he would not have to be the leader of the wagon train, and could spend more time with his family. As long as Father was with us, I felt I had nothing to fear.

I must have fallen asleep there by the campfire, leaning against him. In the morning, I found myself snug beneath my blankets, where Father must have lain me down so gently that I had not awoken.

CHAPTER 12

Personal notes of Jacob Donner, Secretary of the Wolfenrout, July 4, 1846

"I hope this is the right thing to do," George said as we walked through the camp this evening. We halted our westward progress early in the day for once, in observance of the Fourth of July holiday. Everyone was dressed in his or her best. Sweets had been extricated from traveling cases, saved by mothers and fathers for just this occasion. Some of the younger men were creating fireworks displays out of the gunpowder they carried, and the younger children ran around excitedly.

The atmosphere was festive, but George was too worried to appreciate it.

"You mean the detour?" I said. "We all agreed that we wanted to slow the wagon train down, and this is the best way to do it."

"But it is counter to what I'm trying to accomplish," he said, sounding exasperated. "I believe that we should live in peace with humans. It seems an ill omen that we are leading them to disaster."

"It was the price of getting the others to go along," I said. "If you want enough Wolfen to attend the Foregathering to make it a success, you need not only those who believe as you do, but at least a few of those who disagree as well. Otherwise, it will appear to be a scheme by one faction."

George stared at the ground, frowning. It was strange to behold, as he is so practiced at keeping up the appearance of amiability that I rarely see him with a downcast or disagreeable countenance. "Perhaps," he said. "Or perhaps I should never have called the Foregathering of the Clans in the first place; but I saw no choice. We have to find a way to live among mankind or we will be destroyed."

"So why do you doubt?" I asked. It wasn't like him to second-guess his decisions.

"Because once you get all the Wolfen together, there is no telling what will happen," he said. "Imagine the Americans convening a new Constitutional Convention! What a disaster that would be!"

I laughed. It is so like George to pay such close attention to human politics. Most Wolfen barely pretend to be human, doing just enough to pass as normal folks. Many of us still think of mankind as nothing more than livestock; certainly, we have little interest in human institutions like religion or politics.

"Perhaps I should be satisfied with the rules being voluntary," George mused. "That's served us well, most of the time."

A band of children ran between us, screaming, Wolfen and human mixed together. I saw my Mary and Isaac among them, as well as George's girls Frances and Georgia. Some Wolfen families don't tell their young ones what they are until they are close to their first Turning. As far as these children are concerned, they are all the same.

I could see that George was thinking along the same lines.

"I especially regret bringing our families," he said. "I didn't even tell Tamsen why we are on this trip. She believes we are simply moving to the West."

I, on the other hand, have discussed these matters at some length with my wife Elizabeth, who is a strong supporter of George's views. I suspect she'd rather live as a human and never change again, if it was up to her.

"Well, it is too late now, brother," I said, trying to sound cheerful. But we are all of us feeling that something is amiss. For hundreds of years, we have lived by the rules of the Foregathering—well, most of us, anyway. It has never occurred to us that they could change.

"What's he doing?" I heard George murmur.

"What?"

He nodded toward the giant Reed wagon. In the growing darkness, standing perfectly still, was a tall Wolfen. Crouching by the campfire in front of the wagon, cooking alone while the rest of her family enjoyed the festivities, was young Virginia Reed.

"That's Keseberg," I said. The instant his name came out of my mouth, I realized what he was planning to do.

My brother realized it as well. "*Idiot*," George breathed.

As Keseberg bent down, bunched up his muscles, and started to transform, George took off for the campfire at a near-run, speaking loudly as he went. I followed on his heels.

"There you are!" he called out, nearly shouting.

Keseberg froze, then faded into the shadows.

Virginia looked up, puzzled. "Sir?"

"I've been wanting to talk to you, young lady," George continued, lowering his voice as he realized how loud it was. I could tell he was trying desperately to think of something to say.

"Sir?" she repeated, even more confused.

"Virginia… I saw your disappointment when I was elected leader of the wagon train instead of your father," George said, gaining confidence as he went along. "I want to tell you that I think your father is a fine man and would have made a good leader."

She smiled brightly, though the puzzlement never completely left her eyes. "He is a good man," she said.

"Yes... yes, he is," George said, running out of steam. He turned to me. "Isn't he, Jacob?"

"Errr... yes," I stuttered, half alarmed and half amused at my brother's bumbling intercession. "A fine man indeed."

"Well, then! Uh, that's all I had to say... " George trailed off. As neither of us could think of anything further to say, we turned abruptly and walked away, with Virginia Reed staring after us. My brother's face was red, whether from embarrassment or anger, I wasn't quite sure.

"Where is that confounded Wolfen?" he growled. "Keseberg has gone too far."

Whatever Keseberg had been planning—perhaps to snatch Virginia and take her into the woods, never to be seen again—he'd apparently given up. We both knew that the German had been obsessing over the girl since she'd interrupted the Wolfenrout weeks ago. George had warned him then to leave her alone. "That's a brave little girl," George had said. "I don't want her harmed." Keseberg had just shrugged, as if it made no difference to him one way or the other.

We found him back at the German camp, strolling along nonchalantly as if nothing had happened.

George didn't hesitate: he walked up to Keseberg and pushed him roughly against the back of a wagon. "I warned you, you damned fool!" he shouted. "Leave Virginia Reed alone! We need James Reed to be on our side. If he goes along with us, the whole train will follow."

"Who says I was going to do anything?" Keseberg said innocently.

"I saw it in your eyes," George growled. "It looked to me as if you were starting to Turn, and as though you didn't care whether anyone saw you. You cannot do that, Keseberg. You must quit acting Wolfen until it is safe!"

"Quit acting Wolfen?" Keseberg echoed. With a sardonic expression, he looked around at his followers, who were watching from the campfire. The men chuckled. "But that's just it, Donner. That's your problem. You've quit acting Wolfen. Perhaps you've forgotten how."

George snorted dismissively and turned away. One thing my brother has never lacked is confidence in his Wolfen abilities. We were walking away when Keseberg called out after him, "Donner? That's the last time you'll ever push me. You hear? Next time you'll answer for it."

We kept walking.

"That man almost makes me long for the old days," George said beneath his breath. "I swear, a good old-fashioned fight to the death, and half our problems would be solved."

Or all of them, I thought. The problem is, I am not so sure that George can win a duel with Keseberg. I didn't say that out loud, of course.

CHAPTER 13

Virginia Reed, Hastings Cutoff, July 15, 1846

At first, everything seemed fine. The trail was rougher than promised, but we made good time. On some of the steeper slopes, I had to grab at nearby branches as I lost my footing, and I was certain that the men behind me got a good look at my undergarments. I tried not to blush.

When we reached the foothills, instead of finding an easy trail, we were forced to construct our own path over difficult and steep terrain, sometimes mere inches from steep drop-offs. We all helped pitch stones out of our path and down the mountain, and the men struggled to lever huge boulders out of the way.

While we were thus slowed, a final group of wagons joined us, led by the Graves family, whose lead teamster was a man named John Snyder. "We were the last to leave Independence," he declared.

Those of us who had left late in the season looked at each other uneasily.

"We'll be fine as long as we get over the mountains by November," Father said confidently. More and more, he was stepping into the leadership vacuum left by George Donner, who had grown strangely silent and withdrawn, so different from his earlier good-natured manner.

"Then we'd best get on with it," said Charles Stanton. "The sooner we continue, the sooner we arrive."

* * *

I started to spend more and more of my evenings with Jean Baptiste. He was full of stories, and though many of them were questionable, it couldn't be denied that he had traveled more widely than I. He'd been alone since he was a young boy, and he seemed much more mature than most young men I knew.

One night, Jean and I wandered away into the woods. There, he kissed me. My first kiss! He was bold, not hesitant like Bayliss. I let his hand linger perhaps a little too long on my blossoming bosom.

I was thrilled. Having my first real kiss was an experience I'd been longing for since we'd left Springfield. I don't suppose I thought more of it than that: as something to experience, to savor, but not necessarily a promise of anything more. I'm not sure how Jean Baptiste or Bayliss thought of it. I suspect they had higher expectations than I.

We floated back into camp. It was quiet; everyone was either resting or off foraging.

Over the next few days, I caught Bayliss looking my direction. At first, I looked away, vaguely ashamed. *But why?* I wondered. *What do I owe him?* After all, Bayliss had been avoiding me ever since our ill-fated moonlight walk.

Nevertheless, one night I sat down next to him as he sat staring into his campfire. "Hello, Bayliss," I said. "Can we talk?"

He got up and walked away.

* * *

The next day, I found myself walking behind the Donner family wagon that Jean Baptiste was driving. We were slowly climbing a precipitous slope, which had been steepening so gradually that none of us had noticed that the incline had become dangerous.

As it happened, Bayliss was driving the wagon immediately following Jean's. I was walking between the two of them. This infelicitous confluence of the young men in my life had had me wavering unhappily all morning. I was wondering if I should approach Bayliss again. I felt an obligation to tell him about Jean Baptiste. It was clear that Bayliss knew about our relationship by then, but he hadn't heard it from me personally. I felt I owed him an explanation; but even more, I still wanted to be friends with him. I liked him. He'd been supportive of me when I'd most needed it.

Why, then, had I chosen Jean Baptiste? Because I felt an ever-growing fear of the future, and Jean was much better company—and therefore a much better distraction. He was jovial and told funny stories. It was a shallow reason, perhaps, but just as the party preferred amiable George Donner above Father because of his temperament, I chose Jean Baptiste because he was easier to get along with.

Lost in thought, I was barely aware of the steepening slope.

Jean's wagon started slipping backward on the dry sand. One of the oxen fell to its knees, and the other beasts were thrown off their strides. The oxen grunted and made lowing sounds I'd never heard before, as if they were frightened.

It felt as if the entire mountain was moving, and my body seemed to lurch in sympathy with the motion. I caught my breath and heard a strange, panicky sound emerge from my throat. To the left of the path, a sheer drop-off plummeted into a steep gorge, the treetops at the bottom reminding me of daggers.

Jean shouted at the oxen, his whip cracking. The wagon lurched and started to slide sideways, almost going over the precipice. It came to a stop inches from the lead oxen of Bayliss's wagon.

Bayliss motioned urgently to me and I ran to him with my heart in my mouth. Jean's wagon had nearly slid into me, I realized when I was finally able to think straight. I would have gone over the edge.

Bayliss handed me the reins. "Hold the wagon right here," he said sternly. Glowering, he clambered out of the seat and went to the back of the wagon, and I could hear the sound of something being slammed home. The wagon, which had been sliding slowly backward, stopped moving. Then Bayliss marched past me, his boots digging into the steep trail as he assessed the position of Jean's wagon.

"Block the wheels," he commanded, "or we'll end up at the bottom of the ravine."

"I've not been told to do that," Jean Baptiste answered, a stubborn look on his face I'd never seen before.

"Block the wheels, you damn fool!" Bayliss shouted. As if to reinforce his words, the big wagon slid another couple of inches and teetered on the edge of the cliff. Bayliss hurried to the back of the Donner wagon to block the wheels himself.

Jean jumped down, red-faced. "You have no right to interfere," he said angrily.

"I have every right to protect my wagon," Bayliss said, squaring off with him. "Even if I have to do your job as well as my own."

Both of them glanced my way, as if trying to gauge whose side I was taking. It was only then that I realized the fight was about more than the safety of the wagons.

"What's going on here?" It was Father. He was nearly sliding down the slope in his haste. The scree and gravel of the hill was held together by sand, which crumbled at the slightest touch.

"Their oxen are too weak to pull their wagon up the slope!" Bayliss said. "I blocked the wheels, but we need to use the pulleys!"

"That's for Mister Donner to decide!" Jean shouted back.

Father turned around and assessed the situation. He examined the four oxen pulling the Donner wagon, then hopped up on the tail, untied the canvas, and looked inside.

He also examined our wagon. In the middle of the inspection, he glanced up and noticed me in the driver's seat. He was clearly surprised, but said nothing of it.

"We will unload both wagons," he announced finally. "We can come back later for the supplies. Once they're unloaded, we may not need to use the pulleys and ropes."

It is a good solution, I thought admiringly. By including his own wagon as part of the problem, he was avoiding casting blame.

Once the wagons were unloaded, the oxen managed to make it up the hill, and the problem was resolved.

But I noticed that the solution didn't do much to mollify either Jean Baptiste or Bayliss.

* * *

Until this part of the journey, the trails ahead of us had been clearly marked and easy to follow. There was something reassuring in seeing the ruts of wagon wheels, the stumps of trees cut down for firewood, the remains of old campfires, the boulders and timbers that had been moved aside by other wagon trains.

Now it was as if we were blazing a brand-new trail—which, if we had but known it, we were in fact doing. We had been told that Lansford Hastings had left Fort Bridger ten days before with another wagon train, leaving handwritten instructions nailed to the trees for us to follow. We were following their trail into Weber Canyon.

It was the most difficult terrain we had yet faced.

We found a letter from Hastings, hastily scrawled, telling us to wait for him, that he'd show us a new and better route. We wasted two valuable days waiting. Finally, it was decided that Charles Stanton, William Pike, and Father would hike on ahead and see if they could meet our guide along the trail.

Strange as may seem, those of us left behind were still in good spirits when Father and his two companions trudged off, in spite of the previous few days of difficulty and the looming winter. Having days off from the grueling routine of the trail was a little like playing hooky from school.

I would have enjoyed it more if Jean Baptiste and Bayliss weren't acting like spoiled children. They glared at each other if either of them went near me. As a result, they both stayed away, hovering just out of earshot. I tried to mediate, but it was hopeless. The tension in the air made it impossible to have a discussion with them. I shook my head in disgust and used the time to write in my journal.

One night, as I sat with my family at dinner, I realized that for many weeks, I had paid little attention to my siblings. Mother was tight-lipped around me, which was the only sign of how angry she was with me. *I've been off on a cloud*, I realized.

The boys were still rambunctious, but they had taken on a more serious demeanor. They spent most of their time with the younger drivers, who had taken them under their wing. Patty had grown up a great deal in the months on the trail. She was only nine, but was acting like a responsible young woman—more responsible than I, in fact. As I watched my sister help Mother prepare the meal, I realized that I had been completely selfish. Patty had been doing my chores as well as hers.

Led to the Slaughter

"I'm sorry, Mother," I blurted out. "I should be helping you more."

She didn't respond, just continued to ladle the soup into bowls in stony silence. Patty looked surprised, and both of the boys were wide-eyed. Father was staring off into the distance, not really there—planning the next day's route, perhaps, or dreaming of California.

Then Mother's manner softened. "You will not always have the boys chasing you," she said. "I don't mind—and Patty likes to help. As long as you help your father, Virginia, I forgive you."

Tears came to my eyes, and as I went to bed that night, I vowed to do better. But soon, Jean Baptiste came a-calling, and all my promises vanished into thin air.

The days of rest passed quickly. It wasn't only us pioneers who needed the break: the livestock and the horses needed to be rested and grazed. The trip was far more arduous than any of us had expected, despite the warnings, for the warnings had always been presented cheerfully, as if they were of no consequence. The truth was far different.

Every morning, we women rose early, started the fires, and set the kettles to boiling for coffee and morning beans—those of us who still had them. Then we milked the cows and baked the bread, and that was only the beginning. Our days sometimes seemed to end just as we were starting them. We baked and cleaned, hauled water from the streams, gathered firewood, aired the bedding, and sewed up rents in the canvas, and when all these tasks were done and we finally had some leisure time, it was already dark and time to retire.

We'd go to bed with sore backs, for the day's chores required stooping to wash clothes or draw water, and bending over open fires to retrieve burned food and set it back in the pot, the smoke in our eyes and the cold at our backs. We had no chairs or tables to help ease our work.

In this desolate land, we scrounged what food we could and prepared whatever was available. Cooking seemed to take up just as much time as it had when we had plenty. Mosquitoes found us and feasted on us, so at least some creatures in this awful land were eating well.

Would that we had rested less often! Idle days were a luxury we didn't have. We had spent a week resting at Fort Bridger, and would spend several days at the base of the Wasatch Mountains, and yet another week at the foot of the Sierra Nevada. I wish now that we had pushed on, despite our weariness, despite the pleasure it gave us to sit idle.

Perhaps if we had gritted our teeth and pressed on, everything that happened later might have been avoided. But we trusted the advice of those who were supposed to know best, and who we thought wished us well.

64

CHAPTER 14

Diary of Charles Stanton, August 6, 1846

Had I chosen with whom to travel on such a difficult journey, I would have chosen men in the exact mold of my two companions, James Reed and Bill Pike.

I am aware that Reed isn't well liked by the rest of the party, but I've had dealings with men like him many times in my business career. Gruff, honest, and hardworking, such men are reliable and dependable, though not the liveliest of companions in the evenings after work. While they are abed resting up for the next day's labor, I can be found with our less reliable but more spirited peers, drinking and carousing the night away without a worry in the world.

Bill Pike belongs more in the latter camp. He is neither as well off as Reed nor as dour, and he enjoys a good drink. He is an excellent traveling companion, easygoing and energetic.

Me? As it happens, I have an appetite for both hard work and hard play. I like both men.

I am well aware that my arguments probably swayed the Donner Party to take the Hastings Cutoff. What I didn't reveal was my own doubts. In my long business career, I've also had dealings with men like Lansford Hastings, and I know that such men can either break you or make you rich. They are the men who make things happen—despite having a tendency, far too often, to be wrong. I had no choice but to gamble, for I am too far in debt to play it safe.

I've wagered everything I have on this trip. All my wealth is tied up in the trail-worn merchandise in my three wagons. Some of the perishables I'd hoped would be safely in California by now are already too far gone to save, though I made a small profit selling some to the other emigrants—though nothing like the kind of money I would have made in California.

By the time we started off on our little "shortcut," I was beginning to believe it was a mistake. The only question in my mind was whether it was a bigger mistake to turn back or to push on. Did I wish to survive, even if destitute, or did I wish to risk all and perhaps die trying?

It was probably too late to change routes anyway. I suspected I would have difficulty convincing the others to turn back. Once men such as James Reed set their minds on a task, it is nearly impossible to dissuade them.

Nevertheless, my misgivings grew as the route ahead of us was revealed. It was unforgiving terrain, with massive boulders and narrow paths cut off by sharp angles in the sheer cliffs. Fallen timbers and loose shale blocked the path. Steep gullies and waterfalls were around every corner. It was madness.

On the second day, we found Lansford Hastings nailing another one of his inadequate letters to a tree. He was a little man with an impressive mustache, a potbelly, and clothes that were designed more for the boardroom of a bank than for the dusty trail. He seemed surprised and a little alarmed to see us. While the others were talking, I pulled the note from the tree and read it: "Please continue on, I will meet you later with further instructions."

What is his game? I wondered. These notes were both reassuring and distressingly vague. They seemed to be designed to do nothing more than lure us farther on this impossible route.

As hard as it is to believe given our distrust of him, we were about to be bamboozled by the man yet again.

"Of course this isn't an adequate road, I never said it was," I heard him say in response to Reed's exasperated questioning. "I have found an easier route, believe me. Just ahead."

"Tell me, Hastings," Pike demanded, "have you ever gone this way before? With wagons?"

"As it happens," Hastings said, sounding offended, "I am nearly finished leading the Harlan-Young Party to the Humboldt River. But the route we took was too rough and would take you too long. I have, in fact, found a better route and have marked it for you."

"Why shouldn't we go the same way as the Harlan-Young wagon train?" Pike asked.

"You can if you wish. There is a fork up ahead, and if you wish to ignore my advice, you will see which route they took. However, I strongly urge you to take the new path I have marked."

"But their wagon train made it safely; surely we need only to follow them," Pike insisted.

"They did indeed make it, but it was a very time-consuming and exhausting trek," Hastings said. "We were late arriving at our destination. Indeed, I must hurry back. Therefore, I would encourage you to follow this new path I have laid out for you."

"Not so fast, you humbug!" Reed roared. "We've followed your advice at every turn, and yet we seem to be falling farther and farther behind."

Hastings waved his hand dismissively. "I assure you, sir, that you will reach California in plenty of time. Just continue following my instructions."

Reed was glowering. He too has put his reputation on the line, which I know is as valuable to him as my wagons full of goods are to me. He has also brought along his family, so he has loved ones to consider. As for me, I didn't care any more who was right or who was wrong. I only wanted out of this trap.

Hastings was mounting his mule before we realized he was trying to leave. We started to object, but he waved to us and trotted off. "See you in a few days, folks. Follow the path and you'll be fine!"

I wanted to take out my rifle and shoot him in the back. From the looks Pike and Reed were giving him, they had the same impulse. Then the fat little man rounded a curve and disappeared from sight.

Reed and Pike seemed defeated.

"I don't trust that man," Reed muttered. "I don't know what I saw in him."

"After what we've been through, none of us do," I said. "But we are already committed to this road, unless you wish to go back to Fort Bridger. Unless you wish to admit to the others that you have made a mistake."

Reed looked down at the ground as if looking for an answer in the pine needles and dust. He kicked out, and a rock went careening against the cliff face and then over the side of the ravine.

"What now?" asked Pike.

No one answered him. I sighed and turned to Reed. "Why don't you go on back to the main party and present them with the choices, Mister Reed?" I said. *Such as they are,* I was thinking. "Mister Pike and I will push on ahead for a ways and find out if this trail is as satisfactory as Mister Hastings assures us it is."

"Yes, I still think we ought to check out the trail the Harlan-Young Party took and compare," Pike said. "At least we know they made it through."

"We can try both routes for a short ways," I answered. "It should be clear enough which we should take."

Reed nodded. "Very well. We will wait three days for your return," he said. "When you come back with your scouting report, we will put it to a vote before the entire party and choose our path."

I nodded. I didn't think we had any choice but to move forward. The only question was whether to take the proven but difficult Weber Canyon route or the new route that Hastings had assured us was easier.

In every case, we had chosen the unproven "easier" route, and in every case, it had turned out to be much more difficult and time-consuming than if we had followed the more established path. But the farther we fall behind, the more urgent it is to save time.

It's as if we are destined to always choose wrong.

* * *

After Reed left, Pike and I agreed to explore the Weber Canyon route for one full day and then return to the same spot. Then we would investigate Hastings's new route for one more day, and after that, return to the Donner Party. Our plan was for it to take three and a half days in total. We hoped to arrive back at the wagon train in plenty of time to influence the vote.

It was clear from the start that the Weber Canyon path was a difficult one. Yet we could see evidence that much of the debris had been removed and that the previous wagon train had made slow progress. I was inclined to agree with Pike, after only a few miles, that we should go that direction.

We cut short our exploration, went back to the bottom of the canyon, and started up the other trail.

To our great surprise, the route that Hastings had encouraged us to take was much smoother and gentler than the other. We traveled half a day without hitting any major obstacles. We camped that night feeling optimistic, thinking that perhaps luck was finally turning in our favor.

I awoke in the deepest, coldest dark of night. The fire had burned low but I could see Pike sitting bolt upright across from me, his eyes glittering with fear. I wasn't sure what had woken me until I heard the howling again.

The sound seemed to strike directly at my chest, a stab of fear that stopped my heart for a moment. It was a primordial hunting call, the sound of a superstition come alive. A few moments later, there was a squeal, the cry of an animal that was being slaughtered.

"Wolves... " I heard Pike breathe.

Normally, I would have guffawed at his fear and told him to go back to sleep. Perhaps I might've built the fire up a bit, just to appease my more primitive instincts. But I'm not afraid of wolves. I've run into wolf packs before, and they are usually harmless, despite all the tales. They are more afraid of humans than we are of them, and will vanish if they hear or smell us coming.

But this was unlike any howl I've ever heard. There was a savage tone to it, a bloodlust that had nothing to do with hunger or instinct, but everything to do with malevolence. The cries of the victim were even worse, as if a child was being murdered, the sounds forced through a throat constricted with agony and terror. It sounded as though the prey was being played with, and the torment went on for what seemed hours—though it could only have been minutes—as both Pike and I stayed frozen in place. Finally, the anguished screaming was cut short.

Then not just one howl of victory but a chorus of triumph echoed through our small alcove in the cliff side. It sounded like there were dozens of voices, more than in any wolf pack I'd ever heard of. Eventually, the cries started to taper off, not so much as if the entire pack was moving on, but as if its members were going their separate ways. Finally, there was silence.

Without a word, we built up the fire. I lay down in my blankets but didn't fall back to sleep right away. Pike didn't even bother to attempt to sleep. Every time I opened my eyes—for my slumber was fitful—he was stirring the fire, building up the flames and adding another log.

I was sure that in the morning we'd agree to turn back, but when daylight came, it was as if the previous night's sounds had merely been a passing nightmare. When we heard the birds singing and the squirrels chattering as if everything was normal, the fear that had frozen us began to thaw.

We agreed to carry on for one more day, as planned.

The morning went smoothly enough. The path was wide and clear; the incline was shallow. It was a perfect trail, as if it had been built for us. In the afternoon, that all changed. The road narrowed to little more than a deer path. There was one of Hastings's scrawled notes at this juncture, nailed to a tree, assuring us that things got better a few miles down the road.

We passed beneath the trees, and soon we were scrambling over fallen timber and squeezing between boulders. *How did Hastings get his mule through here?* I wondered. The sky overhead was darkening and black clouds were rolling over us like a damp blanket. A drizzle deepened our misery.

Somehow, in the near-darkness, Pike and I became separated.

As I shouted out for him, I sensed something watching me. I stopped, fell silent, and looked around carefully, taking my gun from its holster quietly and cocking the hammer. Then I heard someone scream on the trail ahead.

I poked my head around the huge slab of rock that cut across the path in front of me. I saw Pike's muddy footprints in the few inches of soil between the boulder and the drop-off. I squeezed around the boulder and on the other side found a small glade, little more than a widening in the trail.

Pike lay on the ground, an animal crouched over him with its jaws clamped around his arm. It looked something like a wolf, but it was shifting, changing somehow. Its arms and legs were longer than a wolf's and ended not in paws, but in what looked like hands and feet. Its eyes seemed alien and strange, and I shuddered, realizing they were human eyes. As I approached, the creature's muzzle lengthened and its chest broadened.

I blinked. It *was* a wolf after all. Whatever I'd seen must have been some trick of the light.

Throughout all of this, Pike kept screaming, the mindless, screeching cries of a man who was no longer capable of thought but consumed by fear. I fired my gun without really aiming, and I heard the bullet splat into the wolf's hindquarters. It yowled, releasing Pike, and faced me, a growl rumbling from its chest.

The sound of its snarl was the most menacing thing I have ever heard. The fur around the wolf's shoulders was raised, and, as if in response, the hair on my head and all over my body stood up in terror. All I could see were those ferocious eyes and those fangs, which seemed to take up its entire muzzle, sharp and white, as its lips curled back and foam dripped from its mouth.

It took a single step toward me, and it was all I could do not to run. *I am going to face my death*, I thought, surprised by my own bravery, *and I am going to hurt it before it takes me.*

I didn't bother to try to reload, but pulled my knife and waited for it to charge. The wolf watched me as if amused. It stopped snarling and stared at me with those reddish-orange eyes. Somehow, its silence was even more frightening than its growling had been.

I shouted. I'm not sure what I shouted, only that it was raw and scared and in its own way, fierce. It was a challenge.

The creature flinched, and in my madness, I almost laughed. Then it appraised me for a little longer, as if curious. I stood waiting for it to attack.

Instead, the wolf turned and ran away. I noticed with satisfaction that it was trailing its right hind leg behind it.

Pike was babbling. It sounded as if he was trying to talk, but all that came out were choking, retching sounds. He got on all fours and vomited into the dirt. "Ga ... Gaw ... Gawd!" he finally stammered.

"It's gone," I said, sounding much calmer than I felt. But my words reminded me that the beast might come back, and I picked up my pistol and hurriedly reloaded. Only then did I get a good look at Pike's wound.

The flesh of his right arm was pierced and bleeding profusely. It was frightening, yet I was surprised that not more damage had been done. A grown wolf could have torn it off.

If a wolf is what it was, came the thought. I've had strange nightmares this entire journey, ever since I joined the Donner Party, most of them involving wolves. I wonder if perhaps, in some dark part of my mind, I was already aware of the danger we are in.

I wrapped the wound tightly. Blood soaked the bandage thoroughly and began to drip from it, but it was all I could do. With the loss of blood, Pike would have little chance of fighting off an infection. He was pale in the moonlight, like a ghost.

He tried not to groan every time he moved. I made a sling out of the extra blanket in my pack and helped him to his feet.

"Can you walk?" I asked.

"If it gets me out of here, I can," he answered.

We started back. Sometime that afternoon, we realized that the trail, which had always been hard to distinguish, had disappeared entirely.

We were lost.

CHAPTER 15

Virginia Reed, Wasatch Mountains, August 10, 1846

Father was gone for only a day, and announced upon his return that Mr. Stanton and Mr. Pike were continuing to scout ahead and that they had met up with Mr. Lansford Hastings, who had assured them that he had a new route all laid out for us. All we needed to do was follow the markings along the trail.

Father told them we would wait three days. We waited four. Finally, there was no help for it: a decision had to be made without them. We were running out of time.

"From what I saw of it, the Weber Canyon trail is an extremely difficult one and will delay us by many days," Father said. "Hastings told us that the new route he has mapped is much easier—and I have to say, it can't be any worse."

No one seemed to know what to say. We didn't have enough information. We'd have to trust—again—that Lansford Hastings wasn't leading us astray for some nefarious reason, or using us to blaze his own trail. Dozens of faces turned to George Donner, who blinked, suddenly remembering that as our leader, it was his decision.

"If you think that's best, Reed," he said. I saw Father wince as he realized that the blame would fall upon him no matter what happened. Donner had been useless throughout this portion of the journey, unwilling to venture an opinion.

I still wasn't frightened, cocooned as I was by young love. I assumed such travails were a normal part of traveling across this vast continent. Bayliss had remained distant, but Jean Baptiste had approached me again, and we were once again spending all our free time together.

I was in love, and my thoughts and feelings were directed toward Jean, who seemed to feel the same about me. We barely noticed all the things going wrong around us. When others weren't looking, especially Father, we had begun to hold hands.

Almost every night, we went walking on the trails behind the camp. Jean was trying hard to convince me to do more than kiss, but I had no intention of doing more than some harmless nuzzling and flirting. And I was certain I could handle him, for he was in my thrall. It was a strange feeling of power, and I was a little ashamed of myself even as I indulged in it.

Every night, the temptation grew to let it go a little further, and instead of being alarmed by this, I was thrilled.

I thought I was so grown up.

* * *

On a summer day full of deceptive promise, our wagon train reached the fork in the road. The wagon ruts from the Harlan-Young Party were clear, leading up a narrow, steep, winding trail. On the other hand, the northwest route, the new pass that Hastings had recommended, was flat and wide. We turned onto that trail.

At first, it seemed we had made the right decision, but after the first day, it was as if the road simply disappeared—as if the mountain itself was intent on blocking us. We came to a narrow path, and Father announced that he had found Stanton and Pike's muddy footprints on it. There, we found a damp, smeared letter from Hastings assuring us that the road cleared only a few miles ahead.

Every able-bodied man was rousted from the drivers' seats and those women who had been taught to drive the wagons were given the reins, including, to my great delight, me. I suppose I was too tired to be scared.

We built a road that hadn't existed before. The men were exhausted after the first day, completely worn out. We hadn't traveled more than a mile. The next day was even worse, and we traveled perhaps a half a mile.

We found signs of a scuffle in one of the little clearings and blood smeared on some of the leaves, but there was no sign of Stanton or Pike. It left all of us unsettled. What chance had we, dragging our huge wagons, if two men on foot could be swallowed up by the wilderness?

And where was Lansford Hastings, who had promised to come back and lead us? In the mountains, we found more letters nailed to trees, cheering us onward, deeper into our fate. I believe that if Hastings had dared to appear on the trail before us, there were those in the party who would have strung him up. Instead, the anger turned toward Father, who had advocated this road.

He was grim, even more severe than normal, and for the first time I saw him stooping under the weight of his worries. He never admitted it aloud, but it was clear that this had been a disastrous mistake.

All of us kept expecting the trail to get better after the next turn, but it only got worse. Entire mornings were spent doing nothing but felling trees, and entire afternoons were squandered removing them from our path. One day, we didn't move the wagons at all: we only prepared for the next arduous day, and then the next. What should have taken only days was taking weeks.

The men could barely summon the energy to eat at night, and the women felt helpless. We comforted the men as best we could. Jean Baptiste and I no longer went on romantic walks, not even to the perimeter of the camp. Instead, we sat at our campfire and he leaned his head against my shoulder, sometimes falling asleep sitting upright. Bayliss stared at us, too exhausted to even resent our closeness.

Everyone in the party began discarding anything that was not absolutely essential for survival. Desks and chairs littered the trailside. Some of the poorer families, who seemed to understand before the rest of us that we were not going to be able to come back and rescue our possessions, started breaking up the furniture for the nights' fires, since that was easier than finding deadfall logs and dragging them back to the camp.

We had been spoiled on our journey across the plains because we always had something to burn at night. The women would gather up the dried dung along the trail—buffalo chips, we called them—and that would fuel our fires. But now we were in terrain where buffalo chips were scarce to nonexistent. The wood in these mountains refused to burn, either too green to catch fire easily or too dry to last long.

Each morning, I looked up at the mountains, and each morning, it seemed as if we were nearer the crest of the pass. But every evening, after we passed what I'd thought was the summit, there would be yet another hill to climb. About this time, mosquitoes appeared in thick clouds, buzzing so noisily in my ears that I wanted to scream.

Finally, we reached a broad, flat plateau at the top of the pass. We could see down the other side of the mountains. We were all too exhausted to celebrate, and indeed, that was probably fortunate, because our troubles were far from over.

From the top of the Wasatch Mountains, we could see the white flats of the Great Salt Lake, stretching into infinity. The downward slope was, if anything, even more difficult. The sandy path zigzagged down the mountainside, slippery and perilous. It seemed as though we were nearly there, but it took ten more arduous days before we reached the level surface of the salt flats.

By the time we reached the flats, none of us had the slightest faith in Lansford Hastings and his magical shortcut. We stopped for a day's rest in the scant shade of the barren hillside. Father spent that afternoon walking back and forth among the different families, taking an inventory. He returned to our wagon, grim-faced, and I heard him and Mother talking in low, urgent tones.

It was as if, as we descended the mountains, we were falling into the deepest regions of hell. The heat sucked the breath from our bodies and turned our clothes wet with perspiration, and then dried them into a stiff, salty crust. That oven evaporated what little energy we had left and melted our very spirits. The wagons sank into the lake of salt enveloping us in the blistering heat.

* * *

It was there, in that glaring heat that poor Luke Halloran died. He'd been a charity case from the beginning, that frail young boy suffering from consumption who had been passed from family to family until everyone had lost all sympathy for him. He had trailed along with us like a ghost, and now he was one. We couldn't look at each other as we buried him, for we all felt guilty about neglecting him.

At night, we froze, but at least we could bundle up under our blankets. In the mornings, when the salt flats were still solid, we made good time, but by midafternoon, the water beneath began to seep upward and the wheels sank into the thick, mushy salt. We pushed the wagons onward, but the oxen were beginning to fail.

In the distance, we could see yet another chain of mountains. That might have cheered us, but Hastings's notes informed us they were the Ruby Mountains, not the Sierra Nevada, and that we had hundreds of miles yet to travel. When we determined this, we all seemed to stop in our tracks, as if the entire wagon train was stunned—as if none of us had the will to go on.

I looked around at my companions. They looked as if they had traveled through a dry snowstorm. They were covered by white crystals of salt that hung from their stringy hair and any loose piece of clothing. I tried not to lick my lips, for they were encrusted with salt and I would immediately crave a drink of water. Our water was being saved as much as possible for the livestock, and all of us were thirsty.

"We should unhitch the oxen and drive them ahead to find water," I heard Bayliss urge Father. "We can come back for the wagons."

"No," Father said bluntly. "Push on."

Some of the other families did as Bayliss suggested, though without success. Several times, I heard shouts of joy as someone thought they saw a wagon or the glimmering of a lake ahead of us. Each time, the vision proved to be a mirage, a mere shimmering of heat and the illusion of hope. After a time, we learned to ignore such apparitions.

The oxen were lowing continuously now, piteously. If we had poked them with hot irons, they couldn't have made more noise. Ominously, after a couple of days, the huge beasts stopped lowing and trudged on in silence.

Several of the smaller families were running out of food. I saw Keseberg arguing with the Eddys, who were now destitute, their oxen having died in harness. They had been forced to leave their wagon behind.

"You have enough food for all of us," Mr. Eddy said.

"I don't know that," Keseberg said heatedly. "I may need it all before we get out of here."

"For pity's sake," Eddy implored. "My family is starving—my children! I'll pay you back when we reach California. I sent money ahead."

"No," Keseberg said, turning away. "I can't eat your money. I can't spend your money if I'm dead."

That night, without telling anyone, Father visited the forlorn Eddy campfire and told them to take what they wanted out of our third wagon, as he intended to leave it behind the next morning.

Our family went on with two wagons, but the very next night, as Bayliss and Father unhitched the eight oxen that pulled our giant wagon, the animals bolted and ran into the darkness. The rolling palace that Father had been so proud of, that had caused so much dissent because of its sluggishness and so much resentment over its lavishness, was left behind to rot in the salt flats. We hitched the four remaining oxen to our last, half-empty wagon, and transferred into it what possessions we still wanted to keep. It was surprising how little seemed worth hauling along. Heirlooms that had been so precious at the beginning of the journey were left by the side of the trail.

No one cried or lamented our fate. We simply marched onward.

Father insisted on taking another inventory of the supplies so they could be shared. Since he was one of those who had lost the most, it probably should not have been him to insist, though it needed to be done. It should have been George Donner who made that decision, but the Donner family had gone on alone and was several days ahead of us. Despite the grumbling, most everyone acceded to Father's request.

The Graves family had managed not to lose any of their wagons and still had most of their livestock. John Snyder, their teamster, didn't want to help. "It's not our fault if you folks didn't plan well enough," he insisted.

I could see Father restraining his anger. "It's no one's fault. Some of us have had more bad luck than others."

"Bad luck?" Snyder snorted. "You're the stupid bastard who convinced us to take this route. Why should I share with you?"

"Then don't!" Father shouted. "I neither want nor need your charity. But there are others among us who are desperate. We are companions on this journey. We must help one another."

"Why should I help you, Reed?" Keseberg said. "If you had made it to California with your palace wagon and your two extra wagons of supplies, were you planning to share with the rest of us?"

"We'll pay you back," said Patrick Breen. He had brought seven children with him, and they had consumed his supplies like locusts. He still had his livestock, but his wagon was bare.

The Murphy family also spoke in favor of rationing, and Keseberg and Snyder could see they were outvoted. I saw deep resentment, almost hatred, in their eyes, but they bowed to the will of the majority. That night, everyone had enough to eat. It was one of the last times that would happen.

Finally, we reached the pitiful shade of the Ruby Mountains. We found a tepid pool of water there, and we rested by it for a time. Another couple of days was gone. We all knew we should push on, but none of us had the will or the strength. The livestock was even worse off. The animals could barely stand, and we let them wander far in search of food: too far, it turned out, because they started to disappear, and we found moccasin prints where cattle and horses should have been.

On our second day encamped below the Ruby Mountains, Father asked Bayliss if he would go searching for our lost oxen. Then Father disappeared for a short while and came back with Jean Baptiste following sheepishly. Jean had been left behind by the Donner family to help the Murphy's. Father was either unaware that Jean and Bayliss couldn't stand each other, or he didn't care.

"I've asked Jean to go with you," he said to Bayliss, who was speechless at this turn of events.

I watched them leave the next morning, neither looking at the other—or at me, for that matter.

When they returned the next night, Jean Baptiste and Bayliss were laughing and joking together. They'd found only our lost mule and one of the oxen, but they seemed to think this meager find was a triumph. I watched curiously as they sat near each other by the campfire that night, talking earnestly in low tones. Each of them gave me a quick glance and a shy smile. *So!* I thought. *A conspiracy of kindness!*

The next day, we continued on with a hodgepodge of animals pulling the wagons. Our family had only four oxen left, and in front of them we put our lone surviving mule, and in front of him, the scrawny horse that Father had ridden most of the way from Independence. My pony had vanished hundreds of miles back, and no one seemed to know what had happened to him. Bayliss and Jean Baptiste took turns walking beside me, and I realized that on their little jaunt together, they had decided to call a truce, and that both of them had decided to look out for me.

I didn't know whether to be insulted or flattered.

The Ruby Mountain pass turned out to be the easiest crossing of the entire trip, though we were so tired that negotiating the simple slopes was a struggle. When we saw what awaited us on the other side, our hearts dropped. There was yet another dry, flat expanse of salt ahead.

At the bottom of the pass, we found a worn, dried-up missive from Lansford Hastings, who informed us that we had two more days of hard travel without water, but that there were adequate provisions on the other side.

"Adequate," Jean snorted.

"The old fraud isn't even bothering to pretend anymore," Bayliss agreed. Out of habit, he spit a meager bit of moisture onto the ground, then licked his lips as if he regretted it.

I nodded in agreement, but there was nothing for it: the damage had been done, and we needed to move on. Soon we would be at the base of the Sierra Nevada, with one final push ahead of us. We were close to reaching our new home: the lush, rich, fertile valleys of California.

"Who's that?" Jean said suddenly.

Out of the wavering horizon, two men came stumbling toward us. To everyone's amazement, it was Charles Stanton and William Pike, though they were barely recognizable. The once stout, cheerful Stanton was gaunt and worn. Pike was as skinny as a split rail and so dark that his skin looked like cured leather. He had a dirty bandage on his arm that was stained a dark brown.

It was August 20th. They had been missing for two weeks. We had thought them gone forever.

We gathered together to await the two men. Stanton straightened up when he saw us and walked toward us with a rueful grin. "Bill and I have come with good advice. Best not take the shortcut."

No one laughed.

CHAPTER 16

Diary of Charles Stanton, Hastings Cutoff, August 10, 1846

I don't know how we got turned around. It was overcast those first few days, but even so, we should have been able to see which direction was east and which was west. Pike was feverish, so it was my fault we got lost. My only excuse was that I had my hands full trying to deal with my companion.

It wasn't more than a few hours after I found him that Pike began to utter strange sounds. He thought there were animals and men—they seemed to be mixed together in his mind—attacking him. He stumbled, walking into branches without seeing them and otherwise acting unaware of his surroundings, yet he went in the direction I pointed him in, so I thought it best to continue on. We were making steady progress going downhill, though the trail was harder and harder to make out.

That night, Pike shivered and sweated, crying out with strange, animal-like grunts that sent a chill down my spine. When he started thrashing about, I wrapped him in his blankets and tied a rope around him to restrain him. Even so, between the strange noises he emitted and the fear that he would roll into the fire or get loose and wander away, I got little sleep that night. Frankly, he scared me, and I wasn't sure I wanted to be unconscious in his presence.

The next day, he was completely delirious. There was no way we could move on. As I looked around the campsite, I realized that I couldn't even see the trail we had arrived by, much less where it went from there. In fact, I suspected there *was* no trail, that we'd wandered down deer paths and gullies, thinking we were getting somewhere, all the time straying farther from our path.

That morning, when I saw the sun rise, I realized with a sinking feeling that we were on the wrong side of the mountain pass.

It was getting colder every night. I doubted we could backtrack and find the others easily. I determined that rather than climb back upward blindly, it would be better to follow the stream downward and wait for the others on the other side of the pass. We had a week's worth of provisions, and I was certain we'd be found before they ran out.

Just to be careful, though, I starting rationing our supplies.

Pike wasn't eating anyway. His body was becoming thinner, all stretched out, and yet when he tossed and turned at night and I tried to restrain him, he exhibited a surprising strength.

On the second day, his fever broke. I woke up to see him staring at me with glittering eyes. "What happened?" he asked.

"You don't remember?" I asked uneasily. He was aware of his surroundings, but his eyes still looked fever-bright. "You were attacked by a wolf."

He frowned, looking down at his bandaged arm. "A wolf? I've had the strangest dreams, Stanton. I was hunting with others, but I had four legs. I think... I think I was a wolf."

That would explain the frenzied thrashing about at night. "Can you walk?" I asked.

"I feel strong," he said, getting to his feet. He immediately toppled over, then looked up at me sheepishly. "My balance seems to be a bit off."

"Try again," I insisted, helping him up. After a few wobbly seconds, he stood upright and took some tentative steps forward.

"Feels so strange," he muttered.

I offered him some hardtack, which he tore into, then spit out.

"Any jerky left?" he asked.

"Sure," I said, handing him a handful. I'd been saving the jerky for later, when we'd really need the strength.

He tore into the dried meat, devouring it, though he didn't seem to be enjoying it much. Still, after he was done, some color came back to his face and he was steadier on his legs. When I asked him if he was ready to continue, he hefted his backpack without complaint and followed me down the slope.

"Where are we?" he asked after awhile.

"Damned if I know," I said. "We're lost. Somewhere on the western side of the Wasatch Mountains."

"The western side?" he exclaimed. "How did that happen?"

"Darkness and you raving out of your mind," I answered defensively.

"Sorry," he said. "Where are the others?"

"Safe, I hope." I said. "With luck, they took the Weber Canyon route. We can find them at the bottom of the pass by going south along the base of the mountains and looking for their tracks. Two wagon trains should have left enough evidence of their passing. God help them if they chose the Hastings Cutoff."

"If I ever meet that man Hastings again... " Pike muttered.

We continued downward and reached the bottom of the pass. It grew hot during the day, though it was still freezing at night. We waited a few days beside the stream at the base of the mountains. If we left to search for Weber Canyon outlet, we'd be forced to leave the water behind, but it was becoming clear that we had to go looking.

Before we left, we drank deeply, as much as we could hold, and filled our water bags. The cold mountain water in our bellies was almost enough to make us think we were full. That night, I divvied up the hardtack and jerky. Pike took the meat but refused the hardened cracker. "Won't eat it," he muttered. "Tastes like sawdust to me."

When I woke the next morning, Pike was nowhere to be seen. I spent the morning wavering over whether to wait for him to return or go looking for him. I followed his trail as far as I could, but his tracks disappeared after only a few hundred yards. After that, I could find only the spoor of animals, mostly deer and wolf.

He came back around noon, walking jauntily, grinning with red-streaked teeth. His face was smeared with blood.

"Where were you?" I asked angrily.

"Did a little hunting," he said, shrugging. He threw himself down on his bedroll and acted as if he was going to sleep.

"Did you think to bring anything back?" I demanded. My stomach rumbled at the thought of fresh meat.

He looked surprised and guilty. "It was only a jackrabbit. Not much meat on it—not enough to bring back."

"You ate it?" I asked, suddenly realizing what all the blood meant. "Without cooking it?"

Again, he looked surprised. "Sure. It tasted all right raw. I was hungry."

"How did you catch it?" He'd left his rifle behind and his knife was on his belt, clean.

"It was easy," he muttered. "I ran it down. I could sense when it was going to turn... strange, now that you mention it. It must have been ill, weak or something. I had no trouble catching it."

I stared at him for a few more moments. The story didn't seem to add up. I shuddered at the thought of eating an uncooked rabbit and the parasites he'd probably consumed along with the meat, and yet, I was also jealous. I'd taken care of this man for two days while he was helpless, and in return, he'd gone off and made a kill and hadn't even bothered to share.

"Next time tell me where you're going," I grumbled.

"Sorry, Stanton," he muttered. He sounded contrite. "I don't know what came over me."

After that, we made good time. Trouble was, we were making good progress to nowhere. When we finally found the tracks out of Weber Canyon, they were weeks old. The Donner Party had obviously not gone that way. We decided to backtrack and wait for the wagons at the foot of the mountains farther to the north, near the stream.

It was only by luck that after a few days I happened to look in the opposite direction, out over the desert, and was startled to see the Donner Party wagons receding in the distance. Somehow they had gotten past us. We headed out after them, but didn't catch up before they started ascending the Ruby Mountain pass on the other side of the desert.

We'd been without food for three days by then. We were forced to go back to the foothills of the Wasatch Mountains one last time. There was no way we could attempt the desert crossing without sustenance. We needed to search for food.

We split up. I couldn't find the spoor of a single animal. I couldn't hear or see a bird in sight. I felt as if I was the only man alive.

Late in the afternoon, Pike came back with a rabbit, acting as proud as if he'd bagged a grizzly bear. The rabbit was only half-consumed this time. I cooked what was left and, in gratitude, offered him another bite, but he turned it down with a sneer, as if the sight of cooked meat disgusted him.

In the morning, I stumbled as I tried to stand up. I stood there for a few moments, wondering if my legs would support me. I staggered after Pike, who was already striding off.

The desert was not as harsh as we expected, and we quickly reached the other side. There loomed the Ruby Mountains. I looked up at the slopes, wondering how I was going to make it over them.

That last ascent was a blur of pain. It felt as though my muscles were being torn from my bones and my bones were shattering under the stress. I stumbled after Pike, who seemed rejuvenated. He helped me over a few of the rougher patches. As he clutched me with uncanny strength, I noticed that he had a wild, rank smell about him. I was thankful when he let me go at the top.

The journey down the Ruby Mountains went swiftly, and at the bottom of the pass, we saw the Donner Party not far ahead of us. We finally caught up with the wagons just on the other side of the salt flats.

* * *

My relief at finding the others cleared my mind. Only when I was safe did I realize how close we'd come to perishing.

Strangely, as my companion had recovered from his wounds, I'd felt more uneasy, not less. It was unnatural, how quickly he had healed. He still wore the bandage, but underneath it, the skin was pink and sound.

Though Pike was healthy again, he'd scared me. He would make strange noises at night, and I would startle awake, my heart pounding, only to find that he was gone. As our rations had dwindled, he'd eaten less and less of them, yet had seemed to gain strength as the days went on.

I was relieved, then, not only by finding my friends, but because I was no longer alone with Bill Pike.

Our fellow travelers were astonished to see us. I could see that they'd struggled in our absence. They shared some food with us, but it was clear that they were running low. Several of the wagons were missing, and much of the livestock. The party looked dispirited, if not quite defeated.

The next day, we reached the Humboldt River. We had finally rejoined the regular trail, weeks late. If we had taken the long way, the established route, we'd have passed this spot long before. There wasn't another wagon train in sight: certainly not behind us, nor could we see the dust of any ahead of us. We were alone, the last wagon train of the season.

But just seeing the tracks and knowing others had passed this way was a relief.

We followed the river for several days, reassured by the deep ruts of those who had been smart enough to avoid shortcuts. The greenery seemed to revive everyone's spirits. By some miracle, we caught some fish with our crude poles, and one of the men shot a deer, so we ate well for a change.

On the fourth day after Pike and I rejoined the group, Reed called a meeting. "We do not have enough supplies to reach California," he said. "Someone has to go ahead and bring supplies back."

No one disagreed, but no one volunteered either.

"I've heard that Mister Sutter is generous to pioneers," Reed continued. "He loans them a stake for a small interest if they make it as far as his fort. I propose we send a couple of men ahead to get provisions and bring them back to us before we start the ascent."

No one replied. It was almost as if, because James Reed was suggesting it, no one wanted to agree.

"It's a good idea," I spoke up. "I volunteer to go."

"You, Stanton?" Reed said doubtfully. "You've done quite enough, don't you think?"

I must have been a sorry sight, but strangely, after only a few days of rest, I was feeling strong. The slow pace of the wagon train was maddening to me, and after my experience with near starvation, I knew better than any of them how much jeopardy we were in.

"I arranged credit at Mister Sutter's settlement before leaving," I said. My voice sounded more confident than I felt. "I'll use my credit for supplies and hire some men to bring them back. All I ask is that I get repaid."

Everyone agreed to this plan. William McCutchen volunteered to accompany me, since Bill Pike was still recovering. I hadn't seen Pike much after we'd rejoined the main group. He was spending his time over in the German encampment, though I'd rarely seen him socialize with them in the months before. But his had been a life-altering experience, I thought. Perhaps he was changing alliances.

There was no doubt it was going to be a dangerous trip. There is safety in numbers, we'd been told by all the experts. That's why the larger wagon trains had the best success. We'd been warned by Lansford Hastings before we left Fort Laramie not to wander off alone, as there were hostile Indians in the area—though a warning from Lansford Hastings had little credibility anymore.

McCutchen and I left the next morning with two weeks' worth of provisions. We caught up to the Donner family wagons two days later and gave them the news. They were already camped at the base of the pass. The party seemed in relatively good shape, though obviously worn out.

When George Donner heard our plans, he gave us his blessing. Not that I would have been dissuaded from my goal in any case.

* * *

We encountered few difficulties along the way. Alarmingly, snow started falling on us about halfway up the Sierra Nevada pass, but the white flakes melted upon touching the ground.

We were nearing the summit when I sensed someone watching us.

Have we been followed? I wondered. I couldn't imagine why, or by who, yet I glimpsed movement behind me. Something primitive inside me reacted as if I was being stalked. McCutchen was looking all around nervously. Silently, we checked our rifles and gave them fresh dry loads. From then on, we carried the weapons in our hands, though it was inconvenient and awkward on the steep slopes.

Those last few nights, neither of us could sleep. When night fell, we'd build the fire high, and I swear I saw eyes gleaming from the darkness, though when I tried to focus on them, they disappeared. One night, however, I must have drowsed off, because the sound of a rifle shot took me completely by surprise. I was on my feet before I knew it, my own rifle already at my shoulder. I stared into the darkness as smoke curled out of McCutchen's rifle barrel.

When he lowered the gun, I saw that his face had gone white, his eyes wide with fear. "I could swear I saw… "

"Saw what?" I said, though I thought I knew.

"Wolves," McCutchen said forcefully, as if he expected me to object. "A whole pack of them. But they were not moving right, Stanton. I'm telling you: I've seen wolves before, and they weren't moving right at all."

I didn't answer, but he could tell I believed him.

That was the last of my catnaps. We both stayed awake the rest of the night. McCutchen reloaded his rifle and we sat as close to the bonfire as we could as night eased into morning. We spent it staring into the darkness.

In the first light of day, I spotted wolf tracks surrounding the site, many of them, and huge. Even stranger, we saw human tracks as well. We didn't say anything about that to each other, because it seemed too crazy. We simply exchanged a wondering look.

We reached the summit about midday, without further incident. It was only after we crossed that divide that I felt as though I'd reentered the real world, as if the previous months had been some kind of dream. We slept well that night. We both sensed we were safe.

With civilization near, I vowed to waste as little time at Sutter's Fort as possible and to return with all the supplies I could afford. Between my credit and the cash Donner and Reed had given me, I felt confident of success.

It wasn't until I returned that I found out that things had gone very wrong for the Donner Party.

CHAPTER 17

Personal notes of Jacob Donner, Secretary of the Wolfenrout, July 1846

As I suspected, George is having difficulty keeping a majority of the Wolfenrout on his side. As we progress west, we are being joined by more of our kind, but the Wolfen who are willing to travel so far from home are turning out to be the most aggressive among us.

My brother called the Foregathering of the Clans in hopes of strengthening the rules, of making them mandatory on pain of death. Instead, I fear the opposite will happen: that the Wolfen will renounce the rules that have kept us safe for so long.

* * *

"I don't understand it!" George shouted at me one night, as if it was my fault. "Humans have invented a device that can communicate information with the tapping of a finger. At a time like this, these dunderheads want to rescind the rules that have kept us safe for generations!"

"Only a few telegraph lines exist... " I began to object.

"It's only a matter of time, Jacob!" he shouted. "Humans are far too clever to allow themselves become our victims—not without retaliation. Where are the wolves, the bears, and lions east of the Mississippi? When was the last time a human in England was killed by a predator? You can walk all the roads of Europe, and the most dangerous creature you will encounter is man!"

"You needn't shout at me, brother," I said. "I agree with you."

"Even the frontiers will eventually be settled. Those Wolfen who continue to hunt humans put us all in jeopardy!"

"Our Kind must hunt, George," I said. "If we try to impose too many rules, they'll be disregarded. You must give the Wolfen—and that includes us—the occasional chance to hunt and to kill."

George was venting to me in private as he cannot lose his temper in public, but the decision has already been made.

After much discussion, the Wolfenrout reached a compromise. We decided we will prey upon the humans of this one wagon train while the

Foregathering of the Clans is being held. George agreed, but only reluctantly, probably because he suspected he would be outvoted. If we must kill humans, then killing them while they are isolated is the best solution. We are doing everything we can to delay the wagon train, in hopes that they will get caught in the mountains when the snows come.

I'm not certain that a vote against Keseberg and his confederates would have been honored in any event. But George has decided to try to maintain the illusion of order for as long as possible, hoping that enough moderate voices will arise in time to make a difference at the Foregathering.

Meeting of the Wolfenrout, August 1846

George was compelled to call for a vote of the Wolfenrout for the first time since leaving Independence. Keseberg was out of control, and we needed to reassert our authority. But I fear that even having to call for a vote is a sign that our control is slipping.

The disagreement started over whether a couple of humans should live or die.

"We've almost convinced them to take the Hastings Cutoff," Spitzer said. "But if Stanton and Pike return with reports that the crossing is impassable, they may yet turn back."

"So we kill them," Keseberg said. "Dead men tell no tales."

"No," George insisted. "It is too soon to show ourselves."

"The others will never know." Keseberg growled. The two men glared at each other, and in my mind's eye I saw them in wolf form, hackles raised, lips snarling.

"I think we can confuse them," I offered. "We can trick them into taking the wrong route, make sure they don't get back in time to warn the others."

"That's good," George agreed. "We need to keep these humans in the dark for as long as possible."

"Just as I said," Keseberg said. "All we have to do is kill them."

"I say we let them live," George snapped. "I call for a vote."

When it comes to voting, we mimic the humans. We used a ballot box, with red and white beans.

The vote was a tie, six to six—which meant that George cast the deciding vote. Still, the outcome was a shock. Sometime after we left Independence, he lost a supporter among the Wolfenrout—I suspect Dutch Charley. With the growing influence of the German contingent, I fear it is only a matter of time before George loses another vote; and once that happens, the stalemate will be broken and humans will be fair game.

"I still say we kill them," Keseberg insisted. "Who knows, maybe they'll meet with an accident on their return. And while we're at it, I say we kill the little Reed bitch, too. She's a snoop."

Uh-oh, I thought. *George likes Virginia Reed, as much as he can like any human.*

"You will leave her alone, Keseberg," George said, and the tone of his voice stopped everyone in their tracks, reminding us all that he is leader of the Wolfenrout because he is the strongest.

It is rare these days that we choose our leaders through combat. We don't need to. Everyone knows from childhood play and contests who is strongest. But Keseberg is a full decade younger than my brother, the strongest of his generation. He will have only heard rumors, old and half-forgotten stories, about George's legendary fights.

Everyone but George seems to know that it is only a matter of time before these two Wolfen settle things the Old Way.

"What does it matter?" Keseberg ignored George's warning tone. "We're going to eat her during the Foregathering anyway."

"When the time comes, if that is the way it must be," George said. "But not until then." I knew then that he still hopes to settle things at the Foregathering so that we don't hunt the humans. I shook my head. I am certain that opinions are turning against him.

"You heard the boss," McTeague said. He is the strongest of my brother's supporters and the most hotheaded among us. Keseberg delights in getting him angry.

"You really ought to join our side, McTeague," Keseberg said. "Let a little of that anger come out."

"The vote has been taken," George said. "The Wolfenrout has decided. You will obey."

Keseberg stood stock-still for a moment, then shrugged. "Very well. Lead the humans astray. They'll probably die anyway. It's a waste of good meat."

Personal notes of Jacob Donner, Secretary of the Wolfenrout, September, 1846

We've had our first fight to the death among the Wolfen on this journey. Fights are rare these days. There are so few of us; everyone is aware that we can ill afford to lose any of our number.

Led to the Slaughter

When Stanton and Pike emerged like ghosts out of the whiteness of the salt flats, it was clear that Pike had been bitten. I saw my brother flush and glance at Keseberg, who couldn't quite hide his smirk.

I feared George would attack the German right then and there, with everyone watching, including the humans.

The tension steadily built among the Wolfen as the day wore on. We all know that attacking a human and Turning him is at least as much a defiance of the Wolfenrout's edicts as killing him would have been, perhaps more so. Such insubordination can't go unpunished.

* * *

The Wolfen gathered that night after the humans were asleep. We'd arranged for all the guards to be Our Kind.

We didn't start a fire. Wolfen can see perfectly well in the dark, and it wasn't cold enough for us to need one. Fires are camouflage for us: unnecessary in reality, but necessary for the illusion of humanness. Indeed, the light can be blinding to us when we Turn, and we avoid fire when we can. Humans discovered that weakness long ago.

The two factions lined up behind their leaders, George on one side of the clearing and Keseberg on the other. I tried to do a quick count, but the Wolfen kept milling about, so I couldn't get an accurate number. With a sense of foreboding, I saw that the two sides were about equal.

Keseberg stood waiting for my brother to say something. Everyone expected the situation to explode.

Instead, that hothead McTeague entered the clearing, stomped over to Keseberg and slapped him in the face. It grew utterly quiet, and then there were soft growls of anticipation.

"McTeague, no!" George cried.

Keseberg looked at my brother with what appeared to be regret, and the message was clear: it should be George who was getting ready to fight, not McTeague. But once a challenge was offered, it could not be rescinded. McTeague was on his own.

Keseberg began removing his clothes.

Already Turning, McTeague nearly tore off own his clothes in his haste, and it was obvious that he was afraid. Wolfen can smell fear, and McTeague was filling the clearing with his fright. He didn't wait for Keseberg to completely change, which was bad form. He attacked, obviously hoping to catch his opponent off guard, going for a strike to the head to end it quickly. Keseberg easily dodged the blow, then managed to fend off a second attack.

I was standing next to my brother, and I could smell the aggression on him. It isn't unheard of in such cases for another fight to break out, but I knew George would think it unfair to attack an already exhausted and wounded Wolfen, and George is nothing if not fair.

As I thought this, I realized I was already conceding the battle to Keseberg. He radiates confidence: a healthy wolf sure of his prowess. It is obvious from the scars on his body that he's been in more than one duel.

The two Wolfen circled each other in the clearing, the slimmer, rangier red-furred Keseberg, and the large, almost round gray-furred shape of McTeague. Ordinarily we would have been howling encouragement from both sides, but we were conscious of the humans—and their guns—just a few hundred feet away.

McTeague initiated most of the attacks, trying for the decisive blow and missing again and again. Occasionally, thanks to the sheer number of swipes he took at the nimbly dodging Keseberg, McTeague managed to inflict a few small wounds. What he lacked in technique and size, he made up for in ferocity.

But Keseberg was coolheaded, and I could see he was letting his opponent wear himself down while saving his own strength. With each attack, he sliced McTeague on some part of his body—small wounds, but ones that bled profusely.

McTeague's chest was heaving in exhaustion. He was no longer snarling, and the fierce light of battle had dimmed in his eyes. Blood flowed over his gray fur in so many places that he looked like Keseberg's twin.

Then, in the middle of one of McTeague's most furious onslaughts, Keseberg landed a blow to his enemy's side that seemed to come from nowhere. There was a blur, and suddenly McTeague was staring down at a huge, gaping wound. I glanced at George, but my brother didn't do anything. He looked sad.

After that, McTeague took one blow after another, none of them enough to kill him, but each weakening him further, and I realized that Keseberg was toying with him, delaying the inevitable.

McTeague didn't look angry now. He looked frightened.

End it! I wanted to shout. I could almost hear the other spectators shouting the same thing in their minds.

As if in response, Keseberg shot his claws straight into McTeague's chest, digging deeper and deeper while his victim flailed his arms harmlessly against Keseberg's back. The thrashing became weaker and slower, and then, as if Keseberg had cut his strings, McTeague slumped and fell to the ground.

I looked toward my brother again. I wished George would set aside his respect for the proprieties for once and attack while his opponent was weakened. Not that Keseberg looked weakened in the slightest. The blood that covered him was mostly his adversary's, not counting the small, superficial wounds from blows he had allowed to reach him.

Keseberg stood there with that smirk, staring at George as if waiting for my brother to step forward and challenge him.

Led to the Slaughter

If George had responded, it would have been the first officially sanctioned duel for the leadership of the Wolfenrout since the Foregathering of Clans was created millennia ago. There were fights all the time, of course, but they weren't authorized. We fancied ourselves a civilized species. Disagreements were supposed to be decided by a vote of the Wolfenrout.

In the far distant past, such duels settled all our disagreements. I fear that soon, this will once again be our way of deciding things. If so, the strongest will rule, not the wisest or the most experienced. Such habits nearly led to our extinction in the Middle Ages, and now that wild streak that is always just below the surface is reemerging.

My brother turned away without a word and went back to his tent. I followed him. The Germans were raucous in their celebration behind us, though most of the Wolfen were respectfully silent. I saw George's shoulders stiffen in shame.

We all know, now, that it is only a matter of time before he and Keseberg fight to the death—and the result of this duel will decide the future of not only the Wolfenrout, but the entire Wolfen race.

CHAPTER 18

Virginia Reed, Humboldt River, September 26, 1846

After Stanton and McCutchen left, taking the two strongest horses left to the wagon train, we continued across the salt flats. The trip across this last stretch of desert was long but uneventful. For once, it proved more arduous in our imaginations than in the doing, and it was with a great surge of relief that we made it to the other side, finding shade, water, and grass for the livestock.

The "shortcut" had cost us nearly a month, but we were rapidly approaching the last leg of the trip. I was still optimistic, though I could see my elders were worried.

Tempers were running short.

Father tried to organize expeditions to go back into the desert and retrieve as many supplies as possible. No one wanted to go, and no one wanted to take orders from Father. Only a few small groups ventured out and returned with some of the scattered provisions.

We met a band of Paiute Indians, and they seemed friendly, but that night they stole some of our horses and oxen. From then on, whenever livestock went missing, the Indians were blamed—though I wasn't so sure that blame was always warranted. Most of the Indians I met on the trail seemed kind and helpful, though I'd hear the men sitting around the campfires at night talk about how we were surrounded by fierce savages.

Fear of Indians had accompanied us on this long journey, and now it manifested itself in nightly alarms. The cry would go up: "Indians!" and the men would rise and load their rifles, the women would gather up the children and take shelter behind the circled wagons, and no one would sleep.

After several nights of this, the response became lackluster, and I fear that if an Indian attack had truly been underway, we would have been quickly overwhelmed. Still, in the mornings, we would discover that more livestock had gone missing. Though the Indians were undoubtedly responsible for some of our losses, I suspected there was also a more sinister explanation.

Led to the Slaughter

By this time, our group had splintered into factions, many of whom wouldn't even speak to each other. At a time when we most needed to co-operate with one another, we were divided, sometimes working at cross-purposes.

I was barely aware of these troubles. Two handsome young men were courting me, apparently having decided to take turns and let the best man win. Each night, one of them would arrive to escort me on a walk, and the next night, the other would come calling.

It was very exciting. They were so different, and yet equally attractive in their own ways. Jean Baptiste was talkative, funny, easygoing, and assertive. Bayliss was serious, and when he spoke I had to pay attention, for there was always a deeper current running beneath the surface of his words. We never talked about how he had disappeared on me the night he had nearly kissed me. He muttered something once about how he didn't feel he deserved me, to which I laughed and agreed.

I was too young, of course, to really choose either one of the boys. I suppose one or both of them thought something longer-lasting would come of our flirtations, but it was never my intention to lead them on.

One night, when it was Bayliss who was escorting me, he gave me a short, chaste kiss. It was what I had been waiting for, and I was surprised by how exciting it was. I wanted more, but Bayliss broke away—unlike Jean, who always gave me passionate kisses that I had to curtail.

We were returning from our romantic excursion when we heard shouting near the livestock. We ran toward the tumult.

What I saw then, I will never forget. I had been aware that something strange was happening, but now I saw evidence of it in broad daylight for the first time. There was no denying what I saw, and Bayliss was there to see it too.

Up until then, I had thought our wagon train was having the usual difficulties. We'd been warned how arduous the journey would be, after all. I knew that it was late in the season, and that there was a chance we could run into trouble in the mountains. We had taken a disastrous cutoff, but that was behind us now. We were perilously short of supplies—but we were so close to our goal!

But after that day, nothing went right. From that moment on, we descended into a hell on Earth that few humans have had to endure.

There, at the center of the livestock stockade, was a giant gray wolf that looked as big as one of the mules. But this wolf was standing on his hind legs like a man. He was facing my father, who held only his Bowie knife. Even as I cried out, the wolf leaped for my father's throat.

Father had been in the Black Hawk War. He never talked about his military exploits, but I knew that he had experienced hand-to-hand combat. He managed to sink the blade into the chest of the wolf, which howled in pain and anger, waking the rest of the camp.

The howls brought people running from every direction, but only Bayliss and I had seen the wolf. The others saw only the aftermath.

The Donners, the Breens, and the Reeds surrounded my father, who still held the bloody knife in his hand. At his feet, instead of a wolf, was the naked body of John Snyder, bleeding from the heart.

* * *

"Hang him," Keseberg said.

My father stood in a circle of pioneers, his hands tied behind his back. He had yet to speak. I could see him thinking furiously: I knew that he was weighing all the factors, because I'd seen him with that expression, with furrowed brow and half-closed eyelids, many times before. When he was done thinking, he would make a pronouncement, and that would be that.

"We don't know what happened here," Breen said, almost pleadingly. The crowd was angry because John Snyder had been a friendly, helpful man, while my father was demanding and unforgiving. Now, his stern attitude was being reflected back at him.

"He killed an unarmed man, *that's* what he did." Keseberg and Snyder had been cronies, but there was more to it than that. I saw bloodlust in the German's eyes, surging just below the surface.

"He wasn't unarmed!" I blurted. "And he wasn't a ma—"

"Daughter!" Father shouted in his most commanding voice. "You will stay out of this!"

"But I saw him—"

"No! You came too late. You didn't see anything, understand?"

Keseberg was staring at me speculatively. Then he shrugged. "Doesn't matter what she says. She'll say anything to save her precious father."

"I was here too," Bayliss spoke up. "I saw it too!"

"No," Father said again. He turned and addressed the crowd. "I will tell you what happened. These children only arrived when it was all over. I don't know what they think they saw, but ... " He straightened and cleared his throat. "Snyder was whipping one of my horses because it had gotten into his feed. When I tried to stop him, he turned the whip on me. He was advancing toward me, as if he intended to strike me again." He turned and pointed at a whip handle, half buried in the dust. It was about ten feet away from the body, lying near the fence.

"Look, some of the horses are bleeding!" someone in the crowd exclaimed.

There were red slashes on the hindquarters of two of our horses, but where the crowd saw the marks of a whip, I saw claw marks. I looked questioningly at my father, who was staring back at me with unblinking eyes, as if willing me to go along with his story.

"I... I saw... that is, I heard the horses screaming," I said, and as I spoke, my voice got stronger and more certain. "Both of us did, didn't we, Bayliss?"

The boy looked confused, but seeing my father's glower and my pleading expression, he gulped and nodded.

"How was he going to kill you with a whip?" one of the women shouted. "Why didn't you run away, or try to get help?"

Father flushed. "No man whips me."

At his words, the crowd grew silent. On one hand, it was an admission of guilt. On the other, everyone had to wonder if he or she would accept a whipping without retaliation.

"We are the law here," Keseberg said. "We have no way of imprisoning him. I say we hang him now instead of later."

Again there was silence. I think if anyone had spoken up at that moment, Father's fate would have been sealed. Before anyone could, I ran to his side and hugged him tightly. "Daddy!" I cried. I always used the more formal title "Father," but I knew that the situation was desperate and uncertain. I hoped that those gathered would take sympathy on the poor daughter of the accused.

He laid his hand on my head, and I felt it shaking. Then I was crying and clutching him with all my might—and it was not an act.

"Well, we can't very well haul him along with us," Breen said. "Even the able-bodied are having trouble. But I won't see a hanging."

"So what do we do?" Eddy asked.

"I say we banish him," Breen said. The man with the huge family rarely spoke, so when he did, people listened. There was a murmur of agreement, and I knew it was decided: my father had been spared.

* * *

Mother cried late into the night. I heard Father's low, reassuring voice trying to calm her down. Patty and the boys slept close to me that night, and I woke up with Tommy's head on my shoulder. I got up early the next morning, and with Patty's help did all the cooking and morning chores. I suppose I used too many of our remaining provisions for that meal, but none of us knew when—or if—we'd see Father again.

After breakfast, Father was sent off into the wilderness, alone and unarmed. He was given the weakest of the horses and a few days' rations.

Mother didn't even emerge from the wagon to see him off. Our sense of loss was so great that in a way, it was as if he had actually been hanged. But I was certain that though he'd been banished, he'd find us again soon enough.

What no one knew was that in the night, I had snuck into Snyder's abandoned camp. I knew that the men who had sent Father off would check to see that his rifle remained in camp, so I took Snyder's rifle and what little food he had stashed in his tent. I rode ahead and met Father just out of sight of the camp as he passed by dispiritedly. I trotted out to him with a rifle in one hand and a pack in the other.

"Virginia," he growled. "You take too many chances."

I could tell he was proud of me, so I only grinned.

He shook his head. "If you were a man," he said, then stopped and laughed. "Nay, it doesn't matter. You are one of those people with the strength of will to get what they want. Whatever else happens, I'm proud of you, Gina."

I felt myself blushing with pleasure at his praise. Father was never outwardly sentimental. But it made me sad, too: it was as if he was saying goodbye.

"Why didn't you tell them what really happened, Father?" I asked.

"Tell them what?" he countered. "That I was attacked by a wolf and when it died, it turned into a man?" He shook his head. "They would think me off my head. No... I would rather they believe I am capable of killing self-defense than that I am insane. I fear that before this journey is over, harsh measures will have to be taken, and I want them all to know that I am the one willing to take them."

He reached out and rested his hand on the top of my head. It was the one sign of affection that Father showed, though I never doubted that he loved me. His huge, knobby hand always felt immensely reassuring—never more so than now. "You will be a magnificent bride for some lucky man someday. But, Gina... Jean Baptiste will never be that man. Nor will Bayliss. You will have a dowry, if I have anything to do with it, that will attract a respectable man."

"They are good men, Father."

He smiled sadly. "Yes, they are. Perhaps you're right. I shouldn't judge. I only want the best for you—and I am not sure either of these young fellows can provide that."

I was saddened, because I knew my father was probably right. I hated to think I was merely toying with the affections of a couple of handsome boys, experimenting with them, learning to hold hands and flirt and kiss. It was at times like this that I felt like a child again—and I wasn't ready to settle down. I wanted to explore the world first, to experience it, before I became a wife and mother.

"Best get back to camp before they miss you, Gina," Father advised. "Tell your mother I will rejoin you further along the trail, when the anger has faded. When the trail grows hard, they'll be happy enough to take me back."

"Can't I go with you?" I implored.

"Gina, I'm counting on you to take care of the family while I'm gone. The others aren't as strong as you... not even your mother. You'll have to act as the head of the household Now, off you go."

Reluctantly, I started to ride back to camp.

"Virginia," I heard Father's deep voice call.

I pulled back on the reins and coaxed my horse around.

"There is something very strange going on. You saw it. Keep an eye on the Germans. Especially, watch Keseberg."

He didn't need to tell me that, but I nodded obediently.

"Take care of your mother and sister," he said. "Watch after the boys. Keep them out of mischief."

We spurred our horses in opposite directions, but I kept glancing back. Just before he rode out of sight, Father turned and gave me a wave.

With a sigh, I returned to camp.

* * *

Everything had changed. I had been happy during the first part of the trip, counting its difficulties an adventure. Until recently, we hadn't lost anyone on the journey who hadn't already been sick before we left. Father had always been there, strong and confident. Now, as we neared the Sierra Nevada, I felt a deep sense of trepidation, though I tried not to show it. Father had left me in charge of the family, but I felt anything but strong and confident.

Suddenly, everyone seemed suspicious of everyone else. Even though most folks didn't know exactly what was wrong, they sensed that something wasn't right. Families were closing ranks, shunning outsiders. The single men were told to look after themselves, sent away from family campfires they used to share in the evenings. They set up their own camp, away from everyone else.

The livestock began to disappear in greater numbers, and soon no one was allowed to ride in the wagons. Everyone had to walk on their own two legs.

So I kept my head down and trudged forward. I was almost afraid to look back, afraid that I would see yet another abandoned wagon or dead ox, another family sitting desolate beside the trail.

I started to feel more sympathy for my mother. She'd tried so hard to keep up the proprieties she knew, the civilized customs she thought was her due. But now, she felt as though she was the hired help, and that all that had separated her from the savages was gone.

It would have been easier for her to don men's clothing to do her chores, as a few of the other women had begun to do, but she clung to her petticoats and bonnets. Even then, she attached beautiful ribbons and bows to my sister's clothing, as if the dirty urchins we had become would somehow be civilized by the little touches of color. She always wore a white apron, as clean as she could make it, as if asserting that though she might be doing a man's work, she was still a respectable small-town woman with her dignity intact. She might wear a pair of Father's boots while tramping in the mud, but she saw to it that her apron was still clean.

It was easier for me. I found enjoyment in the company of young men I might not have been allowed to get to know back in Springfield. We sang around the campfires and told each other stories, and to me, the future still seemed promising and full of potential.

On our fifth day out from the Humboldt River, someone noticed that Hardkoop was missing. The Belgian with the thick accent was the oldest man in the party. His feet had been swollen for days. He'd been complaining so much that everyone had ceased to listen to him. He had been riding in Keseberg's wagon, having paid for the privilege, so no one noticed him missing at first.

"I made him walk, just like everyone else," Keseberg said casually when asked about the old man. Now that Father was gone, none of the other men seemed capable of standing up to the German.

"He *couldn't* walk," I objected. "Did you abandon him?"

"He was sitting by a stream when I left him," Keseberg said, shrugging. "He was alive the last time I saw him, looking happy, dipping his toes in the cold water. I'm sure he'll come along any minute now."

All of us had seen Hardkoop's feet and knew the old man couldn't walk far.

Only William Eddy was willing to speak up, despite his lack of influence. "We need to go back and find him."

It had been a particularly hard day. The fodder for the livestock was almost gone. Several of the horses had died in harness, delaying the journey as they were cut loose from the traces and hauled to the side of the trail.

No one had the energy to go back for the old man. Everyone looked down at the ground, as if too tired or ashamed to face one another.

It isn't my problem, I told myself. *I must take care of Mother and the children.* But once camp was made, my conscience got the better of me and I went looking for help. Jean Baptiste was sitting at the edge of the single men's campfire, his boots off, kneading his swollen feet. I ignored the attention I was getting from the other men, though I blushed at the speculative looks they gave me.

"I'm going to search for Hardkoop," I announced. "Will you come with me?"

Jean sighed and started putting his boots back on.

It was dark by the time we left. The wagon tracks were still visible in the light of the half moon. I had taken possession of my father's rifle without asking anyone for permission to do so. Mother had grimaced and looked the other way. I took the rifle with me everywhere. Earlier on in the journey, the men might have thought it amusing and the women might have been scandalized. Now no one raised an eyebrow. All of us had learned that living in the wilderness required some changes.

Jean carried a walking stick. He offered to take Father's heavy gun, but I shrugged him off.

We walked for an hour, covering the same ground that it had taken the wagon train half a day to travel. When we reached the top of a steep hill, we heard the sound of running water. We looked down into the darkness with foreboding. We'd find Hardkoop here if we found him anywhere, but what kind of condition he might be in conjured up visions of horror. Indians followed our wagons, picking off the livestock. Bears and cougars infested these woods. But having come this far, I was determined to press on. Jean's hand found mine, and I could see him nod in the darkness.

We went down the hill quietly, though one might think we'd be calling out by then: after all, we were unlikely to stumble across the old man unless he answered a hail. Yet we stayed silent.

We reached the spot where the stream ran along the side of the trail. The bank was steep. We went to the side of it and looked down.

I couldn't make sense of it at first. I saw the old man, seemingly sitting cross-legged, his back against a huge boulder at the side of the stream. Then I noticed the frenzied motion of something—some creature—tearing at his throat. Hardkoop's body flopped back and forth like a rag doll. I heard snarling, and in the darkness, a pair of red eyes turned our way. There was a splattering sound, as if thick liquid was being splashed about.

Jean Baptiste ran back up the hill, but I stood frozen, staring into those malevolent eyes. There was intelligence there, and a careful, measuring look, as if it was assessing me; but the creature was satisfied with its prey, apparently, because it turned away disdainfully. It went back to tearing at Hardkoop's body, ignoring me.

This was a different wolf than the one I had seen in the mountain glade. *There is more than one*, I thought. *And if there is more than one, there is probably a pack.*

I slowly, stealthily lifted the gun and sighted down it, but the creature wasn't there anymore. In that brief moment, it had disappeared, as if it had caught the slight motion as I raised the rifle. My hair start to lift up, as if charged by friction, and my knees got weak. I started backing away. I had the sense that it was still nearby, watching me.

The trip back to camp was like a whirling fever dream. I started at every sound, and turned and checked behind me, in front of me—then to the side, then behind me again. The wolf followed me the entire way, I am sure of it, though I never saw it.

I was so exhausted by the time I reached the campfires that I didn't even bother to look for Jean, nor did I want to after he'd abandoned me in the middle of danger. That had been a surprise. I didn't know what I'd say to him. I tried to excuse his behavior, telling myself that both Bayliss and Jean Baptiste would fight Indians, or bears, or anything that could be explained, but that all this strangeness had unnerved them.

Also a surprise was the fact that I wasn't affected the same way. I was frightened, of course, but I figured these creatures could be killed, just like any other animal.

Everyone was asleep when I got back to camp, even the two men who were supposed to be guarding the livestock. I was too tired to do anything about that.

I collapsed into my blankets, completely depleted, the rifle at my side. *I wish Father was here,* I thought.

Though only moments before, I wouldn't have believed it possible, I fell into a deep sleep.

CHAPTER 19

Virginia Reed, Truckee River, October 10, 1846

To be truthful, I was disappointed in both my suitors. Both Jean Baptiste and Bayliss had been with me when something unnatural and frightening happened, but neither of them wanted to talk about it. It was as if they wanted to deny it had happened. Jean was embarrassed, I could tell, and Bayliss was angry.

I wanted to shake them, to tell them that their pride and petty rivalry was unimportant now. It was clear to me that dangerous and implacable creatures were stalking us.

Without Father, I felt immensely vulnerable. I tried to corral my family, to keep them within my sight, but I barely saw my brothers anymore—they were always off with the young men, running around underfoot, to the men's mock annoyance. Mother and Patty were a closed circle: they had established a routine that the rest of us weren't part of.

Nevertheless, I felt it was my duty to protect my mother and my siblings, so I refused to go on any further walks with my suitors, who were most unhappy about it. But Father had asked me to take care of the family, and I intended to do so.

We finally reached the foothills of the Sierra Nevada. The mountains rose before us, covered with huge pines. The peaks were capped with snow, but below the alpine heights, there were gray, jagged cliffs and hillsides of loose scree. It seemed impossible that our wagon train could traverse those rocky crags.

Once again, the Donner group had moved on ahead of us, a few days' journey farther into the mountains to Truckee Lake, the source of the Truckee River. They left word that the Donner family had accepted Father into their midst and that he was traveling with them. This lifted my heart, which was in sore need of some good news.

The Truckee Valley was lush and bountiful, but we'd reached it too late for many of us to save what little we still owned. The push over the final stretch of desert had been cruel. Our family's last wagon had broken an axle, and we'd carried what we could the rest of the way. We had but a few head of livestock left in our possession.

The Eddys were in even worse straits, having lost their wagons days earlier. They were without provisions. None of the other families would help them, including us, for we had barely enough for ourselves. They'd been forced to march along carrying their children, who cried much of the time. The Graves family had been obliged to abandon their wagon, having lost their horses to Indians.

Bayliss and Jean Baptiste, who had attached himself to our family, were carrying as much as they could. Even eight-year-old Patty was burdened with a pack. My little brothers had finally come back to our campfire, realizing their own kin were in bad shape, and also carried their share. They never wandered far from us from then on, and I wondered if they had seen something that scared them.

Mother had started setting aside extra food for Tommy and Jimmy, and I didn't object. I noticed that Patty was getting distressingly thin. When I was honest with myself, I realized I had become rather skinny myself. *Just as well Jean and Bayliss are no longer courting me*, I thought. *I must look frightful.*

The fodder was sparse in the days before we reached the Truckee Valley. By necessity, we'd let the livestock forage far from the safety of the camp. The Indians (*and the others*, I couldn't help but think) were merciless, killing dozens of cattle and stealing many of those that were left. Some of the men took to sleeping near the stockades, but even so, animals were gone in the morning, though the guards swore they never relaxed their vigilance. By then, over a hundred head of livestock were missing from our little group of wagons.

We shouldn't have stayed in that little valley for so long, but we were so glad to be out of the heat. To have fresh water! We had been told that it would not snow until late November, so most of us thought the rest and recuperation were worth the risk. I remember how the river was lined with women trying to wash the trail dust from our threadbare clothes with cold water and hard soap.

We didn't know that in the mountains, the snows had already begun to fall. The mountains were shrouded with mist for a few days, and it wasn't until the clouds dispersed that we saw that the peaks were completely white. The Donner family had already tried to push over the mountains but was forced back. We found out, when they straggled back to Truckee Lake, that Father and Walter Herron had gone on ahead, sharing a single horse, in one last attempt to get help before we were snowed in completely. The news lifted my spirits. Father would come back with supplies and all would yet be well.

Stanton and McCutchen had not returned. We were almost out of provisions. We were worn out by the unexpected rigors of the Wasatch Mountains and the Great Salt Lake. We were too tired and hungry to move forward, but time was running out, and everyone knew it. We were told that the last mountain pass was even harder going than the Hastings Cutoff had been, and I think this dispirited all of us. That was why we lingered longer than we should have on the banks of the Truckee River.

Then something happened that convinced everyone to push on.

* * *

I had taken to sleeping outside our family tent, near the campfire, with the rifle by my side. Late one night, a noise woke me. The fire had burned low, its embers providing little heat or light. I threw off my blankets and took up the rifle. I wasn't sure what I'd heard, only that it had sent my blood surging. I was learning to trust my instincts.

I heard the soft swooshing sound again, then a rasping breath. In the dim light of the fire, I saw eyes staring at me from the darkness, unblinking red spheres that took in the sight of my gun and appeared almost amused. I could see a low-slung body behind the eyes, that of some animal, though the eyes had a strangely human aspect to them. I raised the rifle to fire, but the eyes blinked out and the dark shape ran away into the trees.

I sat back down, my heart pounding. I would not sleep another wink till sunrise, I vowed; yet when the shouting started, I had dozed off. I woke with a start at the sound of raised voices, followed by a gunshot. There was some sort of altercation going on in the young men's camp, and I ran toward it.

When I arrived, I saw Bill Foster standing alone in the middle of a circle of men, as if no one wanted to go near him. He was shaking, his hands trembling as he tried to reload his rifle. At his feet lay William Pike, shot through the head. He was naked, though it was freezing cold.

"He attacked me, I tell you!" Foster cried. "He was like a beast. He... he wasn't... himself!"

There was a wound on Foster's shoulder, blood seeping through his shirt.

"He bit me!" Foster said. He gave up trying to reload his rifle. His muscles went slack and his eyes lost focus: I believe he was seeking refuge within himself.

Finally, Patrick Dolan stepped forward and took the rifle from Foster's trembling hands. "Bill, you killed him."

Foster shivered all over and looked around wildly, like someone waking up from a bad dream. "He came out of nowhere and bit me in the neck!" he said hoarsely. "It was like he was some kind of animal. I threw him off me, and he ran into the darkness, but then I could see him coming toward me again, and I... I shot him. I had no choice. He was a... " He stopped and swallowed hard. He'd been about to say something more, but had thought better of it.

"We'll decide in the morning what to do," Dolan said. "We need to think about this in the light of day."

They covered the poor naked corpse with a blanket.

The men moved off reluctantly, leaving Foster by himself by the fire. No one wanted to be near him, though he'd always been a popular man. He looked at me with blank eyes, as if not really seeing me.

I stepped into the firelight and sat down across from him. "What did you really see?" I asked quietly.

He had a hard time focusing on me. His head and arms were twitching, as if he wanted to run away but was trying hard to hold himself in place. "You wouldn't believe me."

"I might," I said. "I've seen some strange things lately."

"I thought I was being attacked by a wolf," he blurted. "Oh, God, that sounds crazy."

"But he turned into back into Mister Pike when he died?" I asked.

Foster nodded spasmodically.

"I saw the same thing when John Snyder attacked my father," I said. "I believe what you say, Mister Foster."

He seemed pathetically grateful for my support, but what I told him next made him frown. "Tell the others you were cleaning your gun and it went off accidentally," I advised. "They'll believe that more readily than that Pike attacked you, especially that he attacked you in the form of a wolf."

He sat thinking for a while, then nodded. "It could've happened that way. I clean my gun almost every night. Everyone sees me doing it. I'll tell them I was so shocked by Pike's death that my mind conjured up a vision of being attacked, but in truth, he startled me and the gun went off accidentally."

"That's right," I said. "It was an accident. Don't worry: you'll be fine."

Perhaps it would have been better if I had tried to warn the others then, using the testimony of Jean Baptiste and Foster to back me up. But I sensed they weren't ready for the truth; that they would deny it and cease to listen to anything I had to say, that they might even blame me for the bad luck that had befallen the Donner Party.

I went back to my own campfire, traversing the darkness with my rifle at the ready, but I couldn't shake the image of the wound on Foster's neck.

I remembered the wound on William Pike's arm after he returned from the scouting trip with Charles Stanton. I remembered the suspicious looks that Stanton kept casting his companion's way, and how after the trip they were never seen together, though before then, they had been friends.

It might be a good idea to keep an eye on Mister Foster, I thought. *He's been bitten by… one of them.* Even then, I was unwilling to use the word, to admit what was happening. It still didn't seem possible. There had to be some other explanation.

I continued to sleep by the fire after that, if sleep it could be called.

* * *

William Pike died by accident: so it was recorded. No one wanted to admit there was another explanation. The sense of unease increased among the wagon train. One by one, the families remaining along the Truckee River loaded up their few belongings and began climbing the pass.

When we arrived at the encampment at Truckee Lake, we discovered that some small groups had already tried to make it over the mountain. Most of them didn't get far. The snow started falling the day they left and didn't stop. A few groups got close to the summit but ran into snowdrifts up to ten feet tall. They turned back, but it wasn't just the snow that stopped them. I heard the word "wolves" being muttered in conversation. No one wanted to believe that we were being hunted, and yet, by then, almost everyone had seen the sleek bodies of the wolves running beside us, winding through the trees with a natural grace that made us humans feel all the more awkward and helpless.

I learned that Father and Walter Herron were the last to leave before the heavy snows. No one would look me in the eye when they informed me of this, and it was clear to me that they believed the two men lost. But I was certain he had made it. I would have felt something if anything had happened to Father. I was sure of it.

Truckee Lake,
November 2, 1846

My prayers were answered. Stanton returned just after we made it to the encampment at Truckee Lake. He brought word of Father.

"He arrived a few days before I left California," he said to my mother and me after the hubbub caused by his arrival began to die down. "He was healthy, but he had had a rough time of it. Both Herron and your father were emaciated and exhausted. I decided it was best not to wait for him to recover enough to join me, but he made me promise that I would give you a message."

He paused, unendurably. *Tell us!* I wanted to shout at him.

"He said not to give up hope; that he would be back for you as soon as possible. That nothing would keep him away."

Those simple words, that promise, sustained me for the next few horrible months. Without them, I might well have succumbed, as so many did.

More importantly to the rest of the party, Stanton brought mules laden with provisions. He was accompanied by two Miwok Indians named Luis and Salvador. They were the first Indians I had seen dressed in white man's clothing. This only served to make them seem even more savage in my eyes. Their bronzed skin, angled faces, almost Oriental eyes and black hair made them seem exotic, no matter that they were clad in shirts and trousers. *Surely*, we all thought, *the Indians will show us how to survive in this wilderness; surely they will show us the way out of here.*

Unfortunately, Mr. Stanton was also accompanied by more snow. It started again shortly after he arrived, and it never stopped.

CHAPTER 20

Diary of Charles Stanton, Sutter's Fort, October 28, 1846

The buildings of Sutter's Fort are enclosed by mud-brick walls painted white, with guard towers at each corner and a main gate in the middle of one wall. Most everyone lives outside the fort and retreats inside only in times of emergency. I expected thick forests in California, but instead, there is low vegetation and grass pastures, as if God has prepared the land to be plowed. The terrain is gently rolling, with red rock outcroppings, small ponds, and a wide, flat road leading up to the fort.

It seems a paradise; but I am leaving paradise to return to hell.

Just as I was preparing to return to the Donner Party, James Reed and Walter Herron staggered into view. Much of the settlement lined the road to stare as they went by. The people of Sutter's Fort were surprised enough when McCutchen and I arrived so late in the season: they obviously did not expect to see anyone else make it through.

I barely recognized the two men, and I could see in their eyes that they barely recognized me. There before me was a vision of what McCutchen and I must have looked like not so long ago, when we arrived here. They are scarecrow men, with thin arms and legs, gaunt faces, and sunken, dark eyes. These are men who have seen horrors, who have endured great hardship; yet they still have hope that everything will turn out all right.

James Reed wanted to join my party, but I convinced him to hold back, to give himself a chance to rest and recover. In his condition, he'd be more of a burden than help.

"Stay," I told him. "Organize a *genuine* rescue party." I waved at my two silent Indian companions. "I was only able to talk Luis and Salvador into going with me. My finances aren't what I thought they were—I've had some setbacks back East. I've barely been able to buy what you see here. Mister Sutter has been kind enough to loan us a pack mule and provisions, but there is only so much I can take."

"Let me pay you," Reed urged. "Buy another pack animal and laden it with supplies. Things have gotten desperate, Stanton."

Reluctantly, I agreed to let him outfit another mule: any more than that, the three of us won't be able to handle. What I really need is more men, but based on what I can pay, only the two Indians have agreed to accompany me.

I am much lower on funds than I expected. It turns out that the markets back East have fallen into a depression. Unfortunately, news of this downturn came by ship a few days before I arrived in the Sacramento Valley; otherwise I'm certain Sutter would've extended more credit. The provisions and transport I can afford are inadequate, but I don't want to wait any longer. As it is, I fear we'll be too late. Apparently, the last stretches of desert decimated the wagons and livestock.

Reed's condition alarms me. I say he looks as I must have looked, but in reality, he is much worse off. I've always had a little fat on me to give back to the rigors of travel: Reed was gaunt in the best of times, and now looks like a man who's been locked in a dungeon for years.

My two Indian companions are stoic and quiet men. I am trying not to second-guess their motivations. I am paying them little, yet they are uncomplaining. I think they are good men, better men than many of those I traveled across a continent with.

I once believed I would have a fresh start in California, with modest wealth. How little I understood about what I was attempting. The country is far larger than I knew. It is both beautiful and harsh. It punishes the ill-prepared and the unlucky.

A fresh start, indeed. I will be starting from scratch, without a penny to my name. Almost everything I had was invested in three wagons abandoned halfway across the Great Salt Lake and undoubtedly looted by now. What little cash I possessed, I've spent on supplies to take back over the mountains.

And yet, it seems of little consequence compared to the needs of my traveling companions. Money comes and goes—I've been rich and I've been poor more than once in my business career—but life is precious. Perhaps one has to lose everything to understand how little it matters. Fear builds as wealth increases; fear that you'll lose it all. But when one is forced to focus on day-to-day survival, there is little time to be dissatisfied or afraid. One simply endures.

Diary of Charles Stanton, Truckee Lake, November 2, 1846

As we reached the summit, it began to snow; not the sparse, cold, wind-driven snow that blew in our faces during McCutchen and my outward journey, but fat, wet snowflakes that clung to everything and slowed us. The snow seemed to want to weigh us down, drive us into the ground. If it had hit as we were ascending, we wouldn't have made it, but as it was, we managed to stumble our way down the mountain. By the time we reached the cabins at Truckee Lake, six inches of snow had been added to the crusty remains of the previous storms, and it showed no signs of diminishing.

I was hailed as a conquering hero. There was a scramble for the pack ponies, but I ordered everyone back quite firmly. Eventually, everyone respected my wishes that the food be distributed in an orderly manner. By the time everyone had taken a fair portion, it looked as if I had arrived with nothing at all. Spread among sixty people, it seemed little more than a meal.

Yet I know that in these dire circumstances an ordinary meal is a feast, and that it can be stretched into two or three or even half a dozen meals. A meal can last a week, if it is apportioned correctly.

I look outside the cabin and see that another six inches of snow has fallen, and a sense of dread comes over me. A week's provisions aren't going to be enough. Not nearly enough.

The Reeds have accepted me into their cabin, while Luis and Salvador have set up camp just outside. I saved an extra pack of food for the Reeds, which seemed only fair as it was their money that paid for much of what I brought.

The cabin is tidy and well ordered, and I quickly saw that Virginia Reed is mostly responsible for that. The girl is a doer: constantly in motion, taking care of her young brothers and even her sister and mother. Reed asked me to look after his family, but this thirteen-year-old girl is already doing so.

She is an attractive girl, appearing older than her years, and she is drawing much attention from the young men in the camp. She relishes the attention, even as she tries—unsuccessfully—to remain modest. She's spirited, and makes me wish I were a younger man.

The young men—there is the problem. There were a few moments, as I distributed the food, when I thought Keseberg and his two confederates, Reinhart and Spitzer, were going to seize the entire supply. If they had tried, I'm not sure what would have happened. I noticed that young Virginia was armed with her father's rifle and was watching the men warily. Where once I might have smiled indulgently at the sight, I now have no doubt of her capabilities and willingness to use that rifle.

The young fellow who is their driver was at her side, looking equally grim, if a little more frightened than she was.

Other than those two and myself, I'm not sure any of the others even saw the danger. Fortunately, the moment passed. I could see Keseberg eyeing Virginia and myself, then relaxing, deciding to make no attempt to take more than he deserved.

It should have been reassuring that he backed down, but I wonder if he isn't simply planning to wait until we let our guard down. Then again, I doubt there will be much food left after this evening. Most of the families will probably consume all their food rather than ration it.

Besides, it occurred to me that the Germans already look well fed. *They don't need the provisions*, I thought. *They have a secret food supply.*

I shudder at the thought.

Virginia knows too, I can see it her eyes; but the rest of the travelers still seem unaware of what lurks in our midst. If this storm doesn't abate, I fear they will soon find out.

CHAPTER 21

Note found with the diaries of Virginia Reed, Undated Entry

So began the days of cold and hunger. At first, it was the cold that was the worst, the bone-chilling cold that seeped into our clothes and our shelters so that we were constantly shivering. In the end, it was the hunger, the constant emptiness at the center of our bellies that tormented us the most.

Days stretched into weeks and then months of misery as we slowly descended to the level of beasts and beasts preyed upon us. God has mercifully granted me forgetfulness of much of that time, but there is also a small irony here, a little joke that the Devil slipped into the record I so dutifully kept throughout my journey: only the pages that detail the events of our agonizing descent still survive.

These diaries and journals are sad and soiled documents. I have an almost-memory of having gnawed on the edges, as if the paper was food, and indeed, as they lie on the desk before me now, I see what appear to be teeth marks. Perhaps I chewed up the rest of the pages. I don't remember.

Diary of Virginia Reed, November 6, 1846

It has begun to snow again. We have all retreated to our cabins and tents. We have taken refuge in one of the three cabins, and the others have vanished behind a curtain of white. It is easy to believe that only our cabin exists in all the world, that we are alone, the only survivors of some worldwide catastrophe.

The sound of the wind is constant, and so is the creaking of the trees. Only these sounds provide relief from the cries of the children and the moans of sick and starving adults.

When we arrived at Truckee Lake, we found these cabins already here, and we embraced them as our homes, grateful that we didn't have to build shelters from scratch. I wonder now if that wasn't a mistake. The cabins are poorly constructed, and perhaps if we had built them ourselves, we might have contrived something better. Now we are too weak and too tired of the pervasive cold and damp to do much of anything but wait out this new storm.

We long ago consumed the supplies Mr. Stanton brought us. He sits in the corner of the cabin, no doubt wishing he had remained in California. I have spoken with him several times, trying to get more information about Father—wanting, I suppose, simply to share the fact of his existence with another. Stanton seemed irritated by my last round of questions. "There is nothing more I can do, girl," he snapped. He apologized later and told me I was a "plucky little thing." I'm sure he is still exhausted from his efforts on our behalf, bless him. I will leave him in peace.

His two Indian friends are camped outside our cabin and seem comfortable enough. They rarely make a sound. Sometimes I forget they are there. I will feel someone watching me and turn around, sure that I'll meet the red eyes of a beast, only to find the still figures of Luis and Salvador staring at me; then they will nod solemnly, as if in greeting. I sense they mean me no harm. In truth, I see Keseberg as more of a savage than these Indians.

It is still early in the winter. Perhaps this is only a premature storm, which will pass and allow us to continue on our way. So we tell each other; but I see doubt and fear in the eyes of my companions.

November 8, 1846

After Father and Bayliss, the man I most trust is William Eddy. He is the most experienced hunter among those who are left. He shot a bear not long after we arrived at the lake, and he shared it with us without asking anything in return.

Unfortunately, the Eddy family is also the most destitute among us. They lost their wagon early on and have used up what supplies they were able to carry. The second least fortunate family is, alarmingly, my own. We have wealth, but it lies in banks in civilized towns. It means nothing here. We too have lost our wagons.

The only family that still has livestock—though the animals are little more than living skeletons—is the Graves family. Yesterday, we had acrimonious dealings with Franklin Graves, who insisted that we promise to pay double the going price for a pair of oxen. In the end, against the protestations of his wife, he took a note of debt from us. We came out better than

William Eddy, who had to pay $25 for a single ox, or three times the normal cost.

We had no choice.

I won't forget this unkindness.

November 10, 1846

It is still snowing, harder than ever. It is a dry, fluffy snow now, because it is getting colder. This storm will not blow over soon, I fear. When the snow first started to fall, we shot the livestock we still had left and stacked their carcasses on the cold ground, thinking that we had created a store of food. By the time we ventured out to hack off portions of meat, it was clear we had waited too long. The thick blanket of snow had covered everything and filled every crevice, making the land flat and featureless. We didn't reckon on the snow blinding us, softening the features of the landscape and causing us to be lost in a sea of white. It never occurred to anyone that the huge oxen and horses could be buried under snow so thick that we can no longer tell where they are.

This morning I found drag marks in the snow, streaks of red and black gore. It appears that wild animals have discovered the stored meat and have dragged it away. After much searching, I was able to find half a horse carcass. I called out for someone to help me butcher the remains, but no one came. I left the meat in the middle of the path and hurried back to the cabin. Bayliss was waiting by the door, looking concerned, having woken while I was gone. By the time we returned, the carcass was either gone or buried again. I noticed a new set of footprints near the trail, and I suspect that someone made off with my discovery.

I dug into two more mounds, but found tree stumps instead of carcasses. By then, my hands were nearly frozen and Bayliss couldn't even grasp anything anymore. We dared not stay out in the elements any longer. We retreated in defeat to my family's cabin without anything to show for our efforts. My mother and sister couldn't hide their disappointment, and I nearly lashed out at them.

It has occurred to me, in these dark days, that I've always been separate from the others, though I've always hidden this fact from myself. Only Father has really embraced me fully in his heart as a member of this family, though Mother loves me, I think, in her vague way. I've always had more spirit than anyone in my family except for Father. Though he is my stepfather, he is the only father I've ever known, and I am closer to him in temperament than any of my siblings are. It is my faith in him that keeps me hopeful, and which will keep me alive.

Bayliss didn't say a word as we returned empty-handed, but I no longer construe his silence as sullenness. I've decided it is the wisdom of a fellow who knows he doesn't have all the answers. In every case, when he has been put to the test, he has come through for me and my family, though we can no longer pay him and though he might have been better off camping with the other bachelors, who seem to be surviving these travails better than the rest of us.

That night, as we sat by the fire, I accidentally nudged him with my knee. When he moved away, I nudged him again, and when he looked at me in surprise, I gave him a shy smile. After that, we sat companionably together. If my mother noticed, she didn't say anything. Perhaps she thinks that I should experience what life I can while I still can. The fear is always there in the background: fear that we are entombed in the snow, that we are running out of food.

Outside is a lake, but no one knows how to fish. Few of the men have ever hunted: on the trail, the women bartered with friendly Indians for meat. Most of these men were shopkeepers back in Illinois and Missouri; a few were farmers. They can tell you the yield of topsoil and which grasses make the best fodder, but throughout our journey, we have had little luck hunting or fishing.

So whether the lake is full of fish, we will never know; nor have we been able to find any of the animals that must fill this forest. We have no knowledge of the local plants. We may as well be adrift in the middle of the ocean on a boat without a rudder, with the continents beyond reach.

November 11, 1846

It is dispiriting that the snow has, if anything, deepened this morning. No one dares to venture out of the cabin. We are trapped.

As I sit and write by the light of the fire, I can see that our hovel will be inadequate to last us the winter—if we even have the food to last the winter. We have piled up a few days' worth of wood, but it is rapidly diminishing. We are constantly melting snow for water. Occasionally, my mother finds some snippet of food to put into the pot to create a thin gruel.

We have begun trapping the poor mice that infested this cabin when we first moved in. It is only fair, as the little creatures were adept at stealing our crumbs of food. Now they are put into the pot and we regain what we have lost. The little animals can't escape. Outside the cabin, they would freeze; inside the cabin, they are boiled. The older children have made a game of catching them.

The younger children do not yet understand how much trouble we are in, and none of us is going to tell them. They will no doubt find out soon enough. For them, it is a vacation from the constant toil of a moving, working wagon train, with its endless chores and tasks to be attended to. They sit and play word games with each other. My mother managed to hold onto a few books. Perhaps she should have carried more food instead, but I find it difficult to fault her for it.

Bayliss has shown surprising empathy for the children, reading to them in an unexpectedly expressive way and coming up with interesting games for them to play. It helps distract them from the boredom of being shut in.

Starting early in the morning, the children ask over and over when dinner will be. We eat once now, at midafternoon, so that we will still have a few scraps of food in our stomachs when we go to bed. When we wake, we are hungry again, and that hunger builds to a crescendo until the afternoon, when we eat whatever meager provisions we have scrounged.

I saw my mother surreptitiously slipping dead insects into our soup, grinding them up so that they were unrecognizable. When it came time to eat, my mind rebelled, but my stomach readily accepted the offering.

November 14, 1846

It doesn't seem possible, but the snow has continued to fall. It is piled so high that we are continuously forced to dig out the small entrance to our cabin and trample out a path for a few yards beyond it.

I should describe our living spaces. The cabins are rectangular blocks made of unstripped pine timbers, which, when we first moved in, were infested with insects. The insects have mostly disappeared or been consumed, which is unfortunate. What in normal times I would have considered a plague, I now devoutly wish for. A soup of dead insects, the carcass of a mouse, the skin of a scavenged rabbit: when you have no food, anything seems edible.

There is one entrance to our hovel, which isn't really a door, but a hole cut low to the ground and covered with a thick hide. Inside, the floor is tamped-down earth with most of the rocks cleared away—though when I try to sleep, I can still feel rocks under me. There are no windows. The only light comes from the fire pit built in the corner farthest from the entrance. Water drips down the nearby walls and freezes into icicles.

In the roof, there is a small hole for the smoke to trickle out of, though much of it seems to prefer to remain within the cabin. My eyes are gritty and red, and to the sound of the wind and rasping branches has been added a third constant refrain: the sound of coughing. Even outside, the smoke can't escape. It floats up a short distance and seems to get trapped by the previous smoke. It is as if the sky is forcing it downward, and it wreaths the trees in halos of white.

The roofs of our cabins are flat, which was a grave mistake in their construction. Their wooden timbers have started to sag from the weight of the piled-up snow. The previous occupants covered the ceiling with ox hides, which have sprung leaks where the heat of the fire has reached them. These little tears in the hides drip constantly. We've dug small channels for the water to escape down, and as it reaches the cabin walls, the water begins to freeze. It has become my job to break up this ice and encourage the water to leave through the small exits I've dug, which then immediately freeze again. My arms are tired from constantly hacking at the ice, but it always reforms. It is the hardest task I have done on the entire journey. If this snowstorm ever abates, the first thing I will do is dig deeper channels to the outside.

Our fire is burning low now, the light too dim to read the books to the children, too dim to even see each other's faces. We've had to poke the snow away from the hole above the fire, and the moisture has almost put it out more than once. Our firewood is mostly gone. Tomorrow I will venture out to try to find some more.

I pray that the snow will stop falling, that the temperature will rise and begin to melt it, and that I will soon see clear blue mountain skies.

November 17, 1846

Some of us are starting to think of escape. We didn't know this until now, but a small party tried to reach the summit yesterday. They floundered in the deep snow and had to turn back. They returned yesterday evening.

There is talk of another attempt in the next few days. I have decided not to join them, for I promised Father I would take care of the family while he was gone. Yet my spirit goes with them, for I yearn to leave this place, to climb to the top of the pass and descend into California and the future that was promised us.

November 22, 1846

The snow has finally stopped falling. I dared to venture outside, found a few loose branches poking out of the sea of white and brought them back, but not before using some of the bigger limbs to push the snow off our roof. Bayliss helped me by lifting me up onto the roof and then clambering up beside me. The roof held, thankfully. We did a sloppy job of clearing it, but it was the best we could do.

The firewood is damp and doesn't burn well, continuously sputtering and belching out more smoke than ever. I'm certain that when our rescuers arrive—and surely Father will arrive soon—we will smell as if we are made of smoke. Our undernourished appearance will no doubt only reinforce the illusion. Perhaps it isn't an illusion at all. Perhaps we are already ghosts who haven't yet realized we are dead and are haunting the pathetic remains of our last dwelling.

Bayliss is staying in our cabin now. All propriety has been forgotten in this time of duress. Men and women cohabit without thought. No one has the energy to care, much less do anything inappropriate with our proximity.

I still feel guilty about kissing Jean first and ignoring Bayliss. It appears I chose wrong. Bayliss is proving to be a rock, while Jean Baptiste Trudeau is nowhere to be seen.

Today, as we were out foraging, I took Bayliss's face in my hands and kissed him on the lips. He was stunned, nearly falling into the snow, but he quickly recovered and was soon kissing me back eagerly.

Since then, we have rarely left each other's side.

There are about thirty adults in this encampment, and a nearly equal number of children. The Graves family has joined us in our cabin as well. The Breens and their large brood of children occupy the next cabin over. The Eddy family occupies the third cabin, joined by the Murphy's. Keseberg and the other Germans have built a lean-to against the side of it. The Donners chose to erect an encampment of tents farther away, near Alder Creek. The single men have been divvied up among all the encampments, though most have chosen to share the tents.

I have seen no one but my own group for the last five days. Bayliss and I have decided we will venture out and visit the others soon, even if the storms continue. We must find out how they are faring, and whether they doing better than us or are worse off.

CHAPTER 22

Personal notes of Jacob Donner, Secretary of the Wolfenrout, November 10, 1846

The turnout for the Foregathering of the Clans is much lower than my brother George expected, barely enough for our decisions to be considered a consensus. Still, any Wolfen who did not make the journey to this desolate spot cannot complain about the results later.

My brother is trying to delay calling together the Foregathering for as long as he can. I suppose he still hopes that some of the more moderate Wolfen will arrive. I know this will not happen. The outcome of the Foregathering, when it is finally called, is inevitable. By hunting humans, the Wolfen have already shown how they plan to vote.

While waiting for the Foregathering, most of the Our Kind have stayed in the wild, not joining us in human form. There isn't enough human food to share, and we are more efficient hunters in our animal form. There is little game in this wilderness. Most of the herd animals sensed the severity of the coming winter and moved to the lower pastures of the western slopes long before we arrived. Of those few animals left on this side of the mountains, many have already perished.

Our brethren are growing hungry and impatient. George will not be able to delay the meeting for much longer. Meanwhile, the humans are becoming warier.

We did not expect that the livestock would be so diminished by the time we reached the meeting place, so it is fortunate that we had the foresight to accompany a wagon train; but none of us could have foreseen how deep the snows would be, and how cold the nights. As hardy as we are, we are forced to huddle together at night to keep warm.

* * *

Discipline is breaking down. Any humans who wander away from the camp are hunted. George has stopped lobbying for his reforms. No one is listening: we're too hungry to care. Despite my brother's views, I am glad of this. We need to be free of rules.

Led to the Slaughter

We have forgotten who we are. It is glorious to hunt these humans, to run through the snow and catch them by their legs, to hold them down and bite through their spines, paralyzing them and devouring them while they still live.

I have hunted every night since we reached these foothills. Last night, I waited with four of my packmates at the end of a well-used trail. The humans are forced to wander out for firewood, sometimes as darkness falls. The sun had just set when we saw a girl walking nervously toward us. While the others circled around behind her, I revealed myself. The girl screamed and ran back down the trail, into the waiting jaws of my friends. I arrived just in time to see the light go out of her eyes as one of my greedy brethren clamped down on her head a little too hard. She was still deliciously warm as we ate her.

I returned to our tents and cleaned myself off. I didn't want to antagonize George by openly defying his wishes. I'd heard something interesting earlier that evening from some of our packmates, a piece of news I knew would set him off.

"They are planning to attack the Reed cabin," I informed him. "Keseberg thinks that if the Reeds and Stanton are killed, the others will be at our mercy."

"I warned him," George growled. He'd been staring morosely into the fire when I found him, but now he arose and began to Turn. He rarely shifts these days, as if to proclaim his allegiance with the humans. Many of our brethren consider him a human-lover, a turncoat. Defending the Reeds would only reinforce this belief, but I could not regret bearing the news, for upon hearing it, he was roused to action at last.

The ancient bloodlust rose in me, and it was all I could do not to extend my fangs. My brother can be a formidable creature when stirred to fight, when he forgets to think like a human and lets himself be Wolfen. As George Turned in front of me, I fought not to do the same. One of us needed to stay human in order to negotiate, I reasoned; yet I could see from my brother's bristling fur and slavering fangs that there would be no peaceful resolution this night. There was going to be a fight.

I felt the call of the pack. I closed my eyes and continued to resist the urge to Turn. My leader was about to fight for his supremacy. My human side was worried, of course: for my brother, and about the political position I had taken. But the Wolfen inside me *wanted* this confrontation to happen. At last, all would be resolved.

* * *

Keseberg and his followers can always be found loitering around the Murphy cabin. The humans cower inside at night while outside, the howls of Wolfen fill the air. Our Kind saw us approaching and began to gather round. Within moments, the clearing was filled with Wolfen. Everyone had been expecting this confrontation.

Keseberg had been sitting on a log, gnawing on a human leg bone. When he saw us, he threw down the meat and began tearing off his clothing. He can Turn in an instant, it seems, which never fails to amaze me, as it always takes me several minutes to complete the transformation. The scars that cover Keseberg's back and chest become thicker and longer in his wolf form, and he has a long, jagged mark running down between his eyes and onto his snout. His red hair is stringy and sparse, as if it has been torn away in fights, but that only shows the wiry muscles beneath his skin.

My brother, in contrast, has thick, black fur, and appears unmarked by violence. His eyes are a deep yellow instead of the usual red of Our Kind. He looks plump and pampered. I tried to remember his last fight and couldn't.

I stayed in human form in case there was to be a ceremonial challenge, but neither of them was in the mood for formalities.

Standing in the middle of the clearing, George waited for Keseberg to finish changing. Keseberg snarled at him, and the foam from his muzzle splattered across the trampled snow.

Until that moment, I'm not sure that I understood my brother might be killed. Had I thought he would change his mind when he saw he was outnumbered? Had I expected him to concede? I felt deep regret about what was going to happen—and a secret guilt. But that regret and shame were buried under my bloodlust.

Keseberg was now fully wolf.

Every Wolfen had Turned by then, all of them wishing they could join the fight. I feared that the violence would spread, that the two factions would tear into each other no matter who won the duel.

The combatants went to opposite sides of the clearing. This time, no one bothered to proclaim their allegiance by lining up beside them; we simply crowded around them, friend and foe mixed together. Silence fell as we stared at the two rivals.

Keseberg made the first move. He charged at George, who deftly moved to one side, letting the bigger wolf go past. They were both so fast that it took a few moments for most of us to realize the fight had started. George snapped at Keseberg as he passed, barely missing his haunch, but Keseberg was already turning to charge again. Again, my brother dodged out of the way and just missed catching him in passing.

It appeared they were equals in speed.

There was a gasp of awe from the other Wolfen. Truly, the two strongest of Our Kind were before us. Then the combatants tired of their cat-and-mouse game of charge and dodge. They rose up and grappled with each other, using their front paws to both defend and attack, almost as if they were human boxers. Keseberg made his first mistake, getting too close while trying to snap at his enemy's neck, and was caught by the swipe of a claw: another scar to add to his collection. He howled for the first time, not from pain, but from rage. Every human within hearing distance must have frozen in fear. It even sent a chill down my spine.

They retreated to either side of the clearing. My brother was unmarked but panting heavily. Keseberg was bleeding from the nose but appeared even more vigorous than before. I'm certain that to him, such a wound was only a reminder that he was in a fight.

They took turns attacking, though they were both slowing down.

Then my brother called on reserves of energy he'd been hoarding. He initiated most of the attacks, and each time, he seemed to get closer to landing a killing blow. He ripped tufts of fur from Keseberg, but he himself remained untouched.

I was beginning to fear that he would wear himself out, and that Keseberg was waiting for that to happen, when George broke off and retreated. He sat on his haunches, as if daring Keseberg to attack him.

To my surprise, Keseberg also sat, and they stared at each other.

Everyone was silent and still.

Then, as one, they rose and charged, meeting in the middle of the clearing with a great clash of tooth and claw. Their movements were so fast and frenzied, it was impossible to tell one from the other.

Then the flurry of movement ceased, and the scene before us became a frozen tableau. George was pinned to the ground; Keseberg had bitten into his shoulder. Slowly, inexorably, he closed his jaws. I heard bones snapping, and my brother made a small, pained sound. Then Keseberg shook him violently, nearly ripping his front leg off, and abruptly let go.

George lay on the ground, stunned, then tried to get up on his good front leg. He could barely stand, much less fight.

"Stop!" I cried.

Both wolves turned and regarded me.

"I beg of you, Keseberg, for all I have done for you, let him live!"

They both began to change back into human form.

"Stay out of this, Jacob!" my brother shouted as soon as he was capable of speaking.

Keseberg smiled. "For all you have done?" he echoed. "I suppose I owe you that. After all, if it wasn't for you, we'd be having a nice civilized Foregathering instead of solving things the Old Way."

"What's he talking about, Jacob?"

"Didn't you ever suspect, George?" Keseberg asked. "Your brother has been working against you the whole time." He turned to me. "What was it you did? Made sure that the invitations to the Foregathering reached only certain regions in time? I never would have thought of it, myself."

"Is this true?" George shrank before my eyes, diminished, an old man.

I didn't say anything. I couldn't look him in the eye.

"Of course it's true!" Keseberg shouted in triumph. "Jacob has figured out human ways better than you have, George. He's learned how to conceal and connive better than most men."

I couldn't deny it. I'd never thought of what I was doing as particularly human, but now that it had been said out loud, I realized Keseberg was right. I'd wanted to return to the Old Ways, to become fully wolf—and in order to do so, I'd become more devious than the humans I hated.

"I'll let you live, George," Keseberg said, "if you surrender to me. If you agree that by the Old Ways, a new leader has been chosen. Do you yield?"

George was looking at the ground. When he looked up, it was at me, not Keseberg. "I yield," he said softly.

It was over. The crowd surged forward; some of our brethren carried George away, while most stayed and celebrated with Keseberg.

George refuses to speak to me.

* * *

The Foregathering of the Clans was held, but it was a mere formality. The vote was a foregone conclusion.

We met high in the mountains, in a ravine near the summit. All of us were in wolf form. The wind cut through our thick fur. Our breath came out in little clouds of fog that floated above us, caught the wind, and joined the clouds.

Every color and size of Wolfen was represented. It was magnificent to see so many of us in one place, though there were hundreds instead of the thousands we had expected. The distance and the weather proved to be too much for many of our brethren. Still, it was a sight I shall never forget. Wolfen are so rare and spread out, I am sometimes tempted to believe that my pack is the only one in the whole world.

George did not even bother to attend. Keseberg was triumphant, and the leaders of the other clans showed him deference.

The vote was nearly unanimous. Wolfen are now allowed to create as many of Our Kind as we wish, and to hunt as we see fit. The rules suggested by the last Foregathering of the Clans have been abrogated instead of strengthened.

The results are the exact opposite of what my brother hoped for. Perhaps George is right and it will lead to disaster. In the meantime, I feel free to be myself for the first time in my life. I will hunt to my heart's content, and if, in the end, I am hunted down and killed in turn, I will not complain.

The clans have dispersed. Most of us escaped these mountains before the next storm arrived—which was fortunate, for otherwise, they might never have left. Some of us stayed, to our regret. It is not only the humans who are starving now.

CHAPTER 23

Diary of Virginia Reed, November 25, 1846

Another storm has descended. The second group has returned, defeated, after nearly reaching the summit.

It sometimes seems as if this storm has always existed and will always exist, and that we will be trapped in our sorry state throughout all eternity. Hell is not a fiery place, I now know: hell is wet and cold and dark.

I informed my mother of my intention to seek help from the other cabins. She nodded, understanding that there was no other choice.

Bayliss went with me, though I could tell he was reluctant. He isn't the beautiful boy I remember. His dark hair has begun to fall out in patches and his high cheekbones are sharp points below his sunken eyes. I have no doubt that I look equally terrible.

I have come to appreciate Bayliss and his steady demeanor. Once, I thought him gloomy and pessimistic, but reality has done much to confirm his appraisal of life. I can no longer argue that he is wrong about the way things are in this world.

I took his hand as soon as we walked away from our cabin and only let go when we reached the next cabin over.

We almost got lost, though that seems impossible, as our destination was such a short distance away. But the snow was blinding, and we had our eyes closed much of the time as we trudged through it. I was light enough to walk on top of the thin crust of ice beneath the latest layer of snow, but Bayliss broke through with every step, sinking up to his waist. Occasionally, I too broke through and was forced to crawl back up onto the crust and try to tread ever so lightly. It was exhausting, and I can only imagine how it must have fatigued Bayliss, yet he didn't complain, and he didn't ask to turn back.

We visited the other cabins, one by one. This was not as easy as it sounds, though they are within a few hundred yards of each other. I'd hoped the others would have more food than us, but if they do, they refuse to share. I choose to believe that no one is holding back, but if the others truly are hiding food, they are being disciplined about consuming it. Everyone looks hungry. Everyone looks equally miserable.

The exceptions are Keseberg and the men who hang around his lean-to next to the Murphy cabin. They seem strangely vigorous. Some of the single men look wild, almost feral. They eyed me in a way that made me feel uncomfortable.

We quickly moved on to the Donner camp, where we were told that George Donner has injured himself cutting up logs and is confined to his tent. The people in the tents seem drier than those of us in the cabins, but also colder, as their fires are outside. They had one main campfire burning in the middle of the circle of tents. A young man sat next to it, looking miserable, and it took me a moment to realize it was Jean Baptiste.

He looked up at Bayliss and me as if he didn't recognize us. He didn't look emaciated, but he did look wild. His hair has grown very long and he has a beard now. His eyes were shining in the firelight, and there was no welcome in them.

"Jean?" I said tentatively.

"What do you want?" he growled at us. "Go away!"

I hadn't seen Jean since the incident with Hardkoop. I'd been disgusted with his running away and had not sought him out. I suppose I thought he'd come crawling to me with apologies. Perhaps he wasn't as reliable as Bayliss, but I still thought of him as a friend. I could hardly believe how much he had changed.

"What's wrong, Jean?" I asked. "What happened to you?" Bayliss was pulling me away even as I spoke.

"Run away, little girl," Jean sneered. "Run away, little boy. There is nothing that can save you."

I was speechless. He sounded so cold, so heartless. Why would he say such things? Where was the cheerful, easygoing boy I remembered?

"Come on!" Bayliss hissed at me. He kept his grip on me until we were out of sight of the campfire.

"What's happened to him?" I wondered aloud.

Bayliss shook his head, looking grim. "There's something wrong with him. There's something wrong with the whole bunch of them."

We trudged on in silence. I wondered whether to express the suspicions I had. I decided that Bayliss was the only one I *could* tell; he was the only other person who had seen the wolf that attacked Father turn into a man.

"Did you notice anything else?" I asked.

"Other than that everyone is suspicious and distrustful and only looking out for themselves?"

"Have you seen John Haven or Jeremiah Stevens lately?" These were two of the Donner family's hired hands, and it had occurred to me that I hadn't seen either of them since we arrived at Truckee Lake.

Bayliss frowned. "Now that you mention it, no. But then again, half the camp is staying in bed these days. They're probably holed up in one of the tents, saving their strength."

Perhaps, I thought. *Or perhaps they are already gone.*
Something is keeping the Germans active and healthy while the rest of us starve.

* * *

That night, I loaded Father's rifle, though I knew that the powder might get damp and it would be better to keep it inside the sealed powder horn. I slept with the rifle at my feet, and once, after waking at the loud crack of a tree limb breaking under the weight of the snow, I found myself standing with the rifle in my hands, pointed at the entrance, before I was fully aware that I'd left my bed.

Bayliss got up, pushed the barrel of the rifle down, and put his arms around me. I turned to him and rested my cheek against his chest. I was trembling, but the strength of his arms and the steadiness of his demeanor calmed me.

Still, I kept the rifle near me as I went back to sleep.

November 26, 1846

More snow. The world now consists of snow and smoke: blinding, stinging smoke inside dark cabins, bright, freezing, spitting snow outside. We are completely out of food; the mice have all been caught, the insects in the timbers consumed. We are filthy, and though inured to the odor, I sometimes catch a whiff of how we would smell to others, and I feel ashamed.

Mother boiled a leather backpack last night, and it was tastier and heartier than anything we have eaten for some time. It has probably occurred to all of us that we may soon have to eat the ox hides that provide shelter over our heads. It is a terrible choice, for the hides can serve as either food or protection, but not both. Hunger will win in the end. Hunger vanquishes everything, even the cold.

Some of us have tried tasting what few plants can be found that aren't stripped bare by the winter. The vegetation tastes bitter, and while sometimes it eases the hunger pangs, more often it causes violent diarrhea. Tree bark is even worse, and grasses seem to pass right through us. We do not have the stomachs of horses or oxen. Experimenting has turned out to be more costly than beneficial, and no one has the energy to test the plants systematically.

Bayliss tried the leaves of one of the few bushes both big enough to still surmount the snows and to still have any growth. He got violently ill and spent two days wrapped in his blankets, getting up only to retch in the corner.

As the days have gone by, most of us have given up eating the bitter vegetation. We stay near our fires and try not to move, and let the miserable cold and hunger cradle us. We rarely speak, much less laugh or tell stories. At times, I fear we are defeated already.

But I still believe Father will return to fetch us. He'll bring food and clothing and his strong spirit, and we will survive this winter.

December 10, 1846

It has been three weeks since I last wrote here. I have had neither the will nor the strength to write further in this diary. We have begun to consume the hides that help protect us from the weather. Even as hungry as we are, the gooey mixture is nearly impossible to eat, but eat it we must. No one would turn down bugs now, or the tails of mice, or the visceral insides of oxen.

We have found the bones of the oxen we purchased and lost to the snows—or to some creature. The meat was stripped away. We have boiled these bones so often that they are disintegrating into the gruel and disappearing.

There is nothing left to eat.

We hear laughter from the Keseberg encampment, and it seems to come from a different world. One night, Bayliss and I ventured out into the dark and watched from a distance, and to our amazement, we saw men dancing in the firelight and heard them shouting.

Bayliss was incensed and has decided to go confront the men who live around the campfire outside the Keseberg lean-to. I have begged him not to, for I fear that those men have lost their minds—and their humanity. I cannot conceive of how they remain so strong and vital when all of the rest of us are failing… unless they are no longer like the rest of us.

CHAPTER 24

Diary of Virginia Reed, December 15, 1846

Bayliss is gravely injured. I cannot believe I am writing this, nor can I believe what happened. I want to hide beneath my blankets and let the world fade away. I didn't realize, before, how much I love Bayliss. Until now, I thought of him as a gentle companion whom I cared for as a dear friend.

He has turned into a reliable and steady man, like Father: someone who always strives to do the right thing.

And I love him.

Three nights ago, I moved my blankets next to his, and since then, we have spent the nights sharing each other's warmth. Nothing improper has happened; nor could it have, for neither of us has had the strength—though Bayliss might have been willing to try.

For a time, I managed to dissuade him from going to Keseberg's camp. The men in the German encampment continued to raise a ruckus at night, as if they were celebrating. With every shout, I could feel Bayliss tensing.

Last night, I woke up to find him gone. "Where's Bayliss?" I inquired.

Mr. Stanton rose from his corner, where he was sitting with his two Indians. "He left a short time ago. What's wrong?"

I didn't answer, but hurriedly threw on the blanket I also use as a poncho and ran out. In my haste, I forgot the rifle, which seems inexplicable to me. All the times I lugged that rifle around camp, prepared for an attack, and the one time I needed it most, I left it behind!

"I'm coming with you," Stanton said. He motioned to the Indians to follow him.

I followed Bayliss's tracks in the snow. Stanton lumbered behind me, along with the two silent Indians.

We arrived just in time to see the fight.

* * *

Keseberg was there, egging the others on, as usual. A group of men surrounded Bayliss: Spitzer and Reinhardt, Dutch Charlie, and several of the

126

Donner hired men. William Hook, Jacob Donner's stepson, was on the fringes, and beside him, I was distressed to see, was Jean Baptiste, who had apparently joined the German contingent.

Bayliss tried to leave, but Keseberg pushed him back into the center of the group. Spitzer stepped out to face him. Bayliss pulled out his knife. It was a nearly useless thing, chipped and dull, but it was all he had.

Spitzer didn't draw a weapon. He simply grinned, and as he grinned, his teeth began to grow and hair sprouted all over his body. He took his shirt off, and I saw that he was covered with fur, and then he removed his shoes and trousers. By then he was fully beast, as big as the wolf that had attacked Father. The muscles of his ropy limbs quivered and he snarled, dripping foam from his muzzle.

I remembered Father facing down just such a creature. That memory gave me hope: these werewolves can be defeated. But Bayliss is a slight fellow, and has been starving like the rest of us. He has never been to war, as Father has. He's probably never been in a fight before in his life.

The Indians were talking in low, excited voices. Stanton seemed to understand them. "Luis and Salvador say they are Skinwalkers, evil spirits," he said. "I believe our European ancestors would call them werewolves."

It was strange to hear that word spoken aloud, though I'd been thinking it for weeks, and in fact, it had crossed my mind mere moments before. *How many of the others know?* I wondered. *And why aren't they doing anything about it?*

But none of that mattered just then.

The werewolf was toying with Bayliss, closing his jaws over his victim's face, then opening them, rearing back, and howling. Bayliss's cheeks were wet with tears, but he was stoic, refusing to cry out.

"Help him!" I screamed at my companions.

Stanton looked at the Indians, who shook their heads. They were very still and quiet, even more so than usual. They seemed to be blending into the darkness; in fact, they were slowly backing away.

"I'm sorry, Virginia," Stanton said. "I didn't bring my gun. Even if I had, they outnumber us."

"You're just going to let this happen?" I cried.

Stanton flushed and looked at the ground. I knew I was being unfair to the old man. Of all the men in the party, only he had escaped and returned with supplies; only he had been willing to put his life at risk a second time. What I was asking was too much, but I didn't care: I had to save Bayliss.

"Get the others!" I insisted. "Surely there are more of us than there are of them."

"Perhaps," Stanton said. "But how do we know which are which?"

It was already too late. The Skinwalker leaped for Bayliss, who stood his ground. He raised his knife, trying to emulate Father, trying to plunge the blade into the monster's chest.

The knife snapped off at the handle. It had barely penetrated the creature's fur. The Spitzer-thing landed on Bayliss, pushing him to the ground.

I ran toward the confrontation and had nearly reached the circle of men when someone grabbed me from behind.

"You can't help him!" a familiar voice said in my ear. It was Jean Baptiste, his breath smelling like a charnel house, his body reeking of spoiled meat.

I fought Jean's restraining arms with all my strength, but I could barely budge them. He pulled me back out of the firelight, but several of the men, including Keseberg, had seen me.

"Leave him alone!" I shouted at the top of my voice. "I will bear witness!"

"Quiet, you fool!" Jean hissed. "They let us live because we are trapped. They want fresh meat, so they pick us off one at a time. Some of us may yet escape this fate, but you mustn't challenge them!"

I stopped struggling, and he let me go. I turned and slapped him as hard as I could. "Why have you joined them?" I demanded.

He rubbed his jaw, looking wounded, though not from the blow I had inflicted. The pain in his eyes was emotional, not physical.

"I haven't!" he hissed loudly. "I'm trying to keep an eye on them."

"Then help Bayliss," I implored. "I thought he was your friend!"

Jean stared at me. I was asking him to risk his life for his rival. Reluctantly, he turned and started to move toward the struggling figures.

Bayliss was trying to get up, but the creature kept casually pushing him back down and huffing into his face. Then, slowly, as Bayliss struggled to hold it off, the werewolf fastened its jaws onto its victim's shoulder and bit down. Bayliss's shoulder blade cracked, and he started screaming. Jean froze in his tracks. The creature seemed to be maddened by the sound, overcome with bloodlust, its eyes rolling and foam dripping from its muzzle as growled and closed its jaws more tightly.

"Let him go, Spitzer," Keseberg commanded.

The werewolf ignored him at first, then shook itself and released poor Bayliss. It stood up on its hind legs and began to turn back into a man.

"Come and get him, girl!" Keseberg shouted. "You can have him back!"

I started toward them. Jean tried to stop me. I shook him off and marched into the center of the circle of men. They were silent, but not out of respect for my bravery, for they were leering at me as if it was all a big joke. By the time I reached him, Bayliss had risen to his knees. Without thinking, I started to lift him on the side with the wounded shoulder, and he shrieked and fell to the ground. His face turned white, and he rolled onto his side and heaved. By then, Stanton had appeared next to me, and between the two of us, we got him to his feet.

We stumbled out of the firelight, not stopping until we reached the dubious safety of the darkness beyond. Only then did Jean come and help us.

We started back toward our cabin. I held off speaking until we were halfway there, then couldn't restrain myself any longer. "Why are you with them, Jean?" I demanded.

"I need to find out what they're up to," he replied.

"Aren't you afraid of them?" I was trying to decide if his actions were the most cowardly or the most courageous I'd ever seen.

"Afraid? You don't know how much! But… they feed me well. They can find the dead livestock: they sniff out the bodies even though they're buried in the snow. And I've discovered that there are factions among them. Some wish to feed only on animals, while Keseberg and some of the others have no qualms about eating humans—indeed, they prefer human flesh. They have hinted that they might try to turn me into one of them, but I will run away before I let that happen."

"Why did they let Bayliss live?" I asked, fearing the answer.

Jean gave me a questioning look, as if to say, *Haven't you figured it out?*

Stanton spoke up. "The Indians are right. We must leave this place. I'm going to organize a party to go for help as soon as possible. It may be a forlorn hope, but we can't simply wait to starve to death… or worse, become a meal for those creatures."

About then, Bayliss stopped moaning and fell unconscious. We made the rest of the trek to the cabin in silence. We carried Bayliss's motionless body inside, and Jean turned to leave.

"Where are you going?" I asked.

"I have to go find out what they're planning," he said.

"They saw you, Jean. They know you helped us."

"I've made no secret of how I feel about you, Virginia," he said, staring at the floor. "They won't hurt me; they'll just mock me for it." Again he turned to go.

"Jean." He looked back. It was the first time he'd looked me full in the face since the incident with Hardkoop. "You are welcome here. You have a place to come when you need to."

He nodded, then ducked through the hole and went out into the darkness.

* * *

The night's travails were not yet over. Later, as the moon dropped below the horizon, I got out of bed. I picked up the rifle and went outside. The night was as cold as any I've ever endured. I heard someone stirring beside the cabin, and in the starlight, I could see that the Indians were awake and watching me.

Near the door, there was a small stack of branches that we had gathered for firewood. I ducked down behind the woodpile, and it gave me some cover from the wind. Though I was shivering violently and my teeth were chattering, I dozed off after a time.

The snapping of a twig woke me, and I strained to see into the darkness. A low-slung shape was moving toward the entrance of the cabin. I lifted the rifle and waited until the creature was broadside to me, then fired at it.

It jumped into the air and ran wildly away, then turned and ran in the opposite direction, as if its body was moving without direction from its head. Then it stiffened, fell onto one side, and lay still. I walked up to it, holding my knife, though I knew if I had missed and it was only playing possum, the blade wasn't going to do me much good.

The pall of smoke that hung over the camp had muffled the sound of the shot, but I had little doubt that it had been heard by the Germans—the werewolf's friends. Would they try to take revenge? Or would they consider their compatriot's death justice for disobeying orders?

I didn't care. I wasn't going to wait to be a victim. I vowed to be vigilant from that moment on, and decided to seek out the others and find out who is part of the threat and who is aware of that threat and willing to confront it. We must act; otherwise we are little more than cattle, waiting to be slaughtered.

When I reached the body, I found a naked man lying motionless on the ground. It was Spitzer. He had come back to finish the job, as I'd expected. I had seen the creature's reluctance to let Bayliss live.

I sensed someone beside me and whirled with knife in hand.

It was Luis and Salvador. They nodded to me, as usual, then went over to the body and dragged it off into the darkness. This morning, there was a fresh layer of snow and no sign that anything had happened.

Bayliss is so still. I had to put my hand on his chest to see if his heart still beat.

Where are you, Father? I cry out inside. *Why aren't you here?*

CHAPTER 25

Diary of James Reed, Sutter's Fort, October 28, 1846

The very day I arrived at last at Sutter's Fort, haggard, buffeted by the wind, and worn down by my fears, Charles Stanton was preparing to head back into the mountains on a rescue expedition. I wanted to join him, but I could barely stand. I had to admit to myself that I was in no shape to conduct a rescue; that indeed, I would likely end up in need of rescue myself if I attempted such a thing.

I helped provision Stanton as much as I could. Two Indians are going with him, but other than that, he is alone. William McCutchen is still recovering from their arduous journey and cannot accompany him.

I clasped Stanton's hands perhaps a bit too tightly as I made him swear he would take care of my family. He little resembles the robust businessman I first met in Independence. He is raw and lean, and there is more determination in his eyes than I would have expected from him. In contrast, my companion Walter Herron, who steadfastly helped me over the mountains, has disappeared entirely. I suspect I will never see him again.

Charles Stanton is a brave man, to return to the depredations of the Donner Party when he has no family there of his own. I am forever in his debt.

Having secured his promise to look out for my family, I released his hands. "It is not only the cold and hunger that stalks our people," I ventured.

He nodded, eyes gleaming, and I could tell he knew to what I was referring. "I am returning with rifles and ammunition as well," he said.

Again I clasped his hands, this time in gratitude. I had the urge to embrace him, for at that moment he was as dear to me as family, but refrained.

And with that, I saw him off.

I have not told anyone at Sutter's Fort about what I saw in the mountains. The everyday bustle of activity in this settlement makes what I witnessed seem an impossibility, a fever dream. They would likely think me mad, but if by some miracle they did believe me, they would assuredly be unwilling to accompany me into the wilderness. Yes, it is better to keep what I have seen to myself.

But I know what I saw, and Stanton has confirmed it. I fear for my family, with such creatures around them.

I am already much recovered, and hope to leave in the next few days.

October 30, 1846

McCutchen has recovered enough to accompany me. I say recovered, though in truth we both look like skeletons with a thin layer of skin stretched over our bones, but food and two days' rest have put me back on my feet, and I cannot sit idle while my family suffers.

We managed to find three mules for sale and weighed them down with supplies before setting forth. The trek up the western slopes was almost easy. It is a much gentler incline than the other side of the Sierra. Near the summit, we encountered snowdrifts that were beyond our ability to push through. We went around them where we could, but a few hundred yards from the summit, we found that the snow was equally deep in all directions.

We have fallen back and made camp, and will make another attempt tomorrow.

November 1, 1846

It is hopeless. A snowstorm blew in overnight, so we made even less progress today than we did yesterday. We need snowshoes with which to tamp down the path; but what we truly need is more men. After only a few hundred feet, I was exhausted beyond all endurance. My heart pounded as though it longed to escape my chest.

It was even worse when I stopped to rest; then the full toll of my futile exertions became clear. Though I am not yet an old man, I felt a tightness across my chest and a weakness in my limbs that left them shaking. McCutchen tells me my face turned bright red and I was moaning as I walked, though I was not aware of it at the time. But I was aware that my companion looked as though he was near death. He couldn't move without grunting, as if taking each step was the most difficult thing he'd ever done.

It is clear to me that this won't do. It was perhaps a selfish endeavor, anyway, for we had only enough supplies to feed our own families. I hadn't thought how that would be for all the others.

We must have help. We need a fully manned and provisioned party that can see the rescue to completion.

November 15, 1846

It has taken me weeks to make any progress in assembling a rescue party. Unbeknownst to us, while our wagon train was crossing the Great Desert, America was preparing to go to war with Mexico. California is the prize, and a Colonel John C. Fremont and his men have arrived in Sutter's Fort under the pretense of being a surveying party.

I know that it is a pretense because I have spoken to Colonel Fremont several times in the last few days, after waiting nearly a week for him to meet with me. He knew what I would ask and was prepared to refuse me.

I had failed to convince any of the men here to join me on my rescue mission, even though I was willing to pay them handsomely. This was incomprehensible to me until one of the teamsters took pity on me and explained that Fremont has forbidden anyone to leave the fort until the situation with Mexico is resolved. When I spoke to Colonel Fremont, it became clear that there will be no resolution without conflict. Fremont is determined to gain the California territory for the United States of America.

Several members of the Harlan-Young wagon train, who are well acquainted with the difficulties of the journey over the Sierra Nevada, finally agreed to help me, but at the last minute, the mules and horses I purchased were requisitioned by the military.

I stormed into Fremont's office, brushing past a rough-looking man who moved to stop me.

"My family is starving," I shouted, "and you play at being a soldier!"

"I assure you, sir," Fremont said in a low, even voice, "I play at nothing."

The lack of emotion in his response drained me of mine. I saw that I could not reach him by appealing to his better nature.

"They call you the Great Pathfinder," I said. "What will they call you if you let an entire party of settlers starve to death without attempting to help them?"

"I have no care for how history will regard me," he said.

I was speechless. I knew it wasn't true. This man cares for nothing so much as his fame, except perhaps his fortune. This thought was a reminder to me to swallow my own pride. I tried to reason with him, then begged for his help, but he was adamant in his refusal.

Walking away from that meeting was the lowest point of my life. I felt I had failed my family. I pictured Margret lying in the snow with Virginia and Patty in her arms and young Jimmy and Tommy at her feet. I closed my eyes and, unbidden, a vision came to me of a pack of wolves with red eyes and bloody teeth slinking toward my loved ones.

"Excuse me, sir," I heard a voice say.

I turned to see the man who had tried to stop me outside Fremont's office. He was dressed in buckskins and wore a floppy, wide-brimmed hat. He was short and weathered-looking, and his blue eyes were bright and lively. He could've been anywhere from thirty to fifty years old. I surmised that he was an experienced traveler and outdoorsman familiar with these western lands.

"I couldn't help but overhear your discussion with the colonel," he continued.

"Yes?"

"If you'll allow me to offer some advice?"

I nodded, curious.

"If you suggest to the colonel that you'll convince the other settlers to join our volunteer military force, I think he might be more agreeable to your rescue effort. Have you had military experience?

"I fought in the Black Hawk War."

"I thought so," the man said. "The colonel needs experienced men. Offer your services and see what happens."

"I will do so," I replied. "I thank you, Mister…?"

"Carson," the man said over his shoulder as he walked away. "Kit Carson." Then he turned back to me. "If I were you, I wouldn't mention to the colonel that I said anything. We aren't on the best of terms just now. He's a great man, and I owe him my life, but he can be a stubborn cuss."

So it was that I joined the volunteer brigade. I was given the rank of lieutenant, for as soon as Fremont heard that I had served in the Black Hawk War, he insisted on promoting me.

"You know Mister Abraham Lincoln, then?" he asked.

"Very well," I said.

"He's an… interesting man. Not quite committed to the cause, I believe. Are you committed to the cause, Mister Reed?"

"If you speak of abolition, then yes, with all my heart."

He examined me closely, as if skeptical. Since I am not accustomed to lying, I was a little offended. Perhaps he saw that in my face, for he seemed amused. "Very well, Reed. We'll get you your rescue party. All I ask is that you return within the month."

"If we haven't succeeded in a month, sir," I said, "then it will be too late."

November 20, 1846

Good news! We have been told that there are emigrants camped at Bear Valley, on the western side of the mountains. We should reach them within a day or two. I long to see my dear wife and children. I hope that we are near the end of our travails.

Past the accursed mountains, California is everything we were led to believe, with mild weather and fertile soil. I have already inquired about purchasing land. We can have a fulfilling life here, I believe, God willing. Soon, dear family!

Colonel Fremont was as good as his word and outfitted us with thirty mules laden with provisions. A dozen men have agreed to accompany us: several of the Harlan-Young Party as volunteers, and three men I have hired to take care of the pack animals, as well as McCutchen and myself.

We are well prepared, and I have every hope of success.

November 21, 1846

Bitter disappointment.

Only a few hours into the trip, McCutchen informed me that six of the mules and two of the mule drivers had disappeared. Just like that, nearly a quarter of our supplies were gone.

We reached Bear Valley only to find that the rumored survivors were a young couple, strangers to us, who had gotten separated from a larger party. They were starving, huddled under a leaky canvas lean-to, and would have died without our help. We left them with provisions and a mule and pushed on.

The others are losing faith already. I am not listening to their complaints, but continuing forward and upward. The others have fallen behind, floundering in the deep snows, but McCutchen and I loaded what we could into our backpacks and continued on to the Yuba Bottoms.

We are a mere ten miles from the summit. We will make a final push tomorrow.

December 2, 1846

I have not had the heart to write further in this diary until now. I fear that my family may already be lost. I will not stop until I reach them, but it appears that the Fates are conspiring against me.

William McCutchen and I tried to reach the pass from the Yuba Bottoms, but went barely a mile before we realized it was impossible.

In my despair, I tried to go on anyway, which would have been the end of me. McCutchen grabbed me and held me down until I came to my senses and agreed to turn back.

We returned to Bear Valley to find that the rest of our party had already departed for Sutter's Fort. It seems that while others may want to help, only those of us with loved ones in jeopardy are willing to risk our lives—save for Charles Stanton, God bless him.

When we reached the fort, we discovered that everyone's attention has been turned to a new danger.

The citizens of the Sacramento Valley in are a state of anticipation. Talk of war is everywhere. Fremont immediately requisitioned the horses and mules we'd taken and insisted that we fulfill our promise to join his expeditionary force. He expressed no concern for the lost Donner Party.

I will keep my word to him, for it is clear that I will have no help until this crisis is resolved. I hope that my efforts will be rewarded. I reject the nightmares that come to me. I think of Virginia—that indomitable little girl—and envision her as the protector of my dear wife and my younger children. She will fight to the end, I know. How I wish I was there to fight in her stead!

CHAPTER 26

Diary of Virginia Reed,
December 18, 1846

This morning, we found Bayliss naked and rolling around on the cold dirt of the cabin floor, having thrown off his blankets. He was feverish, the bite mark on his shoulder festering and oozing yellow pus. All of us were disturbed by the crude animal grunts we heard emanating from him in his fever. I couldn't wake him enough to give him water, but I dribbled some into his mouth and he gulped it unconsciously.

Stanton and the two Indians had an argument in the afternoon, and though I couldn't overhear everything, it was clear that the Indians were insisting that Bayliss be put out of his misery, as if he were a sick ox. I saw Salvador make a savage sawing motion with one hand.

"I will not do anything so barbaric!" Stanton shouted, then flinched when he realized everyone in the cabin was listening.

"What are they saying?" I asked him.

"They say Bayliss will turn into one of them—a Skinwalker."

I realized as he said it that I already knew; that I'd feared just such a thing from the moment I saw the bite marks. "What do they suggest we do?"

"They insist we must kill him and cut off... " Stanton broke off, his voice cracking. "What they suggest is unthinkable, and we will not do it."

"Are they so certain he will change?"

"No," Stanton said, shaking his head. "Apparently, it doesn't always happen. Don't worry, Virginia: we will make our best effort to keep him alive. No one is going to be killed because of superstition."

It is more than superstition, I thought, clutching Father's rifle. *But they will have to get by me first.*

I stayed with Bayliss through the day, and glared at Luis and Salvador every time they came inside.

December 19, 1846

Last night, I stayed awake and tried to soothe Bayliss with soft murmurs of friendship and love. "I'm sorry," I said when I thought everyone was asleep. "You are a good friend, dear Bayliss, please awaken. Awaken, dear Bayliss... "

I saw my mother's eyes gleaming in the firelight and knew she had overheard me. Once, she would have objected to me saying such things to a mere servant, but we are all equals now, all of us destitute and laid bare before God.

The cabin is stultifying at the best of times, but Bayliss's moans and thrashing have become too much for most of us to endure. Today, despite the danger, everyone left the cabin for as long as they could stand to be outside. It was better to hear the howling of the wind than to listen to Bayliss cry out again and again.

This evening, we had enough firewood for once, as everyone returned from their wanderings with a few branches.

December 20, 1846

I couldn't stay awake last night, but Stanton was at Bayliss's side when I fell asleep and was still sitting there patiently when I woke to the sound of Bayliss's screaming early this morning.

This evening, as we supped on the thin soup Mother makes every night, even if it is only hot water with a few pieces of bark in it, Patty informed us that, to escape Bayliss's screaming, she had wandered as far as the Donner camp.

"Don't you ever go there alone!" my mother admonished. She didn't quite shout, for she didn't have the energy, but she showed more emotion than I have seen from her in weeks.

"Luis went with me," Patty objected.

I waited for my mother to become even angrier at this, her second daughter wandering off in the company of an Indian, but instead it seemed to mollify her. "Don't do it again," Mother warned, then cleared her throat and fell silent.

"What is the news?" I asked.

"Mister Donner's arm has become infected," Patty said. "He can't move from his bed. The others are, if anything, worse off than we are."

A mixture of emotions crossed my mother's face: satisfaction that we were not the only ones suffering, quickly followed by more charitable feelings of disappointment and sadness at this news.

In the late afternoon, Bayliss stopped moving for a time and I rushed to his side, fearing the worst. He was sleeping peacefully. His bite marks are healing and his fever is receding.

This should have been reassuring, but when he opened his eyes, he stared at me as if he didn't recognize me. His gaze roamed about the cabin without alighting on anything, and he didn't say a word; then he fell into a deep slumber.

I hope that the worst is past and that he will awake in the morning, but I wonder if he will ever again be the Bayliss I have known, or indeed, whether he will be human at all.

December 21, 1846

Bayliss has disappeared. I let myself fall asleep last night, though I had intended to stay awake at his side. No one saw him leave. His tracks go as far as the tree line and disappear: that is, the human tracks disappear, and animal tracks continue on.

No one has said anything, but much of the tension has left the cabin, as if everyone is secretly relieved. I would be angry with them if I didn't feel something of the same emotion. My last memory of Bayliss is that strangely empty look he gave me when he awoke, as if the person I had known was gone.

Though family and friends surround me, I feel more alone than I have since Father left us.

December 26, 1846

Last night, I dreamed the Donner Party was still crossing the Great Salt Flats. It was silent, without a breath of wind; the sun beat down on me, and I saw mirages of shimmering blue lakes. I was dying of thirst. I woke thirsty and melted some snow to drink, freezing despite being bundled up in the blankets and most of the clothes I possess.

Mother has surprised me with her resilience. I never thought she had such strength, but perhaps she never had to exhibit it before because Father was always there.

On Christmas Eve, she revealed that she had hidden some of the food Mr. Stanton brought over the mountains from California, and she fixed us soup that was far more substantial than anything we'd eaten in weeks. We all agreed it was the best Christmas present she had ever given us. We even invited Mr. Stanton and his two Indian friends to share in the feast.

We rarely stir from our beds now, except to attend to the necessities. Our cabin has become filthy despite my mother's constant efforts to clean it, and it is a blessing that it is too cold for us to smell the filth of our existence. We have to face away from each other when we speak, for everyone's breath smells so foul, it is like speaking to rotting corpses.

On Christmas Day, Salvador motioned to me that he'd like to borrow Father's gun and go hunting. Reluctantly, I let him, and was rewarded for my trust when he returned with a hare. We had another unexpected celebration, and for a few moments that night, amid the flickering firelight and the happy faces of my brothers and sister, it was almost as if nothing was wrong, as if we were simply whiling away the winter in a snug cabin.

That only made our hunger today seem worse. Twice more, Salvador has left with the rifle, but each time, he has returned empty-handed. Luis went out once but had no better luck.

Bayliss remains missing. No one could survive out in the woods for this long.

All God's creatures have abandoned us to a purgatory of suffering.

December 27, 1846

All days are the same now. White snow outside; inside, we are as worms, wallowing in the dirt.

Mother and I have decided to go seek help. That she is willing to leave her other children behind shows how desperate she is, but she knows it is better than waiting helplessly, day after day, while we starve. Certainly, I can better fulfill my promise to Father by trying to bring back help for my family than by staying here and watching them die.

It has not stormed for several days now, though the skies are overcast, and it is a little warmer. Tommy and Jimmy are starting to fail. Though we give my brothers bigger portions of whatever meager sustenance we manage to scrounge, they are suffering the most. They cry at night, endlessly, and seem to have night terrors every hour.

Milt Elliot has agreed to accompany us on our desperate quest to find help, and so has Eliza Williams, who has left the Donner encampment and joined us. We took her in reluctantly, as we do not have enough even for ourselves. She won't say what drove her away from the Donners, to whom she had seemed devoted. She is a quiet, painfully shy girl, and though she is my own age, she seems much younger. When I hesitated to accept her offer to come with us, she looked me in the eye defiantly. "I can't stay here," she said. "I can't stand to watch little Jimmy and Tommy suffer so."

I impulsively hugged her, and she had tears in her eyes when I gave her permission to come along.

We have left our family in the care of Charles Stanton, whom we know to be a good and faithful man.

God help us on our journey.

January 1, 1847

The new year, alas, has not begun well.

It started snowing as soon as we left the cabin, but at first it was only a light flurry, so we kept going. By the time the snow began to fall in heavy, wet flakes, we'd made such good progress up the pass that we continued on.

I was happy to finally be doing something. The miles went by so fast that I wondered if we'd made a mistake in not trying this before. I knew that others had tried, but I told myself that they'd given up too easily, or the weather hadn't been in their favor.

Almost as soon as I thought that, the weather turned. That first night, as the winds buffeted us behind our crude shelter of branches, we realized that our endeavor was probably hopeless. However, we pressed on the next day, and again, it seemed we were making good progress. The snow had frozen hard enough to support our weight, though it was slippery. The winds had died down by morning, and the cold was endurable.

The second night, we managed to start a fire, and though we were all bone-tired, I think we were starting to believe we would succeed.

The creature began to stalk us the next morning.

We caught glimpses of it through the trees, moving faster across the snow than seemed possible. It was low to the ground and dark, and it moved silently. It was following us at first, and then, suddenly, we saw it standing just a few yards ahead of us.

We all stopped dead.

It started to slink toward us. I knew we couldn't outrun it, so I raised my rifle and waited for it to come closer. When it was some ten feet away, it reared up on its hind legs, and its snout twisted into something that looked like a smile painted on a monster.

That moment seemed to last forever.

Then I pulled the trigger.

That same instant, as if it had known exactly when I would fire, it dropped down and dodged to one side. A tree splintered behind the wolf; I had completely overshot it.

I began to reload, knowing I'd be too late.

The creature seemed to enjoy our helplessness. Elliot pulled a knife, but he was shaking so badly that I knew he'd never be able to fight the beast.

The werewolf crouched, ready to spring.

Then, from off to our left, where the vegetation was thickest, another of the creatures came hurtling out and latched its jaws onto the throat of the first werewolf.

The creature who had been menacing us reared up, almost throwing off its attacker, but the second werewolf held on, and I could see its jaws tighten and blood begin to flow. Our would-be attacker thrashed about wildly but could not break free, and its convulsions slowly diminished until it lay still.

It was over. The creature lying dead in the red snow of the trail was turning human, though I didn't recognize him under all the blood.

Our protector stared at us, and I knew that my companions were anything but reassured, but as I met its eyes, I knew we'd been saved by Bayliss, or whatever it was that Bayliss has become.

He vanished back into the foliage.

* * *

The skies disappeared, replaced by a white curtain of heavy snow. We tried to continue, but the footing became impossible. The moisture seeped into every fold and wrinkle of our clothing. The light was flat, so that a hole in the ground appeared to be nothing more than a slight dip, and the trees stretched endlessly into the distance and yet were right in front of us, surrounding us, hemming us in no matter where we turned.

We gave up. No one said anything; there was nothing to be said. We all turned around as one and headed back to the cabin.

January 2, 1847

We have begun to tear down the last of the ox hides that cover the ceiling of the cabin. We are cutting them into strips and boiling them. The stew is an ugly brown, pasty and cloying, and nearly inedible, even as hungry as we are.

This morning, we woke to find a thick frost covering us. The fire had burned so low that it was nearly impossible to rekindle. The Breens have agreed to accept us into their cabin if we are willing to share the ox hides. We are moving over this afternoon. We take nothing but the clothing on our backs and the moldering blankets, stiff with the cold.

January 3, 1847

I can recall a time when I thought my fellow travelers kind and generous. How naïve that now seems!

I believe that all of us are hoarding food. I am ashamed to admit that I am. Though I have given up my portion to my brothers more than once, I always save a little for myself. We have become so wretched and selfish that I fear we are lost to God. He has turned away from us because we are so wanting in virtue.

Today, Mrs. Graves came to our cabin and demanded that we give her the ox hides as payment on what we owe. We argued, but had little energy to resist. After the Graves family left with all the hides they could find, Stanton revealed that he'd hidden some because he'd feared that others would try to steal them.

When these meager scraps are gone, we will have nothing left to eat.

CHAPTER 27

Diary of Charles Stanton, January 1, 1847

I no longer feel the hunger. My body has wasted away, and I am a wraith wandering the woods alone. I am at peace beneath the trees, for nature, in its silence and stillness, is not cruel, simply uncaring. Nature and I are one, and soon I will lie down in the dirt and snow and become nourishment for the earth.

The calendar says that it is a new year. Never has this date seemed so arbitrary, nor had less meaning.

The others are talking about another attempt to leave, this time with the roster to include everyone who can still travel, which is roughly a quarter of those left alive. These are fathers and mothers who are willing to leave their children behind, because all can see that if nothing is done, everyone will die.

I've been asked to go with them and I think I shall, not so much for my own sake, for I can feel that my end is near, but for the sake of the children: for Virginia Reed and her young brothers and sister, for the great brood of Breen siblings, and even for the Graveses, who have become petty and domineering but who only wish to survive, as we all do.

So I will join them. It is a forlorn hope, but I will try one more time to save these people.

There is another reason that I plan to go along. Someone has to protect us from the Things that hunt us. They have us trapped. They don't want us to get away or find help. There are those among us who know that we are being preyed upon, and there are others who are unaware of that terrible fact, but the majority of the Donner Party simply refuses to believe such a thing could happen, even though they have all seen evidence of it.

I have broached the matter with all the different groups, and only the Reeds and the Breens seem both aware of and willing to confront what faces us. To my mind, it is not a coincidence that these are the only two families that have remained mostly intact, and have kept some shreds of their dignity and integrity: the Breens because of their strong Catholic faith and the Reeds because of their strong faith in James Reed, their paterfamilias.

I wish I had faith in either. God I can't speak for. He's never done anything for me. The last time I saw James Reed, he was but a pale shadow of his former domineering, assured self.

I don't know how many of these Monsters there are, or who among us may shift into one at any moment. I sense that most of us are still as we appear, but I don't know for sure.

Virginia Reed has decided to stay, to protect her family, but she took me aside at the last moment.

"William Foster is going with you," she said.

"Yes," I answered. I knew what she was going to say next.

"He has been bitten," she told me.

I nodded and pointed to the pistol at my belt.

I will go along with the others, the witting and the unwitting, and I will keep my pistol and my rifle loaded and close at hand, and endeavor to do my best to protect these poor innocents. I hope that we will draw away enough of the Beasts that the loved ones we are leaving behind will remain unmolested.

January 2, 1847

We have begun our journey. Each of us is armed, and each is carrying a few days' worth of rations—if ox hide and pine nuts can be considered rations. We hope be able to hunt and forage along the way, but thus far we have seen no wildlife, not even their tracks. All God's creatures know better than to venture out into this cold. Well… almost all.

Franklin Graves fashioned some crude snowshoes for most of us. Those few who started out without them quickly gave up and headed back. We now number fifteen souls.

Without the snowshoes, we would make no progress at all, but they are unwieldy, constantly coming undone and needing repair. Our progress is agonizingly slow. None of us is well-nourished enough for this trip, but we cannot wait for help to arrive in the spring. The rescue parties would find us gone, missing like our forebears on Roanoke Island. Vanished. Eaten.

If even a few of us can survive, we will bear testimony to our misery and our struggle.

January...?, 1847

All I can see are the dark vertical stripes of what I think are tree trunks. Everything else is white, sky to ground. We are snow blind. Some of us can't even see the trees, judging by how they keep walking into them. We are walking in single file, each holding onto the person in front of him, and only moving as fast as the slowest among us.

I have seen one other thing: quick flashes of movement among the trees. I fear it will not be long before we are attacked, but we have vowed not to turn back no matter what. I believe we are being herded. It is hard to tell direction, but we climb ever higher, for we know that on the other side of this mountain is California.

The trail, never clear in the first place, has disappeared. We simply follow the easiest route through the underbrush, which means that we encounter dead ends, cliffs, rockslides, and tangled deadfalls, and are constantly forced to double back.

The snow must be twenty feet high. We sleep in tree wells to get out of the wind.

I have no idea how far we've traveled. I've even lost track of the nights. Has it been six, or eight? Such confusion is a result of the hunger and cold we have been suffering. Our food seemed to run out in only a couple of days. We are dying, but no one has proposed that we turn around. No one is giving up. We will not go back.

January...?, 1847

Patrick Dolan has broached the unspeakable. He insists that one of us must die so the others can live. There was a moment of silence after he spoke, but no one objected. Instead, we began rationally discussing how this might happen. Someone, I don't remember who, suggested a duel. Bill Foster suggested a lottery of some kind.

In the end, we were not desperate enough.

Not said aloud but surely thought by all was the fact that soon one of us will succumb, and that person will save the rest of us, giving us the energy that will make it possible to move on a little farther. Perhaps far enough to survive.

Winter,
1847

I am no longer putting dates in this journal. I can't remember what day it is. This accursed journey has been my whole life, and nothing good has ever happened. I am not going to survive this; none of us will.

Unless... unless we do the unthinkable—the forbidden.

Franklin Graves died during the night. Soon after dawn, if the thin light that wended its way through the trees could be called dawn, Antonio also passed on. A blizzard has kept us here for days now. No one looks at the two bodies.

Lemuel Murphy, the twelve-year-old boy, is near death. It was finally decided that some of us—I won't record whom—should cut away strips of flesh from the corpses and feed them to the child, to try to save him. I refused. I told them that once we took that step, we would never come back.

Lemuel need never know what he has eaten, they argued.

I started out on this mission with the intention of saving us from the Monsters. Little did I know we would become Monsters ourselves.

I refuse to partake, knowing that this will seal my fate. I do not judge the others. I cannot judge them, for I am tempted. It is meat, after all. Only meat.

I walked away from the campsite. Luis and Salvador started to follow, but I told them to stay. I watched from a distance as the others—again, I will not say whom—crouched over one of the bodies and hacked at the flesh.

This sight was apparently too much for Patrick Dolan, who got up in the middle of this scene, muttering incoherently. He took off his clothes, the sounds he was making more like those of an animal than a man. He ran directly toward me; I don't know if he saw me or if it was happenstance. As he ran, he began to Turn. He dropped to his hands and knees and hunched his back upward as if in pain. His face elongated and his groans became growls, his hands and feet became claws, and he howled at the gray skies in pain or triumph, I couldn't tell which.

I heard answering howls off in the distance, and I knew that we had been herded to this spot where we could all be consumed.

The creature that had been Dolan started lurching back toward the campsite, where the others stood frozen. I took aim and shot it in the back.

It flopped to the ground, then tried to get up and run toward me, but it covered only a few yards before falling over. I walked over carefully and prodded the body with the tip of the rifle. Before my eyes, the fur faded away, the snout receded, and the creature turned back into a man.

I grabbed him by his ankles and dragged him toward the others. They left off hacking at the corpse and stood silently, watching me.

"If you have to eat someone, you should eat he who intended to eat you," I said; then I walked away.

I will watch them from a distance. I will try to protect them.

But I am no longer one of them.

CHAPTER 28

Diary of Charles Stanton, Undated Entry

I have survived, though the night I left the others, I was certain I would perish. I dug a hole in a snowbank and nestled into the little cave I had made. It seemed a strange thing to do, but almost immediately, I felt relief from the frigid winds. The snow was like a blanket draped around me. A blizzard was building, so I stayed where I was. The next morning, I was surprised to find myself warmer than I have been since this desolate winter began.

The hunger has once again faded away. It is as if my body understands that it shall never again be granted food. This, my body, is all the fuel I have, or will ever have.

I'm just out of sight of the others, and I can hear them clearly. The soft sounds carry far under the glowering sky—nightmare voices devoid of humanity, discussing the unthinkable. I imagine that the doomed souls of hell talk in such a way.

They spoke calmly of what parts of the bodies to cut away next. They organized the flesh in such a way that they could distinguish its origins, so that no one need consume his own relatives, as if it were acceptable to eat friends but not family. I could scarcely believe what I was hearing.

I overheard William Eddy refuse to eat the flesh, and ascertained that Luis and Salvador had likewise turned away in disgust. Later that day, as the blizzard grew, I heard a whispered discussion among the survivors about whether they should kill the Indians. In the evening, I stole to the edge of the camp and caught the attention of my former companions. I felt responsible for them. They followed me to this desolate end. Luis and Salvador turned to look at me with stoic faces. I warned them of the others' intentions. Later that night, they slipped away into the darkness.

I thought about following them or asking them to join me, but I thought better of it, deeming it best for them to get away completely, to use whatever skills they possessed to survive and rejoin their own kind. I let them go. No one was supposed to know I was there. I wanted to remain unseen, unnoticed, a guardian from a distance. I crept away from the camp, back to my snow cave. I could hear the sounds of the Things that hunt us in the woods all around us.

The group managed to get a fire going, and as they began to cook the human flesh, I gagged at the smell—not because it was foul, but because it was so enticing. I breathed through my mouth, trying not to take it in, but well into the night, when the fires had long since burned low, the smell of the flesh still coated my nostrils and throat.

In the morning, I changed my mind and decided to follow after Luis and Salvador. I don't know if I planned to join them in trying to escape or to plead with them to help me save the others.

I'm not certain that I wanted to save the others.

At first their tracks led directly west, but soon they started meandering, and I realized they had become lost. Luis and Salvador had left in a hurry, without the tools they needed to start a fire, without sufficient clothing. This was true of myself as well, of course, but I was possessed of an unusual energy, as if knowing that my end was near had given me permission to expend all my life's spirit in a few days.

I saw depressions where one or the other of them had fallen, and their footprints grew ever closer together, as if they were merely shuffling forward. I feared what I would find.

I was not the first to find them. They were in a clearing, leaning against a fallen log, their heads nearly touching. They were conscious—their eyes were moving—but they were covered with a crust of frozen snow and clearly hadn't moved in hours.

I didn't see fear in their eyes, only acceptance of their fate. They were at peace, for they knew they had tried to do right.

Standing over them was Bill Foster, his rifle cradled in his arms. He was still, his chin on his chest as if he was deep in thought, contemplating the condition of the Indians.

I raised my rifle, ready to fire if he should start to turn into a beast. Virginia had warned me that Foster had been bitten, so I had been expecting this.

"I'm sorry," I heard him say. He pointed his rifle at Luis's face and fired. The Indian's head all but disappeared, chunks flying through the air and splattering against tree trunks.

Salvador gave a low groan. I should have fired at Foster then, but I was so stunned by this unexpected turn of events that he had plenty of time to pull his pistol and shoot Salvador in the chest.

I ran into the clearing. Foster was leaning down, staring into Salvador's eyes as he died, but straightened up when he saw me coming. I didn't see guilt in his face, merely a faint surprise that I was there, and he even began to offer a welcoming smile before he noticed my expression.

"What have you done, you bastard?" I cried. I'd been horrified by my companions' willingness to eat their dead fellows, but until then, none of us had murdered another.

"They're just savages," Foster said calmly. "They were dying anyway. I did them a favor."

I almost shot him then. Perhaps I should have.

He ignored me, got down on his knees, and pulled out his knife. He turned Salvador over and cut away his leggings, took a section of thigh and began to hack it off.

Again he shocked me, because instead of taking the meat back to the others or starting a fire, he took a handful of the raw flesh and began to eat it. He gagged a few times but kept swallowing. As I watched, he began to Turn.

I backed away in horror. I heard the sounds of bones shifting and cracking, the slithering of flesh as it moved to different parts of the man's body and assumed different proportions, the ripping of clothing as muscles expanded. Foster pulled off his clothes as quickly as he could, revealing long black fur.

Backing away, I stumbled over a log and fell over backward. My rifle discharged uselessly into the sky. I heard growling above me, then something landed roughly on my legs. I looked up into the face of a werewolf.

Its fangs were coated in blood, and unlike the other werewolves I'd seen, there appeared to be no human intelligence in those red eyes. This was an animal, nothing more. I felt its claws in my shoulders and thighs, digging into me with the violence of its snarling. It lowered its muzzle and I pushed desperately at its neck, but it continued to press down on me as if it couldn't even feel my resistance. It licked my neck, and then I felt its teeth start to sink into my flesh.

Suddenly, it stiffened. Confusion filled its eyes, and it cocked its head as if perplexed. As I watched, the creature began to turn back into the man I knew as William Foster.

As soon as Foster realized he was crouching over me, he sprang up, startled. He looked down at his torn, discarded clothing and shivered, then began to put the clothes back on. As he did so, he noticed that his hands were covered with blood. He touched his face, his mouth, and pulled away a strip of flesh caught in his teeth and held it out in front of him in bafflement. He tossed it away in disgust. Then he saw the bodies of Luis and Salvador, and he froze in place as the import of what he was seeing sank in.

"What happened here?" he asked.

"You started to turn into a wo—"

"No!" he shouted, drowning out my words.

I tried again. "You were becoming a crea—"

"I don't want to hear it!" he cried. He stared at the two dead Indians, then turned away. I saw him trying to compose himself. "I found them this way," he said.

He looked at me defiantly, as if daring me to contradict him.

I saw no point in doing so. I shrugged, casually picked up my rifle, and began to load it. I wasn't yet sure what I was going to do, but reckoned it was best to be prepared.

Foster didn't look concerned by my reloading. It was as if, as far as he was concerned, nothing that had happened had really happened. He turned stiffly and walked away, back toward the others. By the time I had finished reloading, he was out of sight. I decided not to pursue him.

I stood over the bodies of Luis and Salvador and wept. For the first time since our troubles began, I wept. Yes, I wept bitterly for a couple of savages: savages who had volunteered to help strangers—white men—and had been murdered for their kindness.

I felt something trickling down my neck and touched the place where I'd been bitten. He'd barely sunk his teeth into me before he changed back, but they'd gone deep enough to make me bleed.

I shuddered. So far, everyone I have witnessed get bitten by one of these creatures has turned into a Monster. I looked at the blood on my hand and felt my heart sink, but I shook off my dismay. I never expected to survive this trip anyway; now I've decided to make certain that I won't.

I wished I could bury my friends, or at least cover them, but I could barely move and didn't dare expend the energy. With a last muttered apology, I headed back to my shelter. I hadn't gone more than a dozen yards when I sensed something behind me.

I turned to see five of the creatures approaching the dead Indians with their noses to the ground, sniffing. A couple of them glanced my way, unconcerned, then dismissed me from their attention.

I raised the rifle, then lowered it. At best, I could kill one of them before the rest fell upon me. They began to tear into Luis and Salvador, growling and snapping. The huge male who led them went first, and when he'd torn off enough flesh to drag away, the others started worrying the bodies, tearing off limbs and ripping open stomachs to get at the still-warm entrails.

I backed away, foot by foot, and finally, when I was out of sight of the carnage, I turned and ran.

CHAPTER 29

Diary of James Reed, San Jose, California, December 26, 1846

I shunned all celebrations at Christmas. Indeed, I fasted in sympathy with the poor souls stuck in the mountains of the Sierra Nevada.

The people of San Jose have tried to help me, petitioning the military to mount an expedition. This appeal received little response, so I sent out a call to civilians. Only three men responded, and though some supplies have been donated, I know it will not be enough. I will have to wait until this conflict is decided. The roads have been made impassable by the tide of refugees fleeing local uprisings.

I have bowed to the inevitable and accepted my commission as an officer. As commander of the volunteers, I have been given the cast-off uniform of one of Fremont's lieutenants. I feel ridiculous, as if I am an imposter: even in the Black Hawk War, in the midst of real danger, on real battlefields, my uniform always felt like a costume. But I salute my superiors and follow orders. What's more, I give orders and they are followed.

It is all real enough.

The native Mexicans clearly don't want to fight us. They don't seem to care who claims sovereignty over this beautiful land, far-off Mexico City or far-off Washington; they certainly don't want to die over it.

Fremont, on the other hand, is itching for a fight, so we play soldier while my family starves in the snows. I gave my word that if Fremont helped me in my rescue attempt, I would stay in his service until the conflict is resolved. I didn't foresee that the conflict might never manifest to be resolved.

Even if I wished to break my word, all available resources have been requisitioned and all able-bodied men have been drafted. I have made some contacts among the soldiers that I hope will prove useful when this is all over.

Fremont endlessly drills his regulars as well as the volunteers, but the more he drills, the more frustrated he becomes as he realizes that the civilians are never going to take to military life.

I am not sleeping, which only gives my mind more time to obsess over what might be happening to my family. If the situation here is not resolved soon, I will desert, and even if it means joining my family only to share their doom, I will find them. I cannot let them believe I have abandoned them.

January 5, 1847

The battle—such as it was—is over. For us, that means the Mexican-American War is over. The Battle of Santa Clara, as it is being called in the dispatches, was little more than a skirmish.

The forces facing us were more than sufficient to defeat us on their own, and they had even more resources they could have called upon, but they chose not to fight. Fremont's belligerence is winning battles before they begin, battles whose outcome would have been in doubt if they were actually fought.

All had surrendered to us but one Mexican official, who unexpectedly decided to kidnap six sailors from the sloop USS Warren while they were on shore requisitioning supplies. I suspect the sailors may have been trying to take the supplies without paying. The Californios already don't trust us because of our constant invasion of their ranchos, and what may have been a minor incident turned into a crisis. The Army wanted a fight and was looking for any excuse to start one, and this was their excuse.

I was in the San Jose area when the skirmish started and immediately reported for duty to the local commander, a captain of artillery named Marston. Once again, I'd been trying to organize a relief party. Every available white man was caught up in the coming conflict, so I'd decided to search out Californios who might be willing to help me, for money or for charity. The Mexicans refused to even talk to me, however.

I was certain there would be no battle. No one had the stomach for it. I was therefore astonished to be called into the captain's tent and told that the volunteer troops would be given the honor of leading the charge. I was surprised by that, because I was certain the regular Army would want to take credit for our victory, but then I realized that they would take credit in any case, and no doubt thought that if they could win the battle without any regulars being killed, so much the better.

"Have you sent a delegation to negotiate?" I asked.

"I will not negotiate with hostage takers," Marston declared. "You are to march to the walls of the town and lead the charge. Do you understand?"

"Yes, sir," I said, giving him my best salute.

We had scarcely left the camp before I ordered the column to halt. I took aside the lieutenant who had been assigned to me as liaison to the regulars.

"Woodworth, we aren't going to be charging a fixed position," I told him. "That's suicide. We will approach under cover, and when given the signal, we will fire upon the walls. Then we will ask for negotiations."

"Those aren't our orders, sir." The young fellow needed to be convinced, but I could see he was already wavering.

I grabbed him by his sleeve and stared earnestly into his face. "I've seen what happens when men charge across an open field at an entrenched enemy. Please do as I ask."

"Yes, sir," he said, without further hesitation.

We crept through a mustard field, the high stalks of the plants concealing our approach. When we neared the open area between the field and the walls, a sentry saw us and fired upon us. Woodworth and I were leading the way, and I immediately pulled him to the ground. As I did so, a bullet hit him in the shoulder.

He looked down, stunned, and grasped my arm. "That would have hit me in the heart!" he exclaimed.

My men returned fire, and for a short time, we exchanged volleys with the enemy. Nobody appeared to be hitting anyone, however.

Even with the bullets flying, even with Woodworth bleeding beside me, it still felt like playing soldier to me. I could see the women of the town watching from atop the flat roofs of the haciendas. We crawled toward the walls, firing as we went.

We were ready to charge the last few feet when our foes raised a white flag. The battle was over.

Two of my men had been wounded. Four of the enemy had been killed.

Later, underneath an old oak tree, a temporary armistice was signed. We agreed that we would not take the Californios' property, and in return, our men were released—and just like that, the war was done.

* * *

I walked away, taking off my too-hot coat, though it was against regulations to do so. I swore I would never again fight my fellow man or wear anyone's uniform.

Outside the town walls, an elderly Californio approached me. "Sir, may I have a word with you?"

"What is it?"

"I asked your captain, but he was rather rude," he said in heavily accented English. He looked at my ill-fitting officer's uniform dubiously. "I have a small inquiry. Are you a gentleman of means? Would you be interested in buying some land?"

"I would be very interested in seeing it," I replied.

It may seem strange, but I am still trying to think of what our future will be in this land. With God's grace, my family will join me soon, and it would be a fine thing to have a home already established.

The man, whose name was Sanchez, took me to his home that night and fed me a feast, and even agreed to supply mules and food for my rescue expedition. In return, I gave him most of the money I still had in credit with Sutter.

"Why do you sell your land so cheaply?" I asked him.

"I do not believe in the assurances of the Americanos that they will allow us to keep our land," he replied. "Conquerors always say that. But they *are* conquerors, and sooner or later, they will remember it. I would rather sell now for less than lose it all later."

A wise man, I thought. I drank to this sentiment, which I thought was no doubt true.

Now all that is needed is for the Mexican garrison south of us to sign a more permanent truce, and I will finally be able mount an expedition to retrieve my family.

February 15, 1847

At last! I have assembled a party composed of men familiar with the wilderness, secured enough supplies to feed all whom we will find, and—most importantly—have the determination to see the rescue through, no matter the difficulties. The military has pitched in, grateful for my service. I made an effort to get to know my men and to convince them of my desperation. Woodworth has been promoted to captain and has asked to lead the party. I'm more than happy to let him take the lead if it will bring more help. The people of this beautiful land have finally responded with all their hearts.

I have not said anything about the creatures I saw in the wilderness. No one would believe me, and indeed, at times I'm not certain I believe it myself. California is the paradise that everyone described. The temperature, even in the middle of winter, is mild. The rivers run high with water that will make the valleys fertile. It seems impossible that only a few days away is a land of starvation and horror, a land where creatures out of myth stalk mankind.

Dear Margret, please wait for me, for I will be there soon. Dear, brave Virginia, watch over your brothers and sister. Salvation is at hand!

For Virginia's sake, I will continue to believe what I saw in the shadows, amid the trees. She came to me early on to warn me that something was wrong. Why did I dismiss her concerns, even though I'd seen evidence of the same things? She looked this horrible reality in the face and accepted it for what it was, while we adults ignored or denied the danger. I will not now conveniently dismiss those memories, no matter how difficult it is to believe them. But neither will I bring them up unnecessarily. I don't want to scare off any of the men who can help us, nor would it benefit us if they began to doubt my sanity.

William Eddy is leading a vanguard, and the other members of the expedition will follow them shortly. The rains have swollen the rivers, and already we are delayed. There have been reports, terrible reports, of cannibalism amongst those who crossed over the mountains in early January. I pray that those left at Truckee Lake have not had to resort to such measures.

I cannot think that anyone in my family would do such a thing: surely they would choose death over such an abomination. I cling to the hope that I will find them alive.

CHAPTER 30

Diary of Charles Stanton, Undated Entry

I am in possession of myself, but for how long, I do not know. I am still clothed, and my clothes are covered in mud and snow but not blood. Though I have been dreaming of running through the woods on four legs, leaping over logs with ease, the snow bracing rather than freezing, the small animals all around me waiting to be caught and eaten, I'm still as hungry as ever.

I do not think I have transformed.

I feel as if I am dreaming all of this—my life as a man as well as my life as a wolf—and sometimes I can't tell what is real and what isn't.

I seem to have more strength, to see and smell and hear more acutely than before. The bite mark on my neck has healed already. I have no doubt that in time, I will become one of those Things. I will not allow that to happen. I keep my rifle loaded, and when I feel my humanity slipping away, I will end it.

Until then, I will watch over the others and try to protect them from the creatures. I see the Things in glimpses, smell them passing by, and hear them in the darkness.

It is easy enough to keep up with the party, for they have started to consume the hides that bind their snowshoes, and while that may be giving them strength, it is also slowing them down. Jay Fosdick had started to lag behind, and one night, as I slipped unwittingly into sleep, I heard him cry out. I hastened to his side, but by the time I arrived, Fosdick was already being torn apart by the creatures, who lifted their heads to growl at me— not because they thought I would harm them, I believe, but because they thought I'd try to compete for their meat.

The next morning, Eddy and Mary Graves went off to hunt. I trailed them closely and when they brought down a deer, I stood just out of sight with my rifle at the ready until the pair had packed up what meat they could carry and headed back to the others. I saw several werewolves trailing them, but I warned them away. They trotted off without looking back.

Before we left Truckee Lake, we managed to gather up enough rations for six days. A month has passed since then. A full moon illuminates the night sky. The storms are fading, but without the cloud cover, it is colder than ever.

The party stumbled into a Miwok Indian camp by accident. The Indians scattered into the trees, but when they saw the pathetic remnants of humanity fall upon the scraps of food left for the dogs, they returned.

It was the same Miwok camp that Luis and Salvador had visited on their way to help us. Once, it would have seemed primitive beyond imagining; now it seemed full of life, energy, and beauty.

William Foster stood at the edge of the clearing, apart from the others. Only days before, he had killed two natives; now natives were rescuing him and his companions. The Miwok most likely will never know what became of their friends, but I could see that all the survivors felt guilty. Foster looked completely forlorn.

The Indians began to share their meager food, and I walked away, believing the worst was over.

Diary of Charles Stanton and the Other, Undated Entry

I have wandered the hills for I know not how long. I shun the company of both men and beasts, for I belong with neither. I have not yet put the gun to my head, as I planned. Life is too dear to me, it appears, even now. Sometimes I wake from my dream of being a beast and find blood caking my face, and I know that I transformed. Yet I also know, somehow, that I have not attacked humans; I have hunted only other beasts. Does that make me a cannibal of a different kind?

* * *

I found myself slowly making my way back down the mountains, toward Truckee Lake. I suppose I hoped I might still help the Reeds, the Breens, and the others trapped there. I don't know what I expected to do.

I have begun to control the transformation. When I feel my blood coursing more quickly through my veins and my eyesight becoming sharper, I know it is about to begin.

There is no use fighting it. I am hungry, cold, thirsty, tired—and in my human form, helpless. So I allow myself to Turn. I find a place to remove my clothing and hide my human artifacts from view, then I change. For a short time, I remember who I am even as I run through the woods, hunting the animals I smell hibernating beneath the snow. Then I, Charles Stanton, begin to fade, and I become fully that other creature, which has no name but a distinct smell, appearance, and identity of its own. I am the Other, but I am also myself.

Somehow, in my wildness, I make my way back to the place where I have hidden my clothing. I dress, shivering but alive, fed, and full of energy. I sit with my journal and recount what I have seen and felt.

I have begun to remember my nightly wanderings. I have begun to remember my human self while animal, and my animal self while human. But the opposite is also true: I am forgetting more of my human self when human, and more of my animal self when animal. I am becoming both things, and neither.

I came across one of the humans beside Alder Creek. I don't remember his name—he was one of the drivers for the Breen family, I believe. The poor emaciated soul stood in the trail looking at me, defeated by my very presence. These remnants of humanity, too weak to attempt to escape over the pass, have been preyed upon the whole time I was gone. I feared what I would find at the Reed cabin.

I almost transformed into human then, to stand naked before him, but I had no explanation to give him for what I have become. I was ashamed, I suppose. I turned and ran. Anyway, I'm not certain he would have been reassured by my transformation.

I have come back to my little hiding place, a small cave outside the camp, where I sit scribbling in my notebook, trying to remember words, trying to remember how to shape letters.

The other werewolves avoid me, more afraid of my wolf form than they ever were of my human form. More than once, my presence has stopped an attack. But I can't be everywhere, and from time to time I come across the remains of unfortunate wretches who have been caught by the pack and torn to pieces.

One day, as I patrolled the perimeter of the camp, I saw Virginia Reed emerge from one of the cabins. She was alert and looking about. She didn't appear defeated, already a victim, as so many of the others do. I don't believe she saw me, but she seemed to sense I was there. She grasped her father's rifle in both hands and called out, "Who's there? Jean? Is that you? Bayliss?"

I stayed hidden until she went back inside. It is as if she has a supernatural sense for when werewolves are around. That night, I left a rabbit I had caught at the entrance of the cabin, and ever since, I have left what I could. I have chosen to help the Reeds, because I can't help everyone and because they showed me the greatest kindness, taking me into their cabin, making me a part of their family.

The Reeds and the Breens have retained their cohesion as families, but the other small groups have fallen apart. They huddle together, facing out into the night, but they don't act as if they are aware of each other.

The Germans don't even pretend anymore. Keseberg leads the pack, and all the other single men follow him. I know that Jean has been Turned, though I haven't seen him kill. The others trap and kill any human who strays from the group. Some have wandered away deliberately, tired of living, letting themselves be culled. In several cases, I tried to help them, but the humans simply sat there in the snow, unwilling to move, until I could bear it no longer and left them to their fate.

Until now, the werewolves have been content to pick off the humans one by one, but as the days grow longer and spring approaches, they have picked up the pace. The humans who are left are the ones who truly want to survive. I sense that we are fast approaching a final battle of some kind.

Yesterday, I ran far and high up the mountain, and far below, I saw a rescue party approaching. I suspect that the next few nights will see the monsters try to kill as many as they can before it is too late.

Once again, I have chosen the Reed family to look after. I will be their sentinel tonight, and the next, until relief finally arrives.

Diary of Charles Stanton and the Other, Undated Entry

It is well that I stood guard last night.

I saw the werewolves gather between the cabins and watched them transform. There are at least a dozen of them now, more than I have any chance of fighting off; still, they targeted the other cabins first.

As I watched, I sensed something behind me. I turned to see a gray wolf, not as big nor as well fed as the others, approaching me. As my hackles rose and I growled at the intruder, it transformed, and there, standing naked and shivering in the snow, was the young man Bayliss. He seemed to know who I was. Perhaps, as he has been a wolf longer than me, he determined my identity by smell.

This night, the two of us stand watch together.

Tomorrow night, I fear, will come the final reckoning.

Diary of Charles Stanton and the Other, Undated Entry

Last night, as I stood guard, Bayliss came up to me, and we stood shoulder to shoulder, waiting.

We could hear the others approaching; we could smell their hunger and animal excitement, just as they, no doubt, could smell our fear. But our fear didn't make us any less dangerous.

There were six werewolves, including the giant red one I recognized as Keseberg. It growled at the others, who halted and sat on their haunches as he moved forward.

He transformed into his human form, a tall, wiry man with scars all over his body. His face has the aspect of a wolf even when he is a man. "Why do you help them?" he asked. "Do you think they would treat you any differently than the rest of us if they knew?"

"We still remember what it's like to be human," I said.

"You two are mistakes. Freaks. Don't you understand? You aren't human any more. You never will be. If they discover what you are, they will think nothing of hunting you down. That's why we led them to this place. No one will be allowed to leave unless they join us."

Bayliss stood trembling but defiant. He looked about half the size of Keseberg. "You can't have them," he said. "You'll have to kill us first."

Keseberg sighed. "Have it your way," he said. He stayed in human form but growled orders to the others. Two of the biggest wolves approached. Bayliss and I had already begun shifting, but we had barely attained wolf form when they leaped for us.

I took the lead wolf's charge, and the other slammed into Bayliss.

I suppose we had fear and desperation on our side, and it lent us strength. I was faster than the other wolf, who seemed almost lazy in his movements. He circled me but didn't attack again; then he moved away.

Bayliss had a similar experience, though he ended up bleeding from a bite to his shoulder.

Keseberg waved more wolves forward, and again we blustered and nipped at each other but didn't close for the fight. I realized then that they were working as a pack, wearing us out, and that it was only a matter of time before several of them attacked each of us at once.

That very scenario had begun to play out when suddenly, one of the three wolves stalking toward me turned on the others, clamping down on the neck of one of his companions. The attack surprised everyone.

The injured wolf fell to the ground, thrashing, while his attacker continued to savage his neck; then there was a snap, and the wolf on the ground lay still. His killer turned and growled at the others, then backed away until he stood beside me. I recognized his scent: it was Jean.

I took advantage of the momentary confusion caused by his defection and attacked, and with my new ally's help, I soon drove off my remaining foe. Bayliss, meanwhile, had two wolves of his own to deal with, though he was managing to fend them off.

Then Keseberg transformed and joined them.

I sprang forward as the wolves pinned Bayliss to the ground, one chomping on his back leg, another latched onto his throat. Before I could stop him, Keseberg closed his jaws on the back of Bayliss's neck; bones cracked, there was a final yelp, and then Bayliss went still.

The three wolves turned toward Jean and me.

One of them leaped at Jean, inexplicably flew sideways in midair, crashed to the earth, and lay there, unmoving: only then did I hear the gunshot. I turned to see Virginia Reed standing by the entrance to the cabin. Calmly, she set down the rifle, pulled a pistol from her coat, and aimed it at Keseberg.

Keseberg didn't hesitate; he ran.

The other wolves began to back away, then trotted off after their leader. Virginia held the gun steady until they were out of sight, then turned and looked at us uncertainly. Neither Jean nor I transformed. Though I think Virginia sensed who we were, I also knew that it would trouble her to see us change. We turned and ran into the night, leaving Bayliss behind with Virginia crouched over his naked human form.

I sit in my little cave while Jean huddles under the few extra blankets I have. We haven't said a word to each other. What is there to say? We aren't human anymore, but we still love those we left behind. We will go back the next night, and the next, as long as it takes for rescue to arrive.

And then? I still have my revolver, with a single bullet. I will not live as a beast. I will not hide. I will end it.

But not before the others are safe.

Diary of
Charles Stanton

Jean has returned to Truckee Lake and informed me that he will not let himself Turn again. I admire his resolve, but I don't think he will have any choice. The Beast is so hard to resist. Yesterday, I came across a young boy on the trail, and I almost killed him. I charged at him but veered away at the last second, his screams ringing in my ears.

I ran to the summit and looked down. Below, I saw the rescue expedition struggling against the snow. It took all my willpower not to turn back into my human form and go warn them.

* * *

They have come for me. I can hear them in the darkness, drawing closer. There are at least three of them that I can smell. I fear this is my last night.

I will wrap up this diary as best I can in my woolen clothing, so that it might survive, and lay it at the doorway to Virginia Reed's cabin as a tribute to her bravery. Perhaps she will learn something that will help her.

If, when this is all over, someone else should read this diary, they will not believe it.

But it is a true story.

Goodbye.

CHAPTER 31

Diary of Virginia Reed, Undated Entry

I do not know what day this is. I'm not even completely certain about the month.

It doesn't matter. Bayliss is dead.

I have already mourned him once, and now I must mourn him again. I want to cry, but I don't dare: I don't have the luxury of grief. I want to lose myself in memories, but for the sake of my family, I must stay in the here and now—though in truth, I have nearly given up.

Bayliss saved me.

I have hidden his body from the others. No one in our cabin has resorted to cannibalism, but I fear it is only a matter of time.

When you see someone's body, you know beyond doubt that that person is gone forever. What is left is only a shell. Seeing that body as a source of sustenance when you are starving is not as unthinkable as I would have once believed, though the taboo is stronger for family and loved ones.

I have already decided that I will die rather resort to such measures. I will walk into the woods, find a place to curl up, and let the wild animals take me—but not the werewolves. They will not have me. I will see to that.

Three wolves protected our cabin last night. One of them was Bayliss. I think I know who the other two were. One moved with an old, stiff dignity that reminded me of Stanton... which made me fear for the group that he left with. Are they all lost? Or has only Stanton fallen?

The other wolf... I don't know how I know this, but I do. It was Jean Baptiste.

At night, we block the entrance to the cabin with all the impediments we have, though I know it would be a simple matter for these beasts to force their way in. Whichever of them dares poke his muzzle into the entrance will have his head blown off. I have spoken loudly to the others about my willingness to protect my home. I not only have my father's rifle, I also have two pistols to back it up. So far, the creatures have not dared to try anything.

At night, I hear them prowling outside. They used to jump onto our roof and scramble about up there, but not long ago, one poked its nose in the hole the smoke escapes through and I shot at it. That was the last time I heard them on the roof. They growl at each other and howl, and sometimes they find meat in the snow. When the first of us died, we put the bodies in a snowbank, thinking to preserve them until rescue arrived, hoping we could one day give them a decent burial. We woke one morning to find a dug-up snowbank and red streaks where the bodies had been dragged away. Bones are strewn about the encampment, but I have decided that they are animal bones and do not look too closely.

I'm not sure why the creatures don't attack in the daytime. I know they are mortal and can be killed like any other animal, and I think they hunt by night for the safety of the darkness. It is harder to shoot what you can't see.

* * *

We have become so weak, I wonder how long we can continue. Patty takes the rifle in the afternoons while I sleep: Mother refuses to do so. It's as if she is unaware of the danger. I think she has retreated into her own mind, and all she ever thinks of now is her family and how to feed us. I've shown Patty how to point the rifle and pull the trigger, but I fear she will freeze when the time comes and I will awaken staring into the eyes of a monster.

Eliza vanished from our cabin. No one saw her leave. I hope she has rejoined the Donners, but I fear she has given herself to the snows. I saw her giving her share of the food to my brothers, and during her last few days with us, she barely moved from her bed.

As bad as our situation is, it is much worse in the other cabins. Everyone avoids the Murphy cabin now, for the werewolves are encamped beside it. I'm not certain how many of those poor people are still alive inside the pine log walls.

I have decided to see how the Donners are doing down at Alder Creek. The last I heard, the cut on George Donner's shoulder had become infected. I will have to take a long, looping detour around the Murphy cabin, but I am determined to go. It is time to join forces, to band together against the Things that prey upon us.

* * *

It was bright when I set out, the shadows all dispelled by sunlight, and my night fears seemed exaggerated. Then I came upon the first body. It was in pieces, strewn beside the trail, barely recognizable as human. The head was missing, for which I was grateful. I didn't want to know which of my fellow travelers it had been. I hurried past.

I found George Donner and his sons inside one of the tents at Alder Creek. It was filled with the foul odor emanating from his shoulder, which was oozing pus and slime. He looked up at me and winced.

"Ah, Virginia. I'm glad to see you still among the living."

"I've come to check on you, sir."

He shrugged, then groaned. "I'm fine, as long as I don't move."

"Eliza is gone," I told him. "Did she return here?"

He shook his head sadly. "She was too gentle a girl for this journey. Not like you, Virginia."

The back flap of the tent opened. A werewolf poked its muzzle in and growled.

"Watch out!" I cried, lifting my rifle and aiming at the beast.

"Stop!" Donner cried. He snarled something and the werewolf went away. As I stared at him, dumbfounded, he gave me a lopsided grin. "That was my daughter," he said quietly.

"You're one of them!" Even as I exclaimed it, I realized that I've known this for some time but haven't wanted to admit it. Yet I'm not afraid of him, not like I am of Keseberg and the others.

"I'm sorry, Virginia," he said. "It wasn't supposed to happen this way. I'd have preferred you never found out."

I realized something else then. "You led here on purpose!"

"I didn't mean for this to happen," he said. "Oh, I knew there would be deaths, of both humans and livestock, as on all journeys to the far West. We meant to feed off those deaths, that is true, but we weren't supposed to reveal ourselves. Our Kind survives in the shadows, whispered about but never spoken of too loudly... "

He shook his head. "Some of these young pups have different ideas. They think of humans as livestock. They think we should feed openly and dare humans to do anything about it. They've forgotten that we were once nearly wiped out in Europe before we set the rules in place: to kill animals rather than humans, and never to make more of Our Kind without approval, other than through natural births.

"I support the old traditions. I called this Wolfenrout because I could see the rules were failing. Keseberg challenged me. It was a fair fight: I'm not as decrepit as I look. Still, I lost, so I must give way to the young, though I believe they will lead us into disaster. I fear, Virginia, that you are on your own. No one will defend you. My sons are too precious to me to allow them to fight Keseberg. He's won."

"How many of you are there?" I thought that if I could discover who amongst us were werewolves, I could avoid them, and I would know who I was up against, and how many.

Donner looked at his sons, who were frowning. "Again, I'm sorry, Virginia. You are not one of us. I have sympathy for you, but I won't choose

167

you over my own kind, no matter how misguided I may think they've become."

* * *

On my way back to the cabin, I saw a boy standing on top of a small hill. I didn't recognize him, though I must have once known him. Though it wasn't as cold as it was earlier in the week, it was still freezing, but the child wore only a bloodstained nightshirt. He was holding a severed human arm in one hand.

I thought he would turn away in shame, or drop the arm and run off.

Instead, he looked at me blankly, lifted the arm, and gnawed a chunk of flesh away. He stared at me with dull eyes and chewed slowly.

Perhaps there isn't as much difference between man and beast as I once thought. Perhaps it isn't the form that matters, but what is inside it. We have been tested, and most of us have failed.

The werewolves are feeding on us as if we are livestock. If we cannot defend ourselves—if we refuse to even believe what is happening to us—then perhaps we deserve our fate.

My mother, I suspect, will never admit the truth. She sees the wolves, but she doesn't see the humans beneath the wolf skins. In her mind, it is the wilderness that is killing us. Patty is like Mother in this, and Tommy and Jimmy are too young to make sense of it.

Father would believe. Father would act upon what he saw. But until he comes to rescue us, it is up to me to protect my family for as long as I can.

When I entered the cabin, I was gratified to see Patty with the rifle in her arms, staring at me wide-eyed. The look of relief that came over her face made me even more determined to protect her and my brothers, who sleep most of the day now instead of being their usual wild selves. Mother was sewing a patch on one of my dresses, as if holes in clothing still mattered to anyone.

On the way back, I'd found a large, long bone jutting out of the snow. I was certain it was from an animal, probably a horse. I couldn't imagine it belonging to a human; its shape was wrong for that. I handed it to Mother, who once would have reacted with disgust, but who calmly took the bone and added it to the already-boiling soup.

It is getting dark. I have set aside my diary, and I am wide awake. I sit facing the cabin's entrance, waiting for night to fall.

CHAPTER 32

Personal notes of Jacob Donner, Secretary of the Wolfenrout, January 1847

I write in this journal as if the Wolfenrout still exists, but in truth, there is no Wolfenrout anymore. When Keseberg triumphed, the issue was decided. There are no rules, no organization, only brute force. We may appear to be a pack, but we are all lone wolves.

My brother was right. I should have known he would be. There is complete chaos among the Wolfen. Anarchy is our master now. The strongest among us take what they want; the weakest fall by the wayside.

At first, I was glad. I felt free: I could finally hunt whom I wanted, when I wanted. But the humans are aware of us now and on their guard, either barricaded inside the cabins or heavily armed and traveling in groups. The Wolfen are no longer organized enough to confront these men, or to plan attacks on them. We were wrong to believe that once we had the humans trapped, they would be at our mercy, for even a weakened man—or woman, or child—can pull the trigger of a gun. Some of Our Kind have already fallen to these weapons.

Keseberg has corralled the humans who are at our mercy like so much livestock, but he will only share with his own clan and those who swear allegiance to him and him alone. Most Wolfen are too proud to renounce their family line and heritage. Many of those who traveled here for the Foregathering have dispersed into the wilderness, looking to protect themselves, their own packs, their own clans. Those who waited too long are trapped in these mountains with the rest of us.

We thought ourselves clever, herding these humans to this isolated spot to prey upon them, but we outsmarted ourselves. We are trapped just as surely as the humans are. The winter is killing us all, human and Wolfen alike. There are no animals to hunt: whatever wildlife inhabited these woods has fled, been eaten, or died in the extreme cold and deepening snows.

Such things happened in Europe, once upon a time. It was one of the reasons the Wolfen first began to consider cooperation among the clans instead of constant conflict. Because of the growing strength of the humans and the dwindling of the wildlife, we banded together and created the rules that, until recently, concealed our existence and controlled our numbers.

There is vicious irony in the way we—the way *I*—disregarded the rules just when we need them most. We are being reminded, in the most brutal of ways, that there were reasons the Wolfenrout was created, reasons the first Foregathering of the Clans was called.

George was right all along, but I betrayed him, and in doing so, I have doomed my family to starvation or subservience. I tried to join Keseberg and the others, but they would not have me. They refuse to share their food with a traitor. Once the ruling family of Our Kind, we are now in danger of dwindling into oblivion… because of me.

The humans are beginning to consume each other. This disgusted the Wolfen at first, but I now realize that the Wolfen may not be above such a thing, the eating of one's own kind.

I went out this morning, ranging far in search of prey. I once felt strong and free running through the snow; now it clutches at my legs and tries to drag me down. I followed the trail of a jackrabbit, the first signs of life I've seen in days. I saw a splash of blood on the white crust of ice, and the tracks of other wolves. I followed those tracks to find three of my own kind fighting over a small rabbit. I didn't recognize these Wolfen, fighting amongst themselves though they smelled of the same pack. They turned and snarled at me, and I backed away.

The rules of the Wolfenrout say we are to share food with others of Our Kind; it is unheard of for a pack not to do so. As I ran away, I realized that we can no longer count on any of the old rules—and I understood for the first time what that truly means.

What I remember most about this encounter is that those strange wolves were nothing but skin and bones. I looked down at myself and realized that I am the same. I returned to my wife and children, and saw them clearly. We are dying. We have been cast out of my brother's presence, and were not accepted by Keseberg's clan. It was I who destroyed the Wolfenrout, but it is my family who will pay the price.

Personal notes of Jacob Donner, Secretary of the Wolfenrout, February 1847

I was wrong to believe that the matter of our leadership had been settled. Civil war has broken out among the clans. Keseberg is abusing his power, and many of the clans are too proud to submit to him. Though I have offered to act as an intermediary, none of them will accept my services; no one trusts me.

This conflict is killing us. Any Wolfen caught by the rival faction is killed, and if we dare venture out alone—or even in a small group—to hunt, we are attacked. We can only move about in large numbers, and it is ludicrous for an army to try to catch a rabbit. My family is alone. My wife loathes me and my children refuse to speak to me. I am an outcast in my own tent.

The humans are being all but ignored. The few that survive are hardly worth the risk of trying to kill. Instead, we hunt each other. Though I have not seen it with my own eyes, I'm afraid that some among us have indeed resorted to cannibalism, just as the humans have.

The ironies continue to mount. The most aggressive among us have been led to the slaughter. We are caught in our own trap, and thanks to my treachery, those who might have prevented this were never informed of the Foregathering.

Word of this disaster will reach the others. Lessons will be learned from it, I hope. Sometime in the near future, I predict, a Foregathering of the Clans will meet and the reforms George expected to initiate will be put into place after all. The Wolfen will go into hiding and blend in with the humans. The most aggressive among us will be weeded out. Everything George has hoped for—and more—will come to pass. It must, because if it does not, we will be hunted down and exterminated. Our Kind will disappear.

Either way, I will not be there to see it. I have not eaten in many days. I am too weak to hunt.

I will leave this journal at the entrance to George's tent, and I hope that future Wolfenrouts will take heed of the lesson contained herein: beware your ancient instincts, for they will lead to the extinction of Our Kind.

CHAPTER 33

Diary of Virginia Reed, Undated Entry

I wouldn't have believed our hell could grow worse, or that the warmth of the sun would precipitate our misery.

We had all dreamed of the day when the cold would leave our bones, when the sun would thaw our frozen hopes and bring the promise of spring. But instead of the beneficent warmth of our summer memories, the sun beats down upon us like a furnace. That and the fires inside the cabin have made the indoors unendurably hot; but even that is not what is driving us from our shelters.

The stench of death pushes us out into the open, the smell of decay, rot, and sickness. There are those among us who can't move and lie in their own filth. We have carried those we can out into the open and cushioned them as best we can in the softening snow. Samuel Perkins, whom Father hired as a teamster in Independence, was once strong and vital. He now has the appearance of a decrepit old man, moaning as we lift him.

Despite the warmth, food is no easier to find. The remains of oxen and mules long submerged in the snow are being exposed to the sun, but spoil before we can eat them. The corpses of our fellow travelers—those that haven't been dragged off—are also being unveiled, as if a graveyard has been turned upside down. Some of the bodies have been butchered; some are untouched. All of them are decomposing with an odor that makes us sick. Indoors or out, it is all the same.

We tried to cover the exposed bodies with snow, digging with our bare hands for as long as we could stand, then letting the sun warm our hands before we started again.

The werewolves prowl day and night now. I hear screams from the cabin where the Graves and Murphy families are sheltered and see frenzied movement outside, as if fights are breaking out among the creatures: dark shapes against the white, red streaks on the ground. One evening, I crept as close as I dared and discovered that the werewolves have fully overrun that cabin. There is howling in the distance, down by Alder Creek, but I already knew that the Donners were werewolves.

My rifle is the only thing keeping them away. I sit with my back to the wall so they can't sneak up on me, and I barely sleep. But I need only endure a little longer, for their reign of terror will soon end. The coming of the sun heralds our salvation: our rescuers are drawing ever closer.

So I tell myself, but salvation seems far away, like a dream from another life.

* * *

On the second afternoon of the thaw, I was sitting in my usual spot outside, my back to the cabin wall, watching my brothers and sister wander around the clearing, when drowsiness crept over me, catching me unaware.

I heard a cry and leaped to my feet. I had dozed off. I looked around wildly for my family and saw Tommy and Jimmy sitting near me, staring wide-eyed in the direction of the scream. I could hear my mother moving about inside the cabin.

"Patty!" I shouted, for she was nowhere to be seen. Rifle clutched in hand, I ran toward the commotion, arriving just in time to see three wolves dragging old Samuel into the woods. He was unmoving, his blood spurting onto the snow in wide arcs.

I took aim, then lowered the rifle. It was too late. I'd only expend a bullet and expose myself to attack for no reason. I heard someone coming up behind me and turned to see that Patty had followed me. Mother hustled Jimmy and Tommy inside, the boys protesting loudly that they wanted to stay, that Virginia would protect them. Tears streamed down my face. I couldn't protect them. I couldn't even protect myself. I was weak, and so tired I could barely stay awake.

Since then, we've all stayed within sight of the cabin. Patty sticks close to me, following me wherever I go, and I have delegated to her the task of watching my back.

Perhaps they mean to kill us all, leaving no witnesses, or perhaps they have a different plan—or none at all, for I suspect the werewolves are leaderless. From the beginning, it has seemed that they are simply taking advantage of opportunities as they arise. There has been no order to who they attack and when, except that they prey on the most helpless.

Well, I don't intend to be helpless. They may take me in the end, but I'll take at least one of them with me. I check the powder in my rifle constantly and replace it whenever it seems clotted. I do not have enough powder to do this with the pistols, so I'm not confident they will fire, but I am confident of this: the first werewolf to attack me or mine will pay the price.

* * *

I feel safer at night inside this awful cabin. I put cups and pans and anything else that might make a clatter just inside the entrance. I've tried to talk some of the others into keeping watch as I sleep, though no one is reliable. Still, I must sleep. We remain besieged, but the creatures have not yet dared to attack.

* * *

In the end, they came for us in broad daylight. We emerged from the cabin in the morning, those of us who could still move. I took my usual spot near the entrance and kept watch over my family and friends. Some walked around poking at the ground and peering under bushes as if hoping they would find a cache of food. Others simply sat and soaked up the warmth of the sun.

When the wolves attacked, they first appeared as a solid, dark wave, rolling toward us over the white and red snow. As they came nearer, the creatures separated and I could make out their individual shapes. Rising to my feet, I began counting, but in my fear and anxiety, I lost track. I tried again, and again lost count. I would guess there were at least twenty.

The huge red wolf I recognized as Keseberg was in the lead.

I stood and raised my rifle, waiting. The other inhabitants of my cabin were gone, having rushed inside at the first sight of the wolves. *It won't help*, I thought. *When I am gone, there will be no one to protect them.*

I was surprisingly calm, and firm in my resolve. I'd been expecting to die like this. I had even thought it might be preferable to death by starvation, as long as I didn't come back as one of them. If it had just been me, I might have turned the gun on myself, but I had the others to think of.

Keseberg swung his big head toward me, ordering one of his wolves forward. It began to stalk toward me, approaching as if confident that I wouldn't fire or that I would be so frightened I would miss.

I didn't miss. The werewolf was gathering itself to spring when I fired. I hit it directly in the chest, and it fell to the ground. A second wolf was already leaping at me. I swung the stock of the rifle with all my might and caught it in the side of the head. It rolled away and then rose to its feet, shaking itself and growling.

The rifle was broken in half, useless. I pulled one of the pistols, but instead of taking aim at my attacker, I aimed at Keseberg and fired. He gave a high-pitched yelp, like a dog that's been kicked, then limped away, bleeding. His left hind leg looked as if it was barely attached to his body.

Drawing my other pistol, I turned to face the remaining wolves, but they too were fleeing, tails bobbing behind them as they disappeared amongst the trees.

A moment later, I found out why. With their keener ears, they'd heard before I did the sound I'd dreamed of for months: shouts, the hearty shouts of healthy men, such as I had not heard in a long while. They had heard my shot and come running.

"Father?" I cried, searching anxiously for his familiar form.

A group of men entered the clearing; strong, energetic men, calling out to me excitedly, leading pack mules laden with supplies... with food.

Trembling, I fell to my knees in the slushy snow, heedless of how it dampened my trousers or of who saw me weeping.

We were saved.

CHAPTER 34

Diary of Virginia Reed, Truckee Lake, February 19, 1847

I can once again put a date to my entry. It is weeks later than I thought. Time became one frozen moment of misery for so long that it seemed like eternity.

At first, I was ashamed. I could see the shock and horror in our rescuers' eyes. They went into the Murphy cabin and emerged white-faced and grim. There was a pit near the cabin where body parts were strewn about, and they found a young boy inside the pit, eating the flesh off a human arm.

None of them has said anything to us directly, but their attitude toward us changed from one of pity to one of wariness.

No one in the Reed and Breen cabin resorted to eating human flesh. As this became clear to our rescuers, they regained their sympathy for our small group while retaining their ill-concealed revulsion toward the others.

It isn't their fault! I want to tell them. *The werewolves had them trapped. The werewolves caused most of this carnage.*

I hold my tongue.

They would think me mad, like Mother Murphy, who hasn't stopped babbling since they arrived. When she first emerged from her cabin, she said, "Are you men from California, or are you from heaven?" That was the last coherent thing she said. She raves of monsters, and the men avoid her.

They are so vital, so quick compared to us. It is as if we were frozen and are only now coming back to life. We move like the broken arms of a dropped clock, in jerks and stops, but the men are kind and help us. The leader of our rescuers is named Ben, and though he is a couple of years older than me, he seems but a boy in his enthusiasm. His chivalry toward me makes me shiver with delight. I must look like a smashed doll, but he treats me as if I am a lady of the royal court.

When he told me that Father organized this rescue and will be here in a few days, I cried out, "A few *days*? No!" before I could stop myself.

He gave me a strange look and awaited an explanation for my outburst, but when none was forthcoming, he began again. "Miss Reed, you are weak, all of you... "

"No," I interrupted. How could I explain the urgency? "No, we must leave now, *now,* before… before the accursed snows begin again."

"We have brought ample supplies. You must recover your strength before you travel," Ben said, puzzled by my insistence. They'd been doling out the food slowly, so that none of us could do ourselves harm by eating too much too quickly.

"I assure you, sir, all of us would rather brave the trip," I told him grimly.

"Very well," he said. "Those of you who are strong enough, we'll take back. It is still early in the spring, and there is always the chance of another snowstorm, I suppose."

I let him think that this was what worried me. No wolves have shown themselves since the rescue party arrived—none but Keseberg. The scarred man stares at me with an intensity that frightens me. He is crippled now, and cannot come after me even though he wants to.

But that doesn't stop him from watching me.

When I was alone, I was fearless. Now, among these strong men, I fear the werewolves will find a way to pluck me from their grasp.

Ben seemed to think it strange when I asked for a rifle, but he handed me one without a word. Killing Keseberg is very much on my mind, but I can't murder him in cold blood, nor would the rescuers understand why a thirteen-year-old girl would suddenly shoot an incapacitated man.

None of us has said anything about werewolves. If none of us had resorted to cannibalism, if the wolves had caused all this, perhaps we would speak, but since some are, in fact, guilty of the crime of which they are accused, we keep silent.

I have considered the men and women still left alive and tried to guess which of them are werewolves, but have finally accepted that aside from the Donners, Keseberg, and a few of his friends, I can't tell. Some among us look better fed than the rest, but there is more than one explanation for that.

I saw Jean Baptiste earlier, talking with some of our rescuers, and wondered when he had returned. He wouldn't look at me at all, and when I moved toward him, he moved away, keeping his distance.

I can tell that the others are already denying what they experienced, already attributing what they saw and heard to the hunger and the cold. But I know the supernatural horrors were real, and I will never forget that fact, no matter how comfortable my future. I will always remember that evil stalks us.

February 21, 1847

We have begun our journey to our new home. There are twenty-three of us strong enough to leave. Thirty-three are being left behind to wait for the next rescue party. This is the first count we've taken since being trapped by the snows, and there are more survivors than I expected. There were times, deep in the night, when I thought the few people in our cabin were the last humans on Earth.

Patty and Tommy only made it a few hundred yards uphill before it became clear they couldn't continue. We stood on the trail trying to decide what to do.

"I will stay with them," I said as I saw my mother waver.

"No, Virginia," she said with surprising firmness. "You will leave with us; no arguing."

One of the men in the relief party overhead us. I think his name was Mr. Glover. "I'll stay," he said. "Don't worry, I won't let anything happen to them."

Mother still hesitated. I knew what she was asking herself: should she save those children she could, or should we all stay... and perhaps all die?

"Go, Mother," Patty said. "If I don't see you again, do the best you can."

I looked at my sister in surprise. She had a resolute look on her face that reminded me of Father.

"I'll go with them back to the cabin," I said.

"No!" Mother's was almost shouting, she was so agitated, which was a sign that she was recovering. She wasn't the ghost of a woman she'd been for the last few weeks. "You are coming with us, Virginia!"

"I promise I will catch up," I said. "I promise."

Mother stared at me for a moment longer, then nodded. "I will take you at your word, Virginia. Hurry."

As we walked back to the cabin, Mr. Glover carrying Tommy, I tried to figure out how to broach the subject of the monsters. The men had seen the wolf tracks and heard several of the survivors talk about attacks, but I don't think they believed us. They seemed to think we were trying to cover up what we had done.

"There are wolves in this camp," I said abruptly.

Glover looked over at me but didn't break stride. "Oh?"

"I assure you, I have seen them. They're dangerous. They've lost their fear of man and have preyed on us."

He said nothing. As we neared the cabin, he stopped and looked me in the eye. "I'll be on the lookout," he said.

Mrs. Breen heard us and poked her head out the entrance. "You can't come in," she said emphatically.

"Pardon?" Glover said, perplexed.

"I won't let you in!" she shouted. "The food is ours!"

"Ma'am, I have enough supplies in my pack to feed myself and these two young ones for weeks. Let us in." He turned to me, eyebrows raised in amazement. I stared back at him. He will never know what it was like. He will never understand why Mrs. Breen said that. But I did.

"Please believe me, Mister Glover," I said. "You must stay alert."

He nodded, then ducked through the entrance, carrying Tommy. Patty hugged me tightly, then followed them without a word.

I turned and headed back to join Jimmy, Mother, and the others, carrying my rifle and looking around alertly. *Last chance to catch me,* I thought. *I hope you try.*

There was no sign of the creatures. Perhaps they were planning to follow those of us leaving the camp, hoping to keep us from reaching salvation. Perhaps there was yet to be a final battle. I almost hoped so, because the alternative was that the wolves were staying to finish off those left behind.

I thought of defying Mother and turning back, but she had been adamant, which was unlike her, and I knew that if I disobeyed her, the thread of trust between us—which had long been frayed—would finally and irrevocably be broken.

February 23, 1847

I caught up to the others quickly. Our group can only move as fast as the slowest among us. We are so close to freedom! Just a few more days and we will be out of the mountains. But the clouds once again grow dark. I fear we will not make it. Another storm is coming.

All this time, I've secretly believed we were condemned, though I've been unwilling to admit it to myself. Now, so close to freedom, I seem to have lost my courage. Our bad luck is following us. We ran out of supplies on the third day, but our rescuers are confident. They say there is a cache of food and supplies a short distance away.

February 24, 1847

The food cache is missing, and the supplies are strewn about the clearing. What hasn't been spoiled has been defecated on or stomped into the dirt.

"What kind of animal would do this?" one of the men wondered out loud, though there are wolf tracks all over.

Those of us from Truckee Lake looked at each other uneasily. We know what kind of creatures would do such a thing.

Regrettably, I fear our rescuers are about to find out what it is like to go hungry. The next food station is four days away. It is snowing. The men of the rescue party look around in dismay but talk confidently of the future. Those they have rescued simply put our heads down, hunch our shoulders, and trudge forward. No one has suggested we go back. I think we would rather die.

We managed to start a fire. It is colder than I can remember, even in the depths of winter, even during Mother's and my aborted escape attempt, when we'd been without shelter or fire. The Fates aren't done with us yet. Why fortune favors the foul creatures that stalk us, I cannot understand. Perhaps that which is wild—the mountains and forests—aids those that are wild against the civilized and humane.

In the middle of the night, I heard someone shouting. I woke to find the men dashing about the camp, and I grabbed my rifle and sat up, certain we were being attacked. There was an unusual odor in the air; or rather, it was a familiar odor, but one I'd never expected to smell again: burning human flesh.

I saw one of the men dragging the youngest Breen girl away from the fire. She had put her feet near the fire to warm them and fallen asleep, and her feet were so frostbitten that she had not felt her toes burning in the coals.

The men from California are starting to draw away from us, as if we are cursed. Who can blame them? I see their expressions of alarm and concern, and, yes, fear.

On the third day without food, one of the older boys crept up to one man's buckskin jacket and began snipping off the fringe. The rescuers watched in shock as the boy carefully handed out the buckskin strips to the other children, who began to gnaw on the leather.

You have no idea, I thought as I saw the men recoil. *You will never understand, unless you have endured what we have.*

* * *

That afternoon, we crossed the summit and started down the other side of the mountains.

On the fourth day, we found Jody Denton dead in his bedroll. He'd seemed one of the strongest among us, but as we packed up to leave, we realized he hadn't moved. We left him there, unburied, covered by his blankets.

We arrived at the next supply cache on the fifth day. It had been better concealed and everything was intact, including the food, but it was too late for little Ada Fitzsimmons, who died soon after being fed a morsel or two.

We each ate a small amount, our rescuers insisting that we take it easy. They ate heartily, however. I didn't resent them for it. They are right to keep up their strength.

We left the rest of the supplies for other relief parties, concealing the food as best we could without hiding it completely. As we walked away, I saw that Mrs. Fitzsimmons was carrying her dead baby. One of the rescuers started to speak to her, but I shook my head at him and he fell silent.

Again, it seems our saviors don't know whether to shun us or coddle us.

We descended the slopes all morning, never complaining, for we knew the end of our travails was near. That knowledge gave us strength.

All at once, I heard a familiar voice: a loud, confident voice, drifting up from the slopes below.

My mother cried out and sank to her knees in the snow, sobbing. Father came over the rise, striding confidently like a hero of old, grinning like I'd never seen before. He swept me up in his arms, and I suddenly felt small. All my heavy burdens dropped away, and for a moment, I was his little girl once more. Jimmy grabbed his legs, crying out "Father! Father!" over and over, and then it was his turn to be swept up in Father's embrace.

Father set him down gently and took my face between his hands. "Thank you," he whispered.

He went to Mother then, knelt at her side, and enfolded her in his arms.

February 28, 1847

Father has gone with the rescue party to get Patty and Tommy, but my ordeal is over.

We reached Sutter's Fort without further incident. This afternoon, I was sitting on a log in the sun, almost afraid to believe that what I was seeing was real: happy, healthy men and women bustling about their business; children laughing and playing. I didn't want to move, I felt so serene.

Ben, the young man who first greeted me at Truckee Lake, approached me shyly.

I smiled at him so broadly that I must have looked like a fool.

He stammered for a while, and had to repeat himself three or four times before I understood what he was saying.

He was asking me to marry him.

I looked down at my soiled and tattered dress. I knew I must still look like an abandoned rag doll. If ever I'd begun to have womanly curves, they are long gone now. It suddenly occurred to me that I had turned fourteen in the last month, but it had seemed so unimportant.

I managed to tell him politely that as we barely know each other, it is too soon to think of such things, but once he was out of sight, I couldn't help it: for the first time in months, I began to laugh. I couldn't stop. I laughed until tears ran down my cheeks and my sides hurt. I laughed like the deranged girl I know myself to be.

CHAPTER 35

Diary of James Reed, March 2, 1847

Margret, Virginia, and Jimmy have traveled with my fellow soldiers to Fort Sutter, and I have come to rescue Tommy and Patty. I had a long conversation with Virginia before we parted ways, and she informed me that the situation is dire and that the creatures are still hunting us. I only pray I am not too late.

I want to believe she has begun telling tall tales again, but her stories were not fanciful, nor were they exaggerations, and she wasn't even telling me the half of it. She was trying to spare my feelings, telling me that she was fine, that it really hadn't been so bad.

One look at my wife and I could see—Virginia's stalwart bearing notwithstanding—that it had been much, much worse than I could ever have imagined, and it broke my heart.

I hurried my companions along, and we fought through the snowstorm and reached Truckee Lake a day sooner than anticipated.

Patty and Tommy are still alive, though my youngest boy is very weak. I have not left their side, so I have not witnessed the horrors in the other cabins. The Murphy cabin is apparently indescribable. There are pits outside with body parts in them. It seems Mrs. Murphy has gone insane, and the children in her care, the Eddy and Foster children, are so close to death that they can't be moved.

Keseberg is holed up in the Murphy cabin with an injured leg. It sounds like a bullet wound to me, and I remember Virginia's account of firing upon the werewolves. Each time I hear these stories, I want to deny them, to dismiss them as illusion, products of her vivid imagination, hallucinations induced by hunger and cold—but I have seen these monsters firsthand, and I will not deny their reality for the sake of having a more comfortable view of the world.

The Donners are also in bad shape. George Donner's arm is gangrenous, and I fear he will not last much longer. Jacob Donner is dead. I have heard whispers that his children are alive only because they have been feeding on his body. Elizabeth Donner insists the meat her children are consuming is not her husband.

We are taking back those whom we can. Soon, we will lead the Breens and the rest of my family away from this terrible place. Most of our party will be made up of youngsters; it is judged that with the new rations, the adults left here can stay alive for some time.

I have seen no signs of wolves, natural or otherwise.

March 10, 1847

Our ordeal is not yet over. Young Isaac Donner died during the night. We have been snowed in on the pass for several days. I cannot convince the others to move on, so I am leaving them. I am carrying my children. Yesterday, I met Eddy and Foster and a man named John Stark on the trail and urged them to hurry, for I fear their children are in grave danger back at Truckee Lake.

March 12 1847

We have arrived at Sutter's Fort. I fear Tommy will lose his toes to frostbite, and my hands are bleeding, but we are alive.

So ends our torment.

March 18, 1847

I feel that I must tell the last of this tale, though I was not there to witness it: the tale of this hell that never seemed to end, even when we thought we were free of it. Various parties were dispatched to bring the survivors out of the mountains, but with each rescue, we were forced to leave some people behind, and when we went back for them, we had to leave others behind.

Each time we returned, more were dead and more had been eaten.

Eddy and Foster finally made it to Truckee Lake, having hired four men at Bear Lake to accompany them, only to find their entire families dead. To their great credit, Eddy and Foster stayed to help those left alive.

Keseberg confessed that he had eaten the Eddy children. Though there is more to that story, much more, history will record it as a desperate act of cannibalism.

"Monster!" Eddy cried, and would have done for Keseberg then and there had he not been restrained. It was his four hirelings who stopped him, not truly understanding what had happened.

None of the outsiders truly understand what happened, for there is blame enough to go around, and humans were responsible for much of the misery. After all, not all who killed were monsters, and not all who died were human. Not all who were consumed were consumed by wolves. Such facts have muddled the narrative, even for those who were there.

Indeed, until the end, there were villains in human form. Mrs. Donner hired two of the rescuers to take her children to California, but they took her money and left the children at the cabins at Truckee Lake. But there were acts of selflessness, as well: for instance, if not for John Stark, who took it upon himself to help them though they were not his relatives and he was not paid to do so, the Breens and the Graveses would have died in those mountains.

Still, the nightmare continued. When the final relief party arrived, they found the remains of many poor souls along the trail, partly consumed. They found one-year-old Elizabeth Graves crying beside her mother's body. They came upon pits containing more human remains, and found Keseberg in the Murphy cabin, in possession of the Donners' jewelry and money, and Tamsen Donner missing. There was meat in the stewpot.

Enough. I cannot bear to go on.

Let history tell the rest, though history will never recount the true story of what transpired. I broached the subject of werewolves once with Colonel Fremont, and he looked at me as if I had gone mad. When I pretended I had meant ordinary wolves, I was rebuffed there as well.

"California is a land of beauty and harmony. There are no wolves. There are no monsters. And if there are wolves, they certainly don't eat children," he said.

I've left this record in any case, for those who wish to believe it. There are things in this world that may be denied in the full light of day, but should you find yourself in a winter storm deep in the woods of the high mountains, you will believe, for they are among us.

CHAPTER 36

Final testimony of Virginia Reed, April 1865

It has been nearly twenty years since those terrible events.

I shall be forever grateful that the tragedy was named after the Donner family and that our family's reputation, which suffered enough, was not forever tarnished by the title the Reed Party.

Abraham Lincoln has been assassinated. It is this that impels me to once again put pen to paper. Honest Abe, they called him. I met him once, and in his honor, I have told the true story of the Donner Party.

That people should confess to killing and eating their fellows is terrible enough. Most of the other survivors cannot admit the whole truth about what happened, or they deny it, or have, over time, forgotten the true nature of the horror.

I believe my father, James Reed, remembered everything about those creatures of darkness, but he was a practical, rational man who would never admit to seeing demons, except to me.

When the fateful decision to take the Hastings Cutoff was made, it was Father who spoke most strongly in favor the new route. It was a mistake on his part, but an honest one. We were lied to, manipulated to our awful fate by Lansford Hastings, and later by the famous mountain man Jim Bridger. They were wolves in men's clothing.

Listen to one last testimony.

One day, in that terrible winter, I ventured out of the cabin, hoping to find the carcass of a horse or ox exposed by the wind and the shifting of the snow. Instead, I found five men crouched over the body of another.

I say men, but they were more like animals than men. They stood upright, but were covered with hair, and their arms and legs were unnaturally long. They were bent over the body, and I realized to my horror that they were eating the corpse.

Hiding behind a tree, I continue to observe them, for I wished to bear witness to this atrocity. When the body was completely consumed, those five creatures transformed before me, turning back into men. They were naked, but they quickly covered themselves, talking and laughing as if nothing unusual had transpired.

I was not surprised to discover that three of the men were Keseberg, Spitzer, and Reinhardt, but then the two others turned around, and the sight staggered me.

I saw the man we had met so long ago in Missouri—Lansford Hastings, who had coaxed us to follow the trail that led us into these mountains. And I saw Jim Bridger, who had reassured us that the path was safe. Their faces were red with blood. I sensed that they knew I was watching, but didn't care. Indeed, it seemed to me that they wished for me to witness their depravity.

It wasn't human depravity I witnessed: I am certain of that. People would laugh if I told them this, but these were unnatural creatures, not men.

At first, after our rescue, some of us survivors tried to explain what had happened, but the only thing that made sense to anyone else was cannibalism. I believe now that we humans did not consume our fellows—I myself ate shoestrings and ox hide, insects and tree bark, but never tasted the flesh of another human being—it's just that everyone has been led to believe we did, because no one is willing to believe the truth.

After so many years, that is what I have convinced myself of, at least.

Nonetheless, the history books shall forever damn us.

As I have recounted, my father eventually reached us, and after some further hardship, we made it to California at last. My entire family survived. During our journey out of the mountains, I made sure that we stayed far away from Keseberg and the others.

No one but me ever knew that Hastings and Bridger had been at that camp.

I spent the rest of my life tracking them all down. It was obvious that each of them met an unnatural end, but I made sure to cover my tracks. I killed them with bullets and blades, and made sure they saw my face before they died.

I saved Keseberg for last.

After we returned to civilization, he was nearly tried for murder, but no witnesses could be found. If all of us had coordinated our stories, something might have come of it, but we could not—or rather, would not. He continued to vehemently deny the charges, and eventually the reporters left him alone.

Years later, I tracked him to a small cabin in the woods. He was hiding in the farthest wilderness of Alaska. It was isolated; there was no one around to stop me, no one to act as witness. Boldly, I walked up to the front door and knocked.

The door opened, and there was Keseberg. His long red hair was streaked with white, and he had even more scars on his face than I remembered. He had a crutch under one arm. "Come in, Virginia," he said. "I've been expecting you."

He stepped aside to let me pass, remarking, "You've turned into a beautiful woman."

I ignored the compliment. "You are alone?"

"Of course. I have been alone for years. None of my kind wants to run with an old, lame wolf. Besides, the others blame me for what happened. As many of us died as you humans, you know. Turns out we were as trapped as you were. Ah, that was a winter like no other! We couldn't find prey anymore than your hunters could."

"You ate *us*."

He snorted. "You weren't worth much. One of you barely made a meal."

"That didn't stop you."

He shrugged. "Of course not. I might remind you, it didn't stop you humans either."

This conversation wasn't turning out the way I had planned. The others had tried to fight, or to run. Keseberg was doing neither.

The cabin had a peculiar odor. I made my way into the simple kitchen, keeping my revolver pointed at Keseberg the whole time. There was a rotten haunch of lamb in the sink, reeking of decay.

I looked around the place. It was clear that Keseberg rarely left the cabin, and that nothing was ever cleaned. It reminded me of the cabins at Truckee Lake.

I turned, startled, as Keseberg entered the kitchen behind me. He could barely walk, and I saw that the arm that wasn't grasping the crutch was hanging uselessly.

"I relive those times every day of my life," he said. "I think the Almighty has singled out me, among all the creatures He created on this Earth, to see how much hardship, suffering, and misery a being can bear."

He hobbled to the kitchen table and stared at me. "Go ahead. I've wanted this for a long time. Kill me."

We stood there for a moment, Keseberg and I, regarding one another across the table. Then I lowered the revolver and did something I had never once, in all my years of planning and searching, dreamed I might do.

I walked away, leaving him a tormented, living monument to those days at Truckee Lake.

His screams rang in my ears as I went out the door. "Kill me! Have mercy! Don't leave me like this! *Kill me!*"

* * *

For all I know, he's there still.

About the Author:

Duncan McGeary is the owner of the bookstore Pegasus Books of Bend, located in downtown Bend, Oregon. He is the author of the fantasy novels Star Axe, Snowcastles, and Icetowers, and the author of several horror novels, including Led to the Slaughter and the Vampire Evolution Trilogy. His wife Linda is also a writer; together they attend a writer's group in Oregon. Duncan has two children: Todd, an artist, and Toby, a chef.

Available from
Books of the Dead Press

TS Alan - The Romero Strain
A group of New Yorkers are chased underground by a zombie horde. They gather survivors while traveling to Grand Central Terminal, where they believe help will be found. Their hopes end when they discover the area overrun with the undead, and come face to face with an adversary born from a lab deep below the city.

John F.D. Taff – Kill/Off
When David Benning is blackmailed he's thrust into a world of guns, payoffs and killing ordinary people. As he becomes more enmeshed, he begins to grasp the true motives, and secrets—secrets that must never be revealed. David can trust no one… not even the one person he has grown to love.

James Roy Daley – Authors & Publishers Must Die!
From the mouth of author/publisher James Roy Daley comes Authors and Publishers Must Die! No punches are pulled in this non-fiction title, which is filled to the rim with straightforward, practical advice for writers, while exploring what it's like to be on the other side of the desk. A must read for every author.

J.C. Michael - Discoredia
As the year draws to a close a mysterious stranger makes a proposition to club owner: a deal involving a drug called Pandemonium. The good news: the drug is free. The bad news: it comes at a heavy price, promising much but delivering far more. Euphoria and ecstasy. Death and depravity. All come together, at Discoredia.

Weston Kincade - A Life of Death
Homicide detective Alex Drummond is confronted with the past. His troubled senior year of school unfolds revealing loss, drunken abuse, and mysterious visions of murder and demonic children. Is he going insane? With the help of his friend, Alex must find the source of his misfortune and ensure his sanity.

Julie Hutchings - Running Home
Death hovers around Ellie Morgan like the friend nobody wants. She doesn't belong in snow-swept New Hampshire, at a black tie party—but that' is where she is, and where he is: Nicholas French, the man who mystifies her with a feeling of home she's been missing and the impossible knowledge of her troubled soul.

John F.D. Taff – The Bell Witch

A historical horror novel/ghost story based on what is perhaps the most well documented poltergeist case to occur in the United States. The Bell Witch is, at once, a historical novel, a ghost story, a horror story and a love story all rolled into one.

Justin Robinson - Everyman

Ian Covey is a doppelganger. A mimic. A shapeshifter. He can replace anyone he wants by becoming a perfect copy; taking the victim's face, his home, his family. His life. No longer a man, but a hungry void, Ian Covey is a monster. Virtue has a veil, a mask, and evil has a thousand faces.

Mark Matthews - On the Lips of Children

Meet Macon. Tattoo artist. Athlete. Family man. He's planning to run a marathon, but falls prey to a bizarre man and his wife who dwell in an underground drug-smuggling tunnel. They raise their twin children in a way Macon couldn't imagine: skinning victims for food and money. And Macon, and his family, are next.

Bracken MacLeod - Mountain Home

Lyn works at an isolated roadside diner. When a retired combat veteran stages an assault there her world is turned upside down. Surviving bullets is only the beginning her nightmare. Will she - or anyone else - survive the attack?

Gary Brandner - The Howling

Karyn and her husband Roy had come to the peaceful California village of Drago to escape the savagery of the city. On the surface Drago appeared to be like most small rural towns. But it was not. The village had a most unsavory history. Unexplained disappearances, sudden deaths. People just vanished, never to be found...

Gary Brandner - The Howling II

For Karyn it was the howling. The howling that had heralded the nightmare in Drago... the nightmare that had joined her husband Roy to the she-wolf Marcia and should have ended forever with the fire. But it hadn't. Roy and Marcia were still alive, and deadly... and thirsty for the most horrifying vengeance imaginable...

Gary Brandner - The Howling III

They are man. And they are beast. Once again they stalk the night, eyes aflame, teeth flashing in vengeance. Malcolm is the young one. He must choose between the way of the human and the seductive howling of the wolf. Those who share his blood want to make him one of them. Those who fear him want him dead.

James Roy Daley - Into Hell

Stephenie and her daughter Carrie drive down an empty highway, pulling off at a gas station with a restaurant attached to it. Carrie enters the building first. When Stephenie steps inside she discovers that the restaurant is a slaughterhouse. There are dead bodies everywhere. The worse part: Carrie is suddenly missing.

James Roy Daley - Terror Town
Hardcore horror at its best: Killer on the warpath. Monsters on the street. Vampires in the night. Zombies on the hunt. Welcome to Terror Town. The place where no one is safe. Nothing is sacred. All will die. All will suffer.

James Roy Daley - The Dead Parade
Within the hour James will witness the suicide of his closest friend, be responsible for countless murders, and become a fugitive from the police. In the shadow of his mind, a demon lurks. Bloodlust is a virus and it's infecting his logic. James has become a pawn, and one thing is clear: survival is not an option.

Tonia Brown - Badass Zombie Road Trip
Jonah has seven days to find his best friend's soul, or lose his own, dragging a zombie across the country with a stripper who has an agenda of her own, while being pursued for a crime he didn't commit... and dealing with Satan. 2,000 miles. Seven days. Two souls. One zombie. Satan.

Matt Hults - Husk
Mallory Wiess is a typical teenage girl... or so it seems. When she moves to rural Minnesota she discovers her new home won't be as boring as she'd feared. Who is the dark figure watching her from across the street? What is the shape hanging in the shadows of the old barn? And why has someone begun digging up graves at the ancient cemetery? In the end, one night will decide if the dead will rise.

Tim Lebbon - Berserk
The army had said it was a training accident. But why had the coffin been sealed? On a dark night, in a deserted field, Tom begins to unearth the mass grave where he hopes - and fears - that he will find his son's remains. Instead, he finds one little girl, dead and rotting, who promises to help Tom find what he's looking for...

Best New Zombie Tales - Volume One
Includes Amazing Fiction by: WHC Grand Master Award Winner, Ray Garton / New York Times Best Seller, Jonathan Maberry / Bram Stoker Award Winner, Kealan Patrick Burke / Bram Stoker Award Nominee, Jeff Strand / Micro Award Finalist, Robert Swartwood / British Fantasy Awards Nominee, Gary McMahon / Bram Stoker Award Winner, Kim Paffenroth... and so much more.

Best New Zombie Tales - Volume Two
Includes Amazing Fiction by: Bram Stoker Award Winner, David Niall Wilson / British Fantasy Award Nominee, Rio Youers / Bram Stoker Award Nominee, Nate Kenyon / Authorlink New Author Award Winner, Tim Waggoner / George Turner Prize Nominee, Narrelle M. Harris / Bram Stoker Award Winner, John Everson / Pulitzer Prize Nominee, Mort Castle... and so much more.

Best New Zombie Tales - Volume Three
Includes Amazing Fiction by: Anthony Award Winner, Simon Wood / Bram Stoker Award Nominee, Joe McKinney / New York Times Bestselling Author, Tim Lebbon / Arthur Ellis Award Winner, Nancy Kilpatrick / British Fantasy Award Nominee, Paul Kane / Bram Stoker Award Nominee, Jeremy C. Shipp... and so much more.

Best New Werewolf Tales - Volume One
Includes Amazing Fiction by: New York Times Bestseller, Jonathan Maberry / Bram Stoker Award Winner, John Everson / Bram Stoker Award Nominee, Michael Laimo / Aurora Award Nominee, Douglas Smith / Bram Stoker Award Winner, David Niall Wilson / Bram Stoker Award Winner, Nina Kiriki Hoffman / Golden Bridge Award Winner, David Wesley Hill... and so much more.

Best New Vampire Tales - Volume One
Includes amazing fiction by: Bram Stoker Award Nominee, Michael Laimo / Bram Stoker Award Winner, David Niall Wilson / Authorlink Winner, Tim Waggoner / Bram Stoker Award Winner, John Everson / International Horror Guild Nominee, Don Webb / British Fantasy Award, Science Fiction Award Nominee, Jay Caselberg / Arthur Ellis Award Winner, Nancy Kilpatrick... and so much more.

John F.D. Taff - Little Deaths
Named the #1 Horror Collection of 2012 by Horror Talk
Named top 5 books of 2012 by AndyErupts

You think you've got bad dreams? Consider author John F.D. Taff's nightmares. Taff has the kind of nightmares no one really wants. But it's nightmares like these that give him plenty of ideas to explore; ideas that he's turned into the short stories he shares in his new collection.

James Roy Daley - Zombie Kong
Big. Bad. Heavy. Hungry. While a 50-foot tall zombie gorilla smashes the hell out of a small town, Candice Wanglund drags her son Jake through the hazardous streets in an attempt to get away from the man that is determined to kill them. She wishes her husband Dale was by her side; he would know what to do. The good news: Dale's alive. Problem is, he was eaten by the gorilla.

James Roy Daley - 13 Drops Of Blood
13 tales of horror, suspense, and imagination. Enter the gore-soaked exhibit, the train of terror, the graveyard of the haunted. Meet the scientist of the monsters, the woman with the thing living inside her, the living dead... James Roy Daley unleashes quality horror stories with a flair for the hardcore. Not for the squeamish.

John L. French - Paradise Denied
This is one of the best collections you will ever read. There isn't a single story in this collection that feels like filler. Vampires, zombies, tough cops, faeries, heroes, or super-scientists, John French has got a tale for you and it's amazing. Again and again, readers agree: this is the book you won't be able to put down. A must read.

Zombie Kong - Anthology
Zombies are bad, but ZOMBIE KONG is worse. Way worse. Big. Bad. Heavy. Hungry. This is the most original zombie anthology of all time. In the jungles, in the arctic, in the cities, in the towns -- Zombie Kong rules them all. All other zombies must bow to their god... ZOMBIE KONG!

Paul Kane - Pain Cages
Reminiscent of Stephen King's classic, bestselling book Different Seasons, Paul Kane gives us an unforgettable collection of four novella-size stories. Each story is refreshingly original and delivers an emotional impact that is rarely seen in today's literature. Dark and moody, clever and well-written... Pain Cages speculative fiction at its best.

Matt Hults - Anything Can Be Dangerous
Anything Can be Dangerous contains four amazing stories:
Anything can be Dangerous ~ the simple things in life can kill.
Through the Valley of Death ~ a vampire tale that will make you remember fear.
The Finger ~ zombie literature has never been so extraordinary.
Feeding Frenzy ~ lunchtime in a place called Hell.

Bill Howard - 10 Minutes From Home: Episodes 1 - 4
When a viral outbreak hits Toronto, Denny Collins and his best friend Thom Washington find themselves trapped over 100 km from Denny's home in a town called Pontypool, where his wife and daughter remain. As the streets begin to teem with violence, they must first find safety, then find a way out of the now deadly metropolis.

Bill Howard - 10 Minutes From Home: Episodes 5 - 8
The journey gets bloodier as the group runs into hordes of the infected in a suburban neighborhood. Thom must make some drastic decisions when the survivors encounter a military camp. But does the camp provide safety, or just another hurdle delaying Denny's expedition home?

Classic - Vampire Tales
Includes: J. Sheridan Lefanu / Bram Stoker / M. R. James / F. Benson / Algernon Blackwood / F. Marion Crawford / Mary E. Wilkins Freeman / James Robinson Planche / Johann Ludwig Tieck

Thank you for reading this book!

CPSIA information can be obtained at www.ICGtesting.com
Printed in the USA
BVOW07s1956250914

367964BV00002B/8/P